D1715986

PURPLE Flame

J.S RAIS-DAAL

authorHOUSE®

AuthorHouse™ UK
1663 Liberty Drive
Bloomington, IN 47403 USA
www.authorhouse.co.uk
Phone: 0800.197.4150

Published by AuthorHouse 04/18/2017

ISBN: 978-1-5246-7887-6 (sc)
ISBN: 978-1-5246-7888-3 (hc)
ISBN: 978-1-5246-7886-9 (e)

Dedicated To My Little Guinevere.
I hope you are as proud of me as your Mother is.

A BOY WITHOUT A FAMILY WILL become lost. But even the lost can be found again.

A boy without guidance will lose hope. But hope can always be restored.

A boy who becomes trapped becomes an animal. But even animals can be trained.

An animal boy who becomes a man becomes a monster. But even a monster can be tamed.

A monster left to fester becomes possessed. But even the possessed can be cured.

A possessed man who has no love has a demon within him. Demons can only be expelled by fire and storm.

But if the possessed man chooses between the demon and love, the answer will be unpredictable.

All that is certain is death.

By fire and storm.

The Purple Star: A Book on the Supernatural

CONTENTS

PART 1

FLINT AND STEEL

PROLOGUE TO PART 1

THE INCIDENT WAS REFERRED TO in whispers. It went by one name: the Inferno. It did not go to the plan the rebel leader had wanted, but he had to see it to some kind of end. For too long he had suffered under the gaze of his superior. For too long he had been forgotten by his master. He wanted what was rightfully his, and he was now fighting to claim it. Everywhere was chaos. He thought he had taken everything into account when he met secretly with his supporters, everything but two crucial elements of his superior's character: power and cunning. His loyalists had done their job in securing the guard posts and holding them, but the counter-attack was calculated and vicious. He knew they would not hold for much longer. As he and more of his soldiers moved deeper towards his target, everything became much clearer. His superior had expected this and planned accordingly.

They were ambushed multiple times by screeching fanatics, loyal to his superior. He knew that the orders were to take him and his loyalists alive, for a more intimate punishment. He would avoid that at all costs. With battle cries, wild swings, and stabs, they fought their way through the ambushes. During every fight, another soldier fell, either gravely wounded or taken by the enemy. None of this deterred him. He had sacrificed too much to fail so close to his goal. Fire raged around the complex, an unfortunate by product of his surprise attack. He tried to ignore the turbulent red flames, which spread violently as if they were searching for prey, but as seasoned as he was, the fire unnerved him – especially when it took his soldiers. He thought for a brief moment that the enemy might own the fire now, but he pushed that thought from mind as he continued along the tunnel.

His destination was close. Able to see the spiral staircase ahead, he ordered his men to a flat-out sprint. Then he charged, his gaze watchful and his sword ready. More fanatics leapt from the gloom, grabbing at him and his comrades. With masterful slices, he dispatched some, leaving cleaved and twitching bodies behind. Seeing that his men had dealt with the others, he proceeded. His troop had been decimated. One hundred brave soldiers had entered the complex with him; now only ten remained – and they were battered. He wondered how the rest of his loyalist troops were faring. How many were taken and how many dispatched, he could not begin to guess.

'Hold here,' he spoke, reaching the spiral staircase. 'Anyone who is not with us, dispatch. We can still carry the day, if you give me the time I need.'

His soldiers saluted silently and took up defensive positions, their weapons ready. Knowing he had done all he could, he ascended the stairs. His speed never lagged and his attention never wavered as he ran. A number of fanatics flew at him at regular intervals, but he dispatched them with ease. And then he arrived at his destination. With a deep breath, he focused. Summoning a burst of strength, he kicked the huge iron door in front of him. It buckled and broke instantly, falling onto the stone floor of the roof with a boom. As he stepped through the gap, fire rose behind him, blocking his escape. His adversary would not let him leave so easily. Readying himself, he strode onto the rooftop.

He could hear the sounds of battle below as he marched, the clang of swords, the brave battle cries of his men, and the shrieks of the fanatics. The sound that made him freeze in fear was the drums. Reinforcements had arrived. He had not planned for this. The plan was to localize the battlefield so that no help would arrive. He padded to the edge and surveyed. Reinforcements had entered the various frays. They were his master's soldiers. He then knew his chance of success was minimal, until he heard the chuckling from behind.

'Did you honestly think you would succeed?' the voice asked, making him spin around and prepare his sword. 'Did you honestly think I did not foresee this, Commander?'

He did not answer as his superior approached. The man's ornate two-handed sword gleamed in the light of the fire that raged around; his black and red armour fit exquisitely, as it should have for a lord. He, of lower rank, felt very inferior in comparison. His sword was smaller and less ornate, but it was battle worn and ready like he was. His armour was tattered and blood-soaked, as it had protected him from the countless blows of various foes.

His superior padded towards him, graceful as a cat. His sword rested on his shoulder. He was a head taller and built like stone. The man was greatly older, but his age was not easy to discern. Age did not matter in their world. He was still deadly.

'Surrender now, Commander,' the lord continued, his eyes pulsating, 'and I will see you do not suffer quite as much as your comrades.'

'A soldier does not surrender,' the commander replied, pacing around his lord, 'unlike lords, who leave when they please.'

He had little time to react as the lord roared and slammed his sword to the floor. Dipping, he rolled away from the body-cleaving arc to safety. Rising, he blocked the return strike with ease, but the force of it sent ripples through his body. Not wanting to leave himself open, he went low and sliced, but he hit nothing. His lord vaulted gracefully over him to safety.

'I did teach you well, did I not?' the lord said, raising his sword.

'Some might say too well.'

They attacked together, both attempting to find a weakness. One would attack, the other would counter, and the other would attempt to counter again. It was a deadly dance, a ferocious dance, that matched the chaos below. Neither saw an opening as they moved to safety.

'What was your plan, Commander?' the lord said tauntingly. 'Take my position and my power and use it for your own gain?'

'Why do you ask questions to which you already know the answers?' the commander responded in kind. 'Do you truly have no knowledge at all, apart from what your spies whisper?'

The lord's eyes glowed red at the insult. He roared with rage as he charged. The commander stood his ground and prepared. The lord attacked with ferocity, but he was predictable. Sensing his opportunity, the commander struck. Blocking another crushing strike, he slammed the pommel of his sword into the lord's face. As his lord staggered back in a daze, he wrenched the two-handed sword from his lord's grasp and threw it over the edge of the roof. With the lord glaring at him in primordial rage, the commander charged him. All hopes rested on this attack connecting.

It did not. The lord had seen it coming. He dodged gracefully away from the charge and kicked the commander, who was knocked from his feet and sent into the air. He lost the grip from his sword as it spun away from him. He landed with a thud but continued to roll. Then he felt himself beginning to fall from the roof. Snapping out his hands, he caught the ledge. Below the sounds of battle began to quieten. His troops had lost. He could vaguely see his soldiers being forced to their knees. He was now their only hope.

The commander felt the sulphur being crushed from his lungs as a strong, clawed hand gripped his throat and hoisted him into the air. He looked upon his lord, who wore the fanged smile of victory on his face. Defeat was not the thought that came to the commander's mind first once his lord spoke.

'Commander, you will face the maximum penalty for what you attempted to do.'

'I hope you burn in angel light, Lord Azrael,' the commander spat as he jammed his thumbs into Azrael's eyes. Azrael howled in agony as he threw his commander away like he was nothing. The commander felt himself plummet again. He knew this would not be the end. He always had a contingency. It was what he was known for. Before his body hit the ground, he muttered the words that he had rehearsed on countless lonesome nights.

All his lord and master found was a husk of a corpse, bereft of any being or life force. The commander was gone. Azrael knelt before his master, who strode back to his keep. Azrael knew this was not the end. It was the beginning. Somehow, one of his lowly commanders had found a way to do what he had always been told was the impossible and the forbidden.

CHAPTER 1

THE SKY WAS CLEAR. NOT a cloud was dulling the perfect endless blue that stretched from horizon to horizon. The summer was unseasonably hot, and the convoy of cars that sped down the open motorway reflected the persistent rays of the sun. The convoy was heading south, as it had done every year. Every year, they travelled in the same formation to the same place.

The front car was the largest, its large wheels centred perfectly in the centre lane of the motorway. On the back seat, a single pair of eyes was open. They belonged to a boy. On each side of him were two girls, both asleep on his shoulders. The girl on the right was small with dark brown hair and looked much like the boy. This was his sister, Shana. Dressed in her traditional pink shirt and white skirt, she lay on her brother's shoulder whilst clutching onto her teddy.

The other girl was older than Shana but was still younger than the boy. She looked nothing like the pair she shared the seat with. She had long, flowing red hair with a face covered in freckles. Even though she was not a member of the family, she was very much a part of it. Her name was Laura, and she was the boy's girlfriend. She lay on the boy's shoulder very much the same as Shana and clutched his arm, which was wrapped protectively around her.

The boy in the middle was different in only one way from his sister. Whereas she had dark brown eyes, he had pale blue eyes and light blond hair that seemed to reflect the sun as it shone through the tinted windows of the four-by-four. His name was Zach. He was the oldest child of the Ford family.

Following the black four-by-four were six other cars containing the rest of Zach's family. Every summer, they went down to the coast for a few weeks. It was sort of a ritual that had stuck with the family ever since Zach was born. Everyone enjoyed the occasion. This year promised to be one of the best family reunions they had ever known.

As the convoy passed under a bridge, they came suddenly to a traffic jam. With this not being much of an issue for the experienced driver, William Ford casually braked and stopped behind the car in front of him. Then he watched as the convoy fell in behind him. Looking into the back seat, he smiled upon seeing his son protecting the girls next to him. It reminded William of his childhood with his sister, who travelled a few cars behind his own. Turning to face the immense block of cars, he caught the eyes of his wife, Grace. She smiled at her husband, but there was a sadness that, after thirty years of marriage, William could easily see.

'What's wrong, darling?' he asked her softly, so as not to wake the children in the back seat.

'I'm just sad that Rodger could not come again this year. He was always the life of the house.'

'It is sad, but I am sure that he will come next year.' He knew that was a lie, but it was easier to say than the truth, which was that his once good friend would never join them again. 'Get some sleep. We will be there soon.'

The tired-looking Grace looked at her husband and nodded before falling asleep again.

Looking back at the traffic, William felt terrible for lying to his wife, but it was the only thing he could say without making her worry. He remembered the days when he and Rodger would play rugby together. As a pair, they had scored the most tries and had won many trophies, but since he had become engrossed in his new job, Rodger had no time for his friend or for his godson, Zach. It made William sad that his friend had no time for him anymore, after everything they had done together.

It happened suddenly and without warning. The only part of the motorway that was empty was the slip road, in front of which the convoy was stopped. This was where it happened.

With no warning, a petrol lorry came speeding forward, obviously with no intention of stopping for anything. Seeing the convoy ahead, the driver did not even try to stop. His eyes fixed on the convoy and aimed for Zach's car. With a fiendish smile on his face, the masked driver leapt out of the lorry and landed gracefully in the bushes bordering the slip road. With a loud crash followed by a huge explosion that engulfed the convoy, the lorry went up in a flash of fire and smoke.

The impact was immense. Cars flew across the motorway and landed on the opposite side of the central barrier. The cars of Zach's convoy dispersed in many different directions and landed metres away from the lorry, on fire with smoke filtering through the small gaps in the doors and windows. And then all was silent. It was over.

As people ran from their cars to the wreckage of the convoy, they all stopped and stared in amazement. All the lifeless bodies of the passengers of Zach's convoy lay perfectly next to each other on the side of the road, but one was alive: Zach.

His clothes were burnt and falling from his body, and his face was black with ash. What astounded everyone the most was what he was doing. He cradled and wept over the bodies of Laura and Shana at the same time. Tears fell like rain through his sky-blue eyes as the lifeless bodies lay in his ash-stained arms.

It took five police officers to drag him away and put him in an ambulance. The whole time, he tried to escape their clutches.

Overseeing the carnage below was the lorry driver. His masked face smiled as he drew out a mobile phone and dialled a number. In a voice deep and emotionless, he said, 'It is done, but one survived.'

'Never mind about that,' the voice replied. 'Get out of there. Your job is finished.'

Slipping the phone into his pocket again, the driver disappeared into the forest, out of sight of the people at the crash site. He had no idea what he had unleashed on the world, as anger festered inside a restrained Zach.

CHAPTER 2

ONE MONTH LATER
The heat of the summer left quickly and was replaced by a cold autumn. Leaves abandoned their trees, unable to hold on as the winds stripped the trees bare, turning their plain branches and trunks into skeletons on the roadside. Fields and forests looked like graveyards for the trees, their lifeless forms swaying in the wind.

The wind was unforgiving and ice-cold for everyone waiting at the bus stop. They mostly wore hooded tops and gloves, all except one. He stood six feet tall, his hair was as black as night, and his skin was as white as pure snow. He wore no hat, gloves, or thick tops. He stood in a thin black zipped jumper that was fully open; underneath was a plain black shirt. His jeans were torn and burnt and still smelt of smoke and burning, the stench clinging to him. His black shoes were covered in mud. His ice-blue eyes were fixed on the building in front of him. They never moved or blinked, his gaze piercing and his thoughts dark. The people in the bus shelter could not help staring at Zach. He could feel their traitorous eyes fixed on him. He had known them all before the summer, but now it was autumn. After the event, no one dared go near him. It was as if he had died and there was something else now in his body.

That was closer to the truth than they could ever have imagined.

As the bus pulled in, people slowly emerged from the shelter, being cautious, as they did not want to get too close to Zach. Once the doors opened, Zach climbed aboard and took his usual seat at the back, a hood covering his head. After the last person clambered aboard, the doors shut with a bang. The engine of the bus cracked and grunted into life as it pulled away. It was a small bus, with only a few seats that looked even remotely safe to sit on, but it served its purpose. There was a three-row gap between Zach and the other passengers. New passengers who got on instantly saw the formation and either sat next to someone or stood, fearful of what would happen if they broke the chain.

As the bus slowly made its way along its route, another passenger jumped on at one of the stops and immediately started to talk to his friend, who sat nervously at the front.

'All right, mate,' he called. 'This is the right bus then?'

'All right, mate,' his friend responded. 'Yeah, this is it. Thought you'd never find it.'

'I'm not that dumb, mate,' the new passenger replied, sauntering over to his friend with a look of confusion on his face. 'Why are you sittin' here?' he asked loudly. 'Have you seen all them free seats and the free back row? Come on, Daz, let's get a decent seat.'

Before the standing passenger could move, Daz grabbed him and pulled him back to his seat, his eyes full of fear. Bewildered by his friend's actions, the new passenger spoke with anger. 'What the hell are you doing?'

'Don't go back there,' Daz replied, the fear emanating from his eyes.

'Why?' his friend asked impatiently.

'Cos of him,' Daz said, motioning at the dark outline of Zach. 'Trust me, Phil. Keep away from him.'

Phil turned to look at the shadowy form of Zach and then laughed at Daz. 'What? Cos of that emo?' he shouted. 'Watch this. I'll deal with this filth.'

Phil stood, shrugged off the hands of Daz, and marched over to where Zach sat. Confidence filled his face when he reached Zach. The whole bus watched to see what would happen.

'Oi!' Phil shouted at Zach.

Zach gave no response, continuing to sit with his eyes shut.

With anger building inside of him, Phil struck the seat bar in front of Zach, the boom causing Zach's eyes to snap open and his ice-blue eyes to glare at Phil, who felt an ice-cold shiver go down his spine.

Composing himself, Phil continued with what he had set out to do. 'Why don't you let these guys sit near you?' Phil asked, pointing at the other passengers on the still-moving bus.

Zach did not answer but continued to gaze at Phil. Phil had never had anyone remain silent after he'd asked a question. In his frustration, he quickly drew out and readied a flick knife, pointing it at Zach.

'Answer me!' he shouted, stepping closer to Zach.

It was then that Zach struck. In two lightning-fast strikes, Zach's right hand broke Phil's elbow. With his left hand, Zach caught the knife as it flew out of Phil's hand. As the knife landed softly in the pale hands of Zach, he kicked Phil to the ground and watched as he slid across the floor to the other end of the bus. Hitting the front of the bus, Phil let out a yelp of pain as he saw a bone pointing out of his elbow joint. Phil looked down the aisle at Zach, who stared at him before he spoke in a deep, almost demonic voice.

'I do not force these people to sit where they sit now,' Zach said in a very pronounced accent. 'They choose to avoid me. They choose to stay away because they are wise, whereas you are not.'

Slowly Zach walked towards the slumped body of Phil and crouched in front of him. It was then that Phil's face first showed fear, as he heard the same voice again, but this time in his head.

'Seeing as this is your first encounter with me, I will let you off the hook for the insult.' After hearing this, Phil yelped in pain, as his arm snapped back to its normal form. 'But do that again and no mercy will be shown to you.' With those words deeply embedded in his head, Phil stood and nodded at Zach before walking, clutching his arm, to where Daz sat.

In a flash, Zach was back in his seat. His last action of that journey was to snap the knife in two. The two gleaming metal pieces became ash with one touch. Phil's eyes widened with fear as he saw what Zach did. Then Phil looked at Daz, who peered sadly into his friend's eyes before dropping his gaze to the floor. The rest of the journey continued in silence.

Eventually the bus entered a small village nestled in the middle of a deep valley. The rain had been pouring down for hours and the roads were soaked. Turning down into a small lane, the bus creaked to a stop. Zach slowly stepped off, his hood still over his head. As he heard the bus drive away, he walked up the small slope which led to his house. It was a strange house. Even though it had two levels, it was still classed as a bungalow. The L-shaped structure was built into one side of a stone wall. The lower level consisted of a garage and a large room. Next to the garage there was a small set of stairs, which led to a glass door. This was the front door to the house. Zach slowly ascended the stairs and slid the door open before silently entering. It would be another sleepless night for Zach, and he knew it.

The dusk turned quickly into an ice-cold night, the cloud cover that had blocked out the sunlight now blocking the bright rays of the moon. Zach had stayed exactly where he was once he returned home, sitting on the decking at the rear of the house wearing nothing but his jeans, his snow-white skin almost reflecting the various lights from the houses that surrounded him. As he sat there, the wind blew lightly on his skin. He neither shivered nor put on layers as the night grew colder. It was what he had been waiting for the entire day: the ice-cold breeze that soothed his skin and his forever burning hands. Zach, knowing he was not alone, opened his eyes to behold a dark figure standing in front of him. It was completely black, apart from its blood-red eyes, which stared back at him. Its silver, sabre-like fangs were set in a grin. Showing no fear to the figure, Zach stood and looked at the creature, his fists ready to lash out at the red eyes that remained fixed on him.

'What do you want now?' Zach asked, his voice deep but not demonic. 'Have you not seen enough blood today?'

'Yes, I have seen enough for now,' the creature replied. 'Do you like your new powers?'

'I hate everything you've given me, demon,' Zach answered, anger filling his voice. 'Thanks to you, I have lost everything and am regarded as a monster! I told you on the day I first met you to leave me alone. Maybe now is the time to go.'

The demon smiled, seeing its plaything fill with anger, its silver teeth reflecting the lights of the other houses.

'Soon I will be gone – well, from this form, anyway,' the demon spoke, its words ringing in Zach's ears. 'But mark my words: you will regret telling me to leave. This is just the beginning, Zach Ford.'

With those words firmly in Zach's mind, the demon disappeared in a cloud of dust and was gone from the deck. Zach breathed a sigh of relief. *Maybe now I will be free,* he thought. How wrong his thought was.

As he turned to walk inside, Zach was struck to the ground by an unnatural pain, one which seemed to paralyze him completely. Managing to look up at the sky, he saw the clouds gather over him. Then he saw lightning beginning to build within the clouds. It was then the demon's voice spoke again, but this time in his mind.

'You asked for me to go,' it said as clearly as it had when it was in front of him, 'and I kept my word. I'm going to be you, and you will be more of a monster than you could ever imagine.' As he heard those words, Zach felt himself beginning to levitate towards the clouds. He soon realized he was hovering above the ground, with a lightning storm raging over his head.

As he hovered there, weightless to the world, Zach considered screaming, but he knew that would not help. Either way, the demon would get what it wanted. Having already lost everything he'd ever loved, he knew it would be best to succumb to the inevitable. Zach looked up and saw the purple lightning raging above. With a loud crack, the lightning projected from the clouds and struck him. It was not a normal bolt; this was a prolonged one. It stayed attached to Zach whilst he screamed in agony. The lightning burnt him internally and externally. Zach wanted this to end. All he wanted was to join his family in death, but he knew that would not happen, as the lightning continued to burn him. At that moment, the demon took advantage, appearing in front of Zach. With its silver grin stretching from ear to ear, its red eyes began burning into Zach's. Zach's transformation into a monster had begun. The pain, excruciating, lasted for what seemed an eternity. Zach could feel the demon building in power inside him. He tried his best to resist both the pain from the lightning bolt and the pain from the transformation, but eventually he surrendered. Then it was over. Letting out a roar of victory, the demon plunged its black hand into Zach's chest, making the two of them one. With its final act of victory, the demon caused Zach to roar as it had done. And then all was quiet. The bolt disappeared, and Zach plummeted to the ground.

Landing with a thud on the decking, Zach let out a cry of pain. His shoulder had dislocated. With no warning, it clicked back into place and healed with no pain. Zach slowly forced himself up to his feet and looked at him body. His burns had healed, and he felt no pain from the lightning bolt. He looked at the place where he had landed on the decking. The cracks that outlined his body were filled in and then disappeared.

Zach could sense that something else was wrong. He strode into the large living room and stood in front of a huge mirror. It was there that his fears were confirmed. Standing where his reflection should be was the reflection of the demon that now possessed him. The blood-red eyes and silver teeth still grinned at him as they had done when the demon first appeared that night.

'What have you done to me?' Zach screamed at the unfamiliar reflection.

'I have made you into one of the most deadly beings on this planet,' it replied.

'I don't want this.' Zach continued to scream, saying, 'I never wanted this!' He headed for the wall, yanked one of his fencing sabres from its scabbard, and held it to his own throat. 'I swear to God, I'll do it unless you get out of me,' Zach said, tightening his hold on the newly sharpened blade at his throat.

'Look at what I am giving you,' the demon answered, 'the chance to have revenge on everyone who hurt you and the chance to find out what happened to your family.'

'I don't want any of those things,' Zach hissed. 'Now get out of me.'

'You leave me little choice then,' the demon replied.

Zach relaxed a little bit, which was all the demon needed. Taking control of Zach's arm, the demon threw the sabre across the room. It stuck in the wall above a family photograph. Turning back to the mirror, surprise covering his face, Zach saw the reflection smiling once again.

'We are one now,' the demon said. 'I control you. And you can summon me when you need a bit more … power.' Zach stood defiantly in the face of his possessed self.

'After tonight, you will begin to see things from my perspective,' the demon continued. 'Sleep now, Zach Ford. Tomorrow will be your first day as a possessed being.'

Hearing those word filled Zach with such rage that he swung at the mirror. His fist stopped millimetres away from the glass, and then he flew out of the room and landed on the wall of his own room. This was where he would spend his night. As the cold, damp wall slowly engulfed him, Zach surrendered to his first unnatural sleep in months. His last thoughts were of his lost love and of the day she was taken from him.

…

The motorbike screeched to a halt just short of small wooden door. The rider gracefully dismounted and removed his helmet. Shaking his brown hair free from its constricted form, the tall man walked through a set of doors. Following the corridor around, he found himself standing outside another wooden door. Brushing his hair back, he knocked and waited. The white-painted thick wooden door slowly opened, revealing a large room with a low table and two brown leather sofas flanking it. In the back corner was a computer desk with an active computer humming on the edge. The huge window had its curtains drawn so that no one could see in, the fireplace on the other side of the room compensating for the lack of light. Sitting on the other leather sofa was a tall, thin man. He was still dressed in his work clothes, which made him seem even bigger to the man who entered. His grey eyes closed to give the appearance of sleep, but the man knew that he was not sleeping. With the door slowly closing behind him, he sat on the sofa opposite and waited for the other man's eyes to open.

'The mission was a success, I take it?' he finally said.

'It was, sir, but there was one survivor,' the biker replied.

'That does not matter, James,' the suited man said, 'as long as that bastard William and his family are dead. That is all that matters.'

Fear overcame James as he awaited the question he knew the suited man would ask.

'Who was the survivor?' he eventually asked.

'It was William's son, Zach,' he replied, fear engulfing his voice. 'He was taken to the district hospital along with the rest of his family's bodies.'

'What!' the suited man shouted. 'You did not mention that when you called me!'

'I know. I'm sorry,' James grovelled, 'but I know someone who will help us.'

'Who?' asked the suited man.

Slowly James rummaged through the pockets of his jacket. Withdrawing a card, he handed it to the suited man. Reading what was on the card, the suited man threw the card on the desk and looked at James.

'Get out,' he said calmly, 'now.'

Not waiting to be told again, James flew out the door. Within moments, the suited man heard the roaring of the bike as it disappeared down the school drive. Walking back to his sofa, Rodger Green's mind filled with a thought. His godson had survived the extermination. And if what was written on the business card was true, then this was now a far more serious situation than he had realized. Picking up his glass of Crawford's Scotch, Rodger knew that he would be in danger until his godson left his school. He would sleep in his office again tonight, as he had done for many nights. He knew the order would not be pleased with his failure.

CHAPTER 3

THE SUN ROSE OVER THE hill that bordered the village, its warm rays illuminating the dew that covered every inch of grass in the fields. With the sunlight burning his closed eyes, Zach awoke. Pushing himself free from the wall, he discovered that his head was pounding, as if he had drunk too much cider. Checking the clock next to him, he saw it was 5 a.m., but oddly he did not feel tired. He stretched, his bones playing the melody of clicks and cracks that he was used to, until finally he stopped and walked out of the room. His day was set to be uneventful, a full day of the torture that was school. He walked to the spacious empty living room and looked in the mirror. He had a strange feeling as he looked into it, as if he had been there recently, but he could not quite picture when or for what reason. Leaving behind the site of his déjà vu, he padded into the kitchen. As he began to cut bread to put into the bird feeders, he cut himself. The pain was excruciating and caused him to scream, when he stared down at his finger, he saw that the wound had completely healed. Scared and confused, Zach returned to his room and slammed the door shut.

Thinking it was all a terrible dream, Zach shouted at himself to wake up, but instead he was struck to the floor by a great pain, which felt strangely familiar but different, like a raging fire was burning him. Managing to get to his knees, he looked up at his near empty room. It seemed to be getting hotter. The books on his bookshelves started to shake. As the pain began to grow, he felt something inside of him – and then he remembered all that had happened last night.

'No!' he screamed. The pain grew and grew until it felt like he would explode.

Trying to relieve his agony, Zach clutched his stomach, keeled over, and shut his eyes. Books flew all around his head, creating a dome above and around his pained form. The pain continued to grow, never ceasing, until he lifted his head and screamed. His scream soon turned to a roar as Shangal broke through and began the change. His bones rapidly grew, broke, and set, inflicting more pain upon the agonized Zach. The heat seared him both inside and out as Shangal's powers returned. He now stood eight feet tall, his skin was grey and thick, his eyes were as red as blood, and his teeth were silver fangs and razor sharp. He assessed his form, that of a monster. As the change process grew more violent and painful, Zach's roar became louder. As he did so, the books that surrounded him burst into flame, creating a fiery dome which engulfed his changing form. He now felt no pain. Outside he sensed the family jeep rise off the ground and burst into flame, lighting up the bright morning sky like a second sun.

Zach fought against the pain and his intruder with all his might. But with the constant barrage of the demon's assault and the agony of the change, he faltered. Eventually he lost control of the flames as they spread from room to room of the house. The flames licked the bare walls and ceilings, removing everything upon them, until all was black and ashen. As the fire raged, he felt the demon began to slacken. He also felt the admiration of the destruction it was creating. Zach took his chance. Summoning what little will and energy he had left, he resisted again. Zach caught the demon off guard at a point when it had few defences. After what seemed like an age of mental and physical struggle, Zach pushed the demon back from his body and mind. As suddenly as the flames had caught, they dissipated, leaving only fire-stained rooms that simmered with smoke and embers. Zach could feel his bones break, shrink, and set. He did not even bother to yelp, as he had no energy left.

Zach was now back in his own form. All around him was ash and charred paper. Every book in his room was destroyed. The ash was still warm to his paper-white skin, its warmth singeing his regrown arm hair. As Zach struggled to keep unconsciousness at bay, he heard movement from outside. He tried to heave himself to his feet, but his muscles ached and his legs would not obey him. He heard the front door give and then open, followed by hurried footsteps moving towards his now closed bedroom door. With a crack, his bedroom door broke and opened. Zach sealed his still-red eyes as strong hands helped him roll himself onto his back. He heard a familiar voice that was not Shangal's. Hoping his eyes were no longer red, Zach snapped them open. As his sight recovered and he regarded his destroyed, smoking room, he saw a familiar face. Seeing no sign of shock in his neighbour's eyes, Zach attempted to stand again, his aged neighbour trying his best to help.

Feeling that his eyes and mind were back to normal, Zach looked at his neighbour and smiled.

'I'm sorry, Jon,' he said in his normal voice. 'Do you want anything?'

'No, no, dear boy,' the old man replied. 'I was just worried about you. I'm your guardian now and I have to see that you are OK. I promised your father.'

Hearing those words from the old man touched Zach.

'Thank you,' Zach replied. 'I must get ready now, but thank you for checking on me.'

'It's OK, my boy,' the old man said. Then he walked out of the front door and disappeared down the driveway. Zach sighed. Now that Jon had gone, he could drop his unconvincing charade.

Opening his hands, Zach saw the burn marks and winced in pain. Unlike the other injuries he had sustained, these ones had not healed and seemed permanent – a constant reminder of what he was: possessed. Throwing the remainder of his few possessions to the floor, Zach managed to find a pair of black leather fingerless gloves. He had to hide what he was from everyone. All of his friends had abandoned him, so he knew they would not come near him. Still, he could not take the chance that someone would. Slowly sliding the gloves onto his hands, wincing and gasping from the pain, he thought of what next to do. It was 6:15 a.m. His bus would arrive in fifteen minutes. After throwing on his usual black attire, Zach flew out of the door. He hadn't eaten breakfast so as not to waste any more time. In a flash he was down at the bus stop. The clouds gathered around him and the rain began, the first good thing about his day.

The rain continued to pour as the bus pulled into the Salisbury station, each drop playing a unique note as it hit the sodden ground. People rushed about with coats and jackets draped over them, or struggled with half-put-up umbrellas as the wind began to build. Zach loved the rain. He glided through the town centre, lifting his head up to the sky as the falling water cooled and soothed his face. People around him scurried into the nearest shelter and stared in amazement at him. He continued to make his way slowly to his school.

Slowly ascending the small, thin lane, Zach arrived at the entrance. It was a small main building which still had its Tudor-design front door and roof. Its small wooden doors opened, which led him into maze of small corridors, stairs, and doors. The first door to come across was the headmaster's large white wooden one, Mr Green's office, but Zach always referred to him as Rodger. It was the only thing that would annoy the headmaster, but Zach had never been disciplined for it. He had learnt that the headmaster had some sort of soft spot for him, despite their frequent heated meetings.

Zipping through the maze of corridors, Zach turned into the smallest, darkest one and stopped at the very end, which was where his locker was. When he returned from the summer holidays, it had been moved here at the request of Rodger, but oddly enough Zach did not mind. He liked the darkness and the knowledge that no one would disturb him. Hearing the squealing tone of the bell, Zach opened his old dented locked, took out his tattered black school bag, and walked casually up a flight of stairs heading towards his classroom.

...

Katie Oldman sat nervously at her new desk in centre of the busy classroom, her dark brown eyes taking in the entire room and the people who sat in it, all of them talking animatedly about their weekends. She sat like a statue, afraid of meeting even a single pair of unfamiliar eyes. After being shown here by the receptionist, she had been abandoned. Now she could feel the prying eyes of her new classmates. The phrase *new blood* keep repeating in her head. At the front of the class was a small slender woman, her light red hair bouncing on her shoulders as she rummaged through the pile of papers on her desk, in search of something elusive. Eventually finding what she was seeking at the top of her pile, she called the class to order and began to call out names.

'Carl?'

'Here.'

'Christina?'

'Here.'

'Debbie?'

'Here.'

This continued for a few minutes until she got to the last name. She faltered slightly. Katie could see her teacher's hands shaking, but she called the name as if nothing was wrong.

'Zach?'

There was no answer. Seeing the other pupils look around in fear, the teacher called again, 'Zach?'

Again, no answer. As she was about to make an absent mark beside the name, the heavy wooden door flung open, crashing into a grey metal filing cabinet, which caused a dent, and in stepped a tall boy clad in black. With a quick look from his pale blue eyes, Mrs Wood ticked his name and put down the register.

'Glad to have you back, Zach,' she said. Her broad Scottish accent could not cover up the lie in her voice, but the boy did not seem to care. He took his place at the back of the class, slinging his bag on the floor with a bang, which made everyone else jump in fright. Then he sat down.

Managing to compose herself, Mrs Wood continued to speak, now that all her students had arrived.

'I hope your last summer weekends were enjoyable?' she asked. Nods and smiles came from all around the room. 'But now it's time to learn. And I have three announcements to make.' She inhaled deeply and then continued, trying not to look into the eyes of the boy who had been the last to enter.

'Firstly, I would like to welcome to our class a new member to this school, Miss Katie Oldman.' She gestured with her hand to Katie, who stood up timidly and looked around the room.

'I trust you will make her time here as enjoyable as possible.' Once again the class nodded.

'Seeing as it's your first day here, Katie, I'll have someone show you around for the day.' She looked around the room and selected the perfect candidate. 'Mister Golden will show you around. Alex?' She pointed to a short dumpy boy, who walked over to Katie and shook her hand violently.

'Just stay with him, dear, and you'll be fine.' Katie nodded in reply. Then she sat down as Alex waddled back to his seat.

'Secondly, we welcome back Mister Jones, fresh again from hospital.' The whole class looked around as another boy, roughly the same size as the one clad in black, stood up. He scanned the faces of all those around him and then stopped at the black-clad boy. Their eyes met for a few seconds before he turned back to the teacher.

'I trust there are no hard feelings between you two,' she said, noticing the locking of their eyes.

'I'm sure we can work something out, can't we, Zachy boy?'

The class all looked at Zach, who stood up slowly. Katie detected a rise in tension. Everyone in that room expected something, and Katie would be right in the middle of it.

What a perfect first day, she thought.

She saw Zach suddenly turn to face her. It was as if he had heard her say that, but he just stared at her before turning back to the boy, who was still standing in front of Mrs Wood.

'We both know how this will end, Christian,' Zach said, his deep voice causing everyone's hearts to beat faster. 'I hope you're ready for it when it happens.'

Their eyes fixed again. There was tension as the class sat in silence. It was Zach who moved first. In a flash, he was back in his seat. Mrs Wood saw and felt that everyone instantly had become calm. However, Katie was not calm. She could not help but stare at Zach in surprise.

I wonder what that was about, she thought, feeling his gaze once again.

'And the final announcement is from the headmaster,' Mrs Wood continued. 'Would Mister Jones both Mister Reeses, Mister Bolter, Mister Lyons, and Mister Draper go and see the headmaster now?'

All six boys stood up and left the room, banging the door shut as they went. Everyone started to mutter. Katie, wondering if that was the norm here, noticed that Zach was not being included in the mutterings. Then she was distracted from her thoughts by Mrs Wood's voice.

'And Zach, if you could see him at ten o'clock after your second lesson?' He nodded slowly in response.

'The rest of you, it's lesson time.' The classroom erupted in annoyed groans as Mrs Woods shuffled the students out through the door. Katie looked for the boy called Zach, but by the time she was out the door, he had gone, obviously knowing the labyrinth a lot better than she did. She heard a stumble from behind her. Wheeling around, she saw Alex Golden, her 'guide'. The small dumpy boy looked at her.

'It's chemistry first.' His face was like the others', full of dislike upon hearing about their first torture of the day. 'But,' he continued, a smile beaming across his face, 'you have to be allocated a locker. Let's go and get you one.'

Katie followed behind Alex, trying not to laugh at his weak excuse for walking.

It is more like a pregnant duck's waddle, she thought to herself, trying not to giggle.

After about five minutes of 'duck following', she came to a long row of lockers. On one of them was her name. Opening the locker, she was very surprised to see it was clean and ready for use. Putting her unneeded books and clothes inside, she looked to see what else she could do. The inside of the door was slightly raised. She rummaged inside her bag, pulled out a small mirror, and stuck it to the inside of the door, along with her timetable and some pictures of her dog. She heard Alex sigh to himself with impatience. Finishing off her interior design, she resumed following him.

The school was not big compared to the other schools in the area, but it was still a maze. The corridors were so thin that if anyone came in the opposite direction, it became a gridlock of students and teachers, all shouting for dominance in the small corridors and walkways. But somehow Alex fought his way through the crowd, followed quickly by Katie. Soon they were out of the congestion. They climbed numerous flights of stairs, finally reaching the science labs, which were of simple design. There were three rooms, one for each type of science class offered at the school. Outside the classroom there was another thin walkway, as well as a small bench crammed full of bags. The lessons had already begun. Finding her pencil case, Katie followed Alex to the end lab, where she heard some animated talking. After Alex knocked on the door, they both entered. The room was wide and set out with three rows of long wooden desks which looked in dire needed of replacement. At the front there was a small teacher's desk and a whiteboard. The classmates Katie had registered with were all there, still discussing their various weekends. Katie was immediately greeted by a man who looked like Alex, just much taller and wider.

'Hello, new one, and welcome to the wondrously strange chemistry lab.' Katie laughed at the energy and the strangeness of the greeting, but she took the man's large hand and shook it.

'My name is Doctor Bark. I will accompany you through the magical world of chemistry.' His face was still animated. Rather than being scared, Katie continued to laugh.

'What's your name, child?' he asked, still with a lot of energy.

'Umm, Katie.'

'Do you have a nickname, Umm Katie?' Doctor Bark joked.

'No. Just Katie,' she replied.

'Well then, Katie,' the doctor continued, 'go and take a seat anywhere you choose and we'll get you started.'

Nervously turning, she faced the class. All of them were still talking about various topics and did not seem to notice that she was searching for a seat. It was then that she realized something peculiar: the entire front row was taken up by the whole class. The middle row was empty, but the back row had one person sitting there. It was Zach. His long black hair covered his forehead. His pale blue eyes were focused on a point outside the window – the spectacular view – whilst his gloved hands stayed motionless on the table. Katie was intrigued and confused as to why everyone was sitting so far away from him. As she headed over to him, she heard her name being called.

'Hey, Katie, over here.' It was Alex. The boy had found the seat next to him empty and was beckoning her to sit there. Turning her head to and fro, she made her choice and went to sit next to Alex. With one last glance at the mysterious-looking Zach, she faced the front. The lesson began.

...

The lesson and the rest of the day would be like any other for Zach. He sat alone, answered questions rarely, and took down notes faster than anyone else. No one made comments about him or even looked at him. He wanted this day to be over quickly so that he could get home and be away from people. Since that morning, he had felt an anger building within him. He fought to control it and for now was winning. He was not sure how long he could hold out, though. Katie intrigued him, as she seemed to have no fear of him. That was probably because she had not had the traditional welcome from the headmaster. He had heard all about those welcomes, and yet he still did not have to desire to ask Rodger about why he chose to warn other students about him. Not yet, anyway.

The squealing of the school bell sounded. Everyone immediately stood up and began heading out, with Zach zipping out and making it to his locker before anyone else. Opening his locker, he took out his bag and began to fill it for the home journey. The day had been difficult for him. It was hard for him to concentrate with Shangal blocking his thoughts by whispering in his mind. The mental warfare was already taking its toll. He could not even remember the meeting he'd had with Rodger. He knew what it would have been about, but he could not recall the specific words. It was lax of him.

Zach's hands were still searing with pain. He was convinced he would catch on fire. Not even the continuing rain seemed to cool his hands. But not matter how bad it got, he still had control and at some points could even block out and hold back the demon. The only thing he couldn't block out was the pain of his branded hands. Sensing he was being watched, he marched out of the school and headed for home.

CHAPTER 4

THE NEW DAY FOR KATIE had started with a lot of confusion. After being thrown a sports kit and practically dragged to the girls' changing rooms, she managed to get talking to some of the squealing girls in her class. She stayed close to a group of three girls. One had long curly blonde hair and was the tallest of the group. She was called Taylor. The other was the complete opposite, with short brown straight hair and a very short frame. She was called Eli. And the last was the odd one out, as they called her. She had short red hair and green eyes and was of medium height and build. She was called Stephanie. Astonishingly Katie found out that all of them had once been friends of Zach, but now they were not for some reason. Katie did not have the confidence to ask why. Instead she listened. She found everything confusing and pondered why for a brief moment before joining in the current conversation.

'So what do we do in PE?' she asked, her demeanour reeking of nervousness.

'Not much, really,' Taylor replied, throwing on her shirt. 'We mostly watch the boys do what they do. It's more fun that way.'

'Oh, right,' Katie said. 'Who will you all watch today then?'

The three girls looked at each other in thought.

'Hmm, that's a tough one,' Eli replied, seeming still to be thinking as she spoke. 'Football's on. That's always a good laugh. Or we can see who's going to get crippled by Zach.'

'What do you mean?' Katie asked, shocked.

'Zach's one of the best fencers and martial artists in the county,' Stephanie whispered to Katie, 'but everyone in the school tries to take him on. No one has ever won. And with him talking to the headmaster again today, you can guarantee it's going to get ugly. I think I'll stick to the football.'

Nods came from the two other girls, but Katie was intrigued to see such talent in action.

'I think I'll watch Zach,' she finally said with growing confidence.

The other three girls looked at each other in amazement and showed her to the sports hall. With a smile of thanks, she entered, not knowing what to expect.

The hall was the largest room in the school. To Katie it was huge. Along the floor was a long white fencing mat, and on either side there were benches where pupils and teachers alike could watch the spars. Katie went and sat on the back row of benches, which were gradually elevated so that all could see. The sports coach stepped onto the mat, his loud voice echoing around the hall numerous times.

'First match will be between Richard Lorton, year twelve, against Zach Ford, year ten.'

Mutters went up around the hall as the tall thin frame of Richard and the large muscular frame of Zach met on the white mat. The two boys walked up to each other and shook hands before going to their allocated ends and checking their weapons. Richard's suit was the traditional white, whereas Zach's suit was completely black. This looked to Katie like a cliché battle of good versus evil. She laughed to herself when she thought of it.

Having chosen their weapons, the boys approached each other and took position. Sliding the visors over their heads, both raised their weapons. Seeing both contenders were ready, the big PE teacher stood up again and signalled for the spar to begin. It was Richard who attacked first, with a clumsy thrust at Zach's chest. Reacting instantly, Zach batted the weak attack away and slashed at Richard's chest, winning the first point in seconds. Both contenders then eased back towards their starting points and waited patiently. Round two began in the same way. Richard placed weak attacks, which Zach parried with such fluency that it looked like he was using no effort. Parrying one such weak attack, Zach took the offensive. Targeting Richard's weak spot, Zach placed many short power thrusts and jabs directly in the centre of Richard's chest. Seeing the pattern emerging, Richard tried to protect himself, but instead he was pushed back by the sheer power of Zach's attack. Seeing a small gap of hesitation, Zach struck.

Doing a feint slash, Zach brought down Richard's sabre and slashed at his chest as the latter tried to raise his weapon for his own attack. The match was over in less than ten minutes. There was not a scratch on Zach's perfect night-black suit.

Katie stared in amazement as Zach went back to his corner and took off his armour, showing just a black undershirt. He gestured to the teacher, who waved at the other fencers sitting on the bench at one end of the mat. Two eventually stood up and made ready. The mat was moved out of the way so the entire hall's floor space was made available. Everyone looked at each other in amazement as Zach stood in the centre of the floor and held his sabre above his head. Katie looked into his eyes. They were not the ice-blue she remembered from yesterday, but she did not get a long look, as the spar began.

Zach whirled round and blocked both strikes aimed at his head, pushing his opponent's sabre away with little effort. His lack of armour gave him far more manoeuvrability than his opponents. Targeting the fencer closest to him, he sent three powerful, precise strikes, which caused the boy to move back far enough for Zach to block the incoming attack from the other fencer behind him. The crowd gasped as Zach effortlessly parried every attack from both opponents, as well as creating counter-attacks out of what seemed to be nothing. Katie thought he was looking bored by the obvious lack of challenge as he finished off the round. Parrying both weak attacks from his adversaries, Zach zipped over to one of the swordsman and slashed at him precisely in the chest. The boy was now out. Turning around, Zach saw the lunge from his other opponent. Stepping out of harm's way, he twisted down the blade of the other fencer's sabre and ripped it from his hands, leaving him weaponless. With a grunt as he hit the floor, Zach's opponent turned over and stared in disbelief as Zach dropped his sabre next to him and strode back to his own corner. Not a speck of sweat ran from his head.

Once Zach reached his corner, Katie watched as he took off some layers until he stood in just his tattered sports trousers and vest. His feet were bare, his visible white skin reflecting the beaming rays of the sun that shone through the windows. Looking at the PE teacher with an expression of disappointment, Zach stood and stretched his muscles, anticipating another spar. Looking back at the bench of fencers, the large teacher pointed at the four contenders who were left. The four stood, sauntered over to the floor, and took their positions. Seeing the challenge in front of him, the vastly unprotected Zach drew his other sabre, glided to the centre of the floor again, and made ready. The crowd were talking in full voices now. Never had someone fought four people from the fencing team, never had anyone done this with minimal armour, and never had anyone done this whilst wielding two sabres in complete unison. But Zach was doing it now, against four of the best fencers in the school. Everyone in the crowd looked on with concern.

Katie once again stared into Zach's concentrating eyes. But something was different. She could swear that his eyes were blood red. Looking closer at him, Katie jumped as Zach's now reddened eyes stared back at her. She saw no pupils, just a continuous sea of red, like two cauldrons of blood fixing on her. She looked around. No one else seemed to notice the anomaly, as everyone was still talking about the unreal scene that was being played out in front of them. Looking again at Zach, she caught one last glimpse of the sinister eyes before the spar started.

Katie had trouble following Zach's movements. He moved so quickly and with such precision that the other fencers had trouble parrying his strong and fierce attacks. And when they tried to counter, he zipped out the way and appeared somewhere else on the floor.

Finally, he was still. The fight had lasted only a couple of minutes, but the four other fighters looked like they had been sparring for hours. Composing themselves, the team of fighters attacked as one, each one carrying out a different attack on a different part of Zach's body. Every attack was powerfully parried by Zach, causing all the other fencers' sabres to fly wildly around. Zach's sabres moved like lightning, each attack causing the sunlight to dance off the newly cleaned steel. Composing themselves again, the team once again tried to defeat Zach. They threw attacks erratically at Zach, but he did not seem to notice. Parrying the last of the blows, Zach took the offensive. Almost flying through the air, he soon placed himself in front of one of his opponents. Blocking a lunge at his chest, Zach wrapped his other arm around the fencer and threw him to the floor. With one of his opponents lying unmoving on the strong wooden floor, Zach chose his next target. Moving himself to the centre of the floor once again, Zach held both his sabres out to his sides and waited for the attack. Sure enough it came, a powerful one aimed at Zach's chest. Seeing the attack early, Zach blocked it with the sabre in his left hand and then slashed twice with the one in his right. From behind him another attack came. Whirling around, he caught the one sabre of his opponent between his two. With his adversary perfectly still, Zach brought his opponent's sabre down with one of his sabres and hit the back of the fencer with the other.

There was now only one opponent left. Fear completely gripped the boy as he saw the rest of his team lying around him. Letting out a cry, he charged at Zach, sabre aimed low. Zach was prepared. When the charge reached him, it was too late for his adversary. In quick succession, one of his sabres thwacked his opponent's out of his hand, causing it to fly across the room and become buried in a wall, and the other sabre slashed twice at the boy's stomach. The spar was over as the four of the fencers lay on the floor, all of them gobsmacked at what had happened. Katie was mesmerized. She had seen no hits on Zach after three spars and no sweat running down his body. He did indeed have talent, but there was something more to it than met the eye.

...

Moving his head from side to side, hearing the melody of clicks and cracks that came from his neck, Zach began to walk away. As he moved away from the hall's centre, he heard something from behind him. It sounded like it was moving fast. Spinning around on his toes, he smashed the sabre out of the hand of one of the downed fencers with his right sabre, and placed the sabre in his left hand at his opponent's throat. Staring at the culprit with enraged red eyes, Zach felt a wave of fear come over his defeated opponent. All Zach needed to do was push and the boy would be dead. It would be so easy to do.

'Ford!' a voice shouted from the end of the hall, causing everyone but Zach to jump out of their skin. Zach turned, his sabre still aimed at the fencer's throat, to see a group of four prefects waiting at the main doors of the hall. It was the tall one at the head of them who had spoken. He was thin and had short blond hair. Zach knew he was the headmaster's son, Carl Green. The other three prefects behind him stood nervous, apprehensive of what they were witnessing.

'It's time for your talk with the headmaster,' Carl said, watching Zach's hands with fear. 'Grab your kit and follow us.'

Turning back to the fencer at the end of his sabre, Zach paused for a moment before withdrawing his weapon. Then he padded back to his corner. Sheathing his sabres and putting the rest of his clothes back on, he strode towards the prefects. As he did so, he caught the eyes of Katie. He had felt her eyes on him throughout the entire session, which had seemed strange but also normal. Something about her intrigued him, but with images of Laura still fresh in his mind, he stopped himself from taking the matter further than intrigue. He walked past the prefects and flew out the door, the troop of prefects turning and struggling to keep up.

Zach had been subjected to this drill hundreds of times before this day. He strode towards the headmaster's office, the troop of prefects still struggling to keep up with his long, powerful strides. Reaching the large white-painted wooden doors, Zach was met by another two prefects. This was standard for him, although no one else in the school was given this treatment, not even Christian and his friends. He stopped as all six of the prefects made a perfect circle around him, all tense and ready for whatever Zach might do. Carl stepped in front of Zach and held out his hands. Zach knew what it meant. As quick as a flash, he drew both of his sabres. All the prefects jumped and took steps back, but Zach was not in the mood for fighting. He placed the weapons into the hands of Carl and then stood stone still, waiting for the doors to open. Carl handed the gleaming sabres to another prefect and turned to the still Zach, who could feel the fear grip the prefect. Even without his sabres, Zach was very dangerous. He resisted Shangal's urge to attack and kill, noting that he had already come too close to killing today.

Carl took a step forward and pressed a red button next to the door. Shortly after, the door opened with a creak. Zach and his entourage entered the room in total silence. Zach knew the room as well as he knew his own house. The fire was still burning in the corner, just like the last time he was in the room, and the two leather sofas were newly cleaned. The group stopped just inside of the door. Rodger was standing at the window.

'Leave us,' he said, still facing the window.

All the prefects looked at each other in confusion. It was Carl who eventually broke the silence.

'Fath … I mean, headmaster, are you sure?' Carl asked.

Rodger turned, annoyance filling his face. Zach could almost taste the frustration. Feeling like he could feast upon it, he suppressed Shangal, who continued to stir within him.

'You two, wait outside,' Rodger replied, composing himself. 'The rest of you, including you, Carl,' he continued, glaring at his son, 'go back to your lessons – now.'

Still looking confused, all of the prefects filed out of the door. Zach saw Carl look back at his father and then shut the door quietly.

Zach looked at the headmaster. Even though he was confused by what had just happened, he did not show it. Rodger looked at Zach for a moment. Moving over to one of the sofas, Rodger sat down and beckoned Zach to do the same. Slowly Zach sat on the sofa opposite, his now normal blue eyes fixing on the headmaster. Zach saw his headmaster struggle under his gaze. The man was obviously uncomfortable being alone with him. *Then why was I summoned?* Zach's eyes were filled with anger and hate. He fought against Shangal, who desperately tried to break through.

'How are you today then, Zach?' Rodger asked, breaking the deathly silence that just a second before had filled the room.

'Say what you want to say and let's get this over and done with,' Zach hissed, his resistance failing.

'Very well,' Rodger said, fear taking hold in his voice. 'Why do you think you are here?'

Zach sat back upon the leather sofa and waited for Rodger to answer the question for him. He always had a tendency to do that with Zach, so the boy just waited for his headmaster to continue rather than waste valuable air. As Zach predicted, Rodger did indeed continue to talk.

'As you know, I have talked to Christian Jones and his friends. They have agreed to leave you be if you leave them to do what they do. Does this sound acceptable?'

Zach stared into the eyes of Rodger. He saw the lie behind his grey eyes and began to laugh loudly.

'You have never been very good at lying, Rodger,' he said, after finally stopping his laughter. 'You did not talk to Christian about that. I know what you use him for.' His humorous tone instantly turned dark and aggressive. Zach could feel Rodger's breaths increase and hear his heart beat faster. The young man tried to calm himself but found that could not, so he stood and walked around the table, positioning himself in front of the frightened headmaster, crouching in front of him, their eyes meeting. Zach, able to feel the quick shallow breaths of Rodger, grinned.

'And how would you imagine,' Zach continued, 'the board of governors, the PTA, and the county council will react when they find out that a trusted headmaster was recruiting bullies to terrorize his pupils, whom he promised would never experience bullying, to leave the school?'

How could he know that? Rodger wondered.

Zach heard Rodger's thought but chose not to reply. Instead, he smiled to himself.

Zach sat back down on the sofa and waited for a response. He could see the headmaster's fear continue to grow. Simultaneously, Zach felt the power inside him grow. His hands began to burn as they had done that morning. Under his fingerless gloves, he could see that the pentagrams on each hand glowed orange. He felt Shangal wanting to burst out of him, but he fought him back, not knowing how much longer he could keep the demon at bay.

'Whatever you know or think you know, Ford, is not so,' Rodger eventually said, still looking at Zach, who began to shift in pain. 'And I have no knowledge of Christian bullying other pupils.'

'Liar!' Zach shouted, his voice demonic and deep, causing Rodger to jump. Zach began to shake violently. His eyes turned blood red, and his teeth grew into fiendish fangs. His hands felt like they were aflame. The brands glowed brightly under his gloves. Once again, Zach spoke, his voice demonic.

'I've seen what he does, every person he has hurt. Every student who has not returned was something done in your name. To deny it is to practically abandon your own students!'

Hearing the raised voices from inside, the two prefects posted outside burst into the room. They gazed in horror as their eyes fell on Zach. He was losing his control no matter how much he fought back. Zach turned quickly and began to growl like a trapped beast. The nails on his hands grew into razor sharp claws, and his fangs grew in length until they slid out of his mouth. He took up an aggressive stance towards the prefects, who were close to cowering in fear. Then Zach opened his arms. He resisted the urge to rip them all apart then and there. He had to regain control. All around him he felt negative energies and emotions. He felt Shangal feed off it and revel in it. The pain was excruciating, but Zach held firm and fought Shangal back.

'Have this victory, mortal,' Shangal seethed in his mind. 'You will not always be strong enough to resist.'

With that, Shangal retreated and Zach began to return to normal. Seeing the fearful faces of Rodger and the prefects, Zach knew he had to go. He swiftly took his leave. None of them dared to stop him as he left. He flew out of sight, Shangal whispering to him as he strode.

Regaining their courage and strength, the prefects stood and checked to see that Zach had left. Rodger stood with a similar expression of amazement and disbelief. His heart fell as he now knew that his own godson, who knew nothing of his real relationship to him, was a monster. He looked at the prefects and gestured at them to leave. Not needing to be told a second time, they both flew out of the door and disappeared down the corridor. Rodger returned to his desk and fell into his chair, still traumatized by seeing his godson in that form. He looked down at his desk and saw the card that James had given to him. Picking it up, he moved his fingers over the elevated letters, which read, in bold gold print, 'David Alexander'. Looking out the window, Rodger contemplated what to do. Should he call the order for help, or should he wait and see what fate had in store?

The door flew open. Carl ran to his father, worry posted across his face.

'Are you OK, Dad?' he asked, putting his hand on his father's shoulder. Shrugging the hand off, Rodger walked across the room to the table that held his diary. He looked at his last appointment of the day. Raising his head slowly, he turned to his son.

'Go to lunch, Carl,' he said quietly. 'I'll see you at the end of the day.'

He heard his son inhale as if to speak, but instead Carl left and slowly closed the door behind him. Rodger often wondered if his son would pay for his mistakes, mistakes that his son did not even know existed.

...

Katie's arms were linked with the arms of the three girls she had met in the changing rooms. Already she felt like part of the school and of the class. As the girls skipped to the field together, Katie still thought of Zach. Her breathing had just now returned to normal after watching him in the sports hall. Her thoughts keep drifting to when she saw his eyes – in both their colours. As the girls got to the edge of the path, Katie stopped and stared at the field. It was the length and width of a football pitch. All along the left and top sides, the pitch was covered by dense woodland, and the other two sides were fenced off. Everyone was outside under the sun, soaking up the rays like sunflowers. Every so often the mass of people lying down would turn over in unison. But in this apparent Eden, there was an anomaly. One of the corners that the woodland had claimed was in constant darkness and decay. Even the ground was dead. Nothing grew there except for an old oak branch, which stretched through the fence, on the other side of which was a mini gorge.

As Katie peered closer, she could swear she saw a figure in there. Trying to discern who or what it was, she felt a hand clasp her shoulder. Jumping and turning, she found the head boy, Carl Green, smiling at her.

'Sorry if I startled you.' His voice was calm. 'I'm here to show you around the field if you want.'

Katie, still trying to recover from her startle, replied, 'No, no, it's fine.' She took a breath. 'I was just going to have a look around the field.'

'Well then,' Carl replied, 'I shall leave you to it.' He smiled and then walked off to the centre of the field, where he was wildly greeted by his friends.

Katie looked back at the decaying space and began to walk towards it. As she got closer, she could feel the eyes of everyone on the field upon her. She heard the cries of Stephanie, Taylor, and Eli, but she choose not to pay them heed as she crossed onto the dead ground. It was a cold and dark place. Katie shivered as she went deeper into the trees. She looked around her at the dead or dying flora. The branches that extended from the trees were like the fingers of a skeleton. The ground was hard and coarse; obviously nothing had grown there for a while. She finally came to an old rusty fence. The metal almost crumbled once she touched it. On the other side was the mini gorge, which was filled with dead leaves and plants that had desperately clung to life but eventually succumbed to death. Looking down the gorge, Katie could see that it led to a hollowed-out tree which looked almost like a cave. She turned back to the light of the opening from which she had come, checking to make sure it had not gone. She felt a chill down her spine as she thought of what did live or dwell in this place.

Katie knew that she did not have to leave for a while. Scanning the area again, she turned to walk back when she heard a rustling from above her. Taking a step forward, she looked up and saw a figure sitting high up on the oak branch. She instantly recognized the figure of Zach. He looked like he was almost crouching on the rapidly decaying branch as if he was going to pounce, but he merely stared back at Katie. Even though she had seen what Zach was capable of, she did not feel fear. Instead, she looked into his eyes, checking to see if they were their usual pale blue colour. Seeing that they were, she took a timid step closer. In a flash of black, Zach leapt off his perch and landed behind Katie. She felt his eyes look her up and down whilst he circled her, taking in everything. Her brown shoulder-length hair was still even though it was windy out. Her dark brown eyes tried to follow his own ever-searching eyes. As Zach continued to circle her, she heard him begin to sniff deeply as if he taking in her scent. She felt uncomfortable but tried her best to remain still as he continued. The fact that she always chose not to douse herself in scented perfumes or sprays added to her confusion about why he was sniffing her. He touched her hair as if sensing her discomfort, and immediately she calmed. After he finished survey her, he positioned himself in front of her. Their gaze again connected, and once again Katie found herself lost within Zach's eyes.

Zach broke the silence, his voice soft and his words clear and precise. It made her heart flutter.

'If you don't know me already, I'm Zach,' he said.

Trying to get her heart under control, Katie thought of what to say, still fearful of scaring Zach. 'Hi. Yeah, I know who you are,' she said quietly. 'I'm Katie.'

She extended her hand in a panicked greeting, but Zach instead bowed to her. Katie was surprised at the greeting, but she smiled, not wishing to be rude. It was the most polite thing anyone had done for her on her first day at her new school. As he rose from the bow, their eyes connected again. She became lost in his eyes once more.

'Are you enjoying your day here?' Zach asked, his voice still soft.

Trying to stop her heart from fluttering, Katie's reply was almost a whisper. 'Yeah, it's quite a maze here.'

Zach chuckled. 'It is quite, but with time I'm sure you will get the hang of things here.'

'I hope so,' Katie replied. 'I kinda like it here.'

...

Zach looked into Katie's eyes. He did not see a trace of a lie. Smelling the air, he concluded that her scent had not changed. Seeing that she was telling the truth, he motioned her to follow him. She did so without a hint of nervousness. She followed him to the entrance, where the sunlight shone on the dead ground. Zach looked with disgust upon the field, where he saw Christian and his henchmen select a target and begin to move in on him. Katie saw it too. Her face filled with equal disgust.

'You may have to change that opinion,' Zach said. 'This place is not like any normal school.'

Katie looked at the bullies as they struck, pinning the young boy to the fence and beginning to taunt him.

'Why doesn't anyone stop them?' she asked, turning to Zach. She noticed that everyone was now looking in fear at Zach's lair. Zach saw the realization hit her. It was he who usually took action, but he showed no intention of doing so today. Effortlessly, he hopped up onto his perch and looked out over the field.

'Why won't you stop them?' she insisted.

'I've always dealt with them. Today I do not want to.' He felt Shangal writhe with anticipation.

'But they are obviously afraid of you. You could be known as a good person, not a loner.'

Zach glared down at her. He could feel his eyes begin to change as Shangal tried again to gain control.

'As it is your first day,' Zach spoke, his voice now low and demonic, 'I will show you what happens when I take action.'

In a flash Zach, leapt from his branch, not snapping a single twig. His form flew through the air, and then he landed gracefully in front of Christian. All of Christian's henchmen backed away as the two boys stared at each other. Everyone on the field stopped what they were doing and watched as Zach moved towards closer to Christian. Catching a glimpse of Katie running to the centre of the field, Zach kept his attention on Christian. It was Christian who made the first attack. With the hockey stick he held in his left hand, he swung at Zach's head. With little effort, Zach dodged the attack and caught the hockey stick in his right hand. With his left hand, Zach uppercut Christian's chin, sending the boy flying to the ground. Picking himself up, Christian stared back at Zach, anger filling his face. Composing himself, Christian charged at Zach, trying to tackle him to the ground. In another lightning move, Zach vaulted over the charging Christian. As he landed, Zach grabbed the now falling Christian's leg and yanked him back along the ground to the place where he had started charging. As Christian landed, Zach again leapt into the air, this time landing by Christian's head. Christian was now weak and in pain as Zach lifted his head and looked into his eyes. Seeing the weakness and pain, Zach roughly dropped his adversary's head and strode towards the dead zone. All the while, Shangal fed on the violence and hate. Zach felt the eyes of the whole school on him as he marched. He could feel their fear, but he did not care for any of them. All he had to do was resist another of Shangal's attempt to gain control. Shangal was more persistent than before as the battle of wills began. Zach could feel a presence approaching and heard a voice call out. He had to escape. His legs were not his own as he ran.

...

Everyone looked away with mixed feelings, some in horror, as Christian was a good friend to them, and others with a sense of satisfaction as Christian's henchmen carried their leader inside. Katie did not know what to think. She stood still like a statue as everyone else continued on with their lunch, obviously forgetting what had just happened. Katie did not know what to do. Once again composing herself, she marched back to the dead area, again oblivious to the shouts of warning from her classmates. Walking back into the lair, Katie looked around. Zach was nowhere to be seen. Still scanning the area, she heard footsteps from behind her. She turned, expecting Zach, but it was Taylor standing at the edge of the dead area.

'Katie, are you in there?' Taylor shouted, fear gripping her.

Seeing that Zach was not there, Katie turned and walked out of the area. Taylor took her back to a group of people who were bathing in the sun. She introduced them all to Katie. It was then that Katie felt more at ease, but even so she had to see Zach before the day finished.

...

Zach had fled to the front of the school, where there was another area the pupils could go to during their breaks. It was not as big as the playing field, but it was dry and clean. Pupils still chose not to go there. It was simply three little areas of grass, each surrounded by a high hedge and with huge fir trees growing in the middle. The hedge was not just a border for each little area; it was also a system of paths which linked all the areas together. It was deathly quiet, as no one was in anyone of these little areas. The only sounds were those of the birds as they scurried through the branches of the fir trees.

Zach appeared out of the woods and quickly surveyed the area. It was empty, but he was not alone. His legs ached after the run, and his eyes were still blood red. Shangal was only partly summoned, but that was enough for the demon. Zach had managed to retract his claws on the way there, but nevertheless he wanted Shangal completely gone.

'Why did you run?' Shangal asked through Zach's mouth. 'You coward.'

'I will not kill anyone,' Zach replied, still fighting to take control of himself. 'I will not use you. Why are you still here?'

'Because of this!' Shangal roared.

Zach's hands burned orange again. The pain was excruciating, but there was nothing he could do as Shangal pointed them at a nearby tree. Zach tried to fight it, but Shangal would not give in. With Zach's hands aimed at the tree, Shangal jerked them forward. Out of both of them flew balls of fire, which pounded the trees, causing them to catch fire. Zach's face contorted in shock as he looked at the sky. Then he had a thought. He stretched his right arm up to the sky and the left to the now burning trees. Instantly the rain fell. In seconds, the trees were doused and started to regenerate. Smiling to himself, Zach began to walk away, but then he was flung across the area and hit one of the regenerating trees. Shangal then appeared in front of him. Zach showed no fear. Instead, he smiled.

'Didn't expect that, did you, demon?' Zach laughed.

Shangal's face was full of anger. Never had his own powers been used by any of his former hosts. This boy was smarter than he had thought. He now smiled back to his mortal host.

'No, I did not,' he replied. 'Maybe this new life for us could be a bit more interesting now that I am here. But hear me, human,' he continued, 'you do not control me; I control you.'

'We'll see who controls who when the time comes,' Zach replied.

With that, Shangal disappeared back into Zach. This time there was no pain, as Zach had gotten used to it now. The rain continued to fall. It got heavier and the wind grew fiercer. Zach did not care. It soothed his burned hands and cooled his aching body.

Hearing rustling from behind him, Zach slowly turned and saw the figure of a thin girl, her long blonde hair waving in the wind, her dark blue eyes staring in fear at him. He knew then that she had witnessed everything and now feared of speaking. The girl's name was Katherine White. She was one of Zach's oldest friends, but lately she had remained distant from him. This was the first time they had met alone in months. Stepping forward timidly, she spoke. Her voice was soft and quiet.

'I saw everything you just did,' she said fearfully. 'What's happened to you?'

Zach looked into her eyes, remembering the days when he and she had been inseparable, the days when they swam in the rivers near to where he lived. But those days were long gone. It killed him to know that there was no going back. Composing himself, he responded, 'I don't know. For your own good, Kat, leave now and don't look back.'

Saying those words burned a hole deep within Zach, but he knew it was better than hurting Kat. He had lost much more before losing her. What was another person to add to that list? Seeing that this was her only chance to go, Katherine walked quickly away from her old friend, and as he requested she did not look back. Zach stood in the centre of the area. His tears began to fall, and with them came the storm.

...

Everyone on the playing field began to run inside. No one had expected a storm to come up that quickly, but no one cared as they ran for cover. Taylor dragged Katie all the way until they were well inside the building. Everyone was then ordered by the now soaked prefects to go to their form rooms to be registered. Before she could catch her breath, Katie was grabbed by Taylor and dragged to the form room. It would have been helpful if Taylor had held onto her upper arm instead of taken her by the wrist. The pain was mild but still very annoying. In what seemed like seconds, Katie was flung through the form room door, where sat in the back row with Taylor and her friends.

'Where the hell did that rain come from?' she shouted to Eli.

'Do I look like a weatherman?' she screamed back.

Katie was equally as afraid as the others. Never had she seen a storm of that magnitude build up that quickly. It was almost supernatural.

The form room door crashed open again as Mrs Woods came through, looking equally as wet as her students. She again began to call the register. So far, everyone was there. When she called out Zach's name, there was no reply. Everyone look around the classroom. He was not there. The storm was getting more and more fierce. Pupils now began to cower underneath desks. Katie looked out the window and saw the figure of Zach. He was moving as if oblivious to the raging storm above. The wind was now blowing with a force that shook the cars and rattled windows. The rain turned to hail, which sounded like whistle bullets as they flew past the windows. Katie rose from her seat, banged on the window, and shouted at Zach, but he could not hear her and instead stood on the open ground and spread his arms. The storm raged even more as he did so. Katie stared at him as she heard him speak to the storm.

'You do not control me!' he shouted.

With those words echoing in the wind, the storm broke up and almost seemed to evaporate. Then all was call. The sun once again shone, all evidence of the storm now gone.

Inside the building, people picked themselves up off the floor and looked outside. They all saw Zach. He was standing like a statue. His arms had fallen to his sides, and his hands were curled into fists. But other than that, his body seemed lifeless. Katie looked into his eyes. They were not the pale blue or the blood red that they usually were; they were now jet-black, no irises, no scleras. They were completely black. He looked around as if he could feel the many pairs of eyes staring at him. Katie knew something was wrong.

Zach appeared strange as he strode towards the school. Katie saw him move back through the main doors. Everyone was shocked by what they saw. Zach did not just stop the storm; he commanded it. The PA speaker in the corner of the room burst to life, causing everyone in the room to jump as the familiar voice of the headmaster blasted through it.

'Due to unforeseen circumstances, all students are to leave the school grounds and return at the normal time tomorrow. All teachers are to report to the staff room immediately.'

All of the students looked at each other and cheered loudly once the announcement finished.

'Sweet,' Christian boomed from his desk, his face covered in plasters. 'The freak should do that more often. Think of everything I can do with a half day with no homework!' He and his friends shot out of the room without another glance back. Soon it was only Katie, before she was grabbed by an unfamiliar person and led out into the gardens. Once Katie was eventually let go, she looked upon someone whom she recognized from the school but whose name she did not know. She regarded her long blonde hair dancing in the calming breeze.

Managing to catch her breath, Katie asked, 'Do I know you?'

The girl shook her head slowly.

'Do you know what happened today?' Katie continued slowly, knowing that scaring the already frightened girl would be disastrous.

'All I know is that you are the only one who can cure him.' The girl's voice was very quiet as she spoke.

'Cure him?' Katie frowned. 'What do you mean?'

'He hasn't been the same since the holidays,' she explained. 'Ever since his accident, it is like he is not him anymore. And with all the rumours being spread about him and what the headmaster is doing, I don't think anyone is safe here.'

Katie did not know what to think. This young girl who looked like she had seen the future was telling Katie that she was the only hope to stop a disaster that she did not know of. Worst of all is that Katie had seen what Zach was capable of. At the same time, she knew that what she had witnessed was just the embers of the fire that was burning. Katie looked up, the clouds from the thunderstorm gone and the sun still shining through. She knew Zach would be long gone, but she had to try to save him, not just for the terrified girl who stood before her, but for everyone. As Katie she regained her thoughts and stood there, she saw that the girl had gone.

CHAPTER 5

KATIE TURNED THE KEY IN the lock of the large door and opened it without a sound. She was instantly greeted by a barking dog who, after seeing her master, lay on her back with her tail wagging.

'Hey, Rosie.' Katie bent down and stroked the excited collie–Labrador cross who was clearly enjoying the attention. Katie's house was big. It was the largest in the row, both in height and width. The grey colour on the outside was only a mask for the bright colours and unique patterns of each room on the inside. There was a crash of movement as a tall young boy sprang down the stairs, landing on Katie. It was her younger brother, Tyler. He had all the same features as Katie but was much taller. Even though he was only eleven, he stood at six feet tall, with already broadening shoulders. Picking his now out-of-breath sister off the ground, Tyler hugged her again. He hated it when his sister had to go to another school away from him, but now that she was back, he was jumping with excitement and happiness.

'You have fun today, Katie?' he asked, still embracing his sister.

'It was OK,' she replied with her face firmly implanted in her brother's chest. 'It was a bit of a drag.' She laughed at the private joke she had made with her brother, whose embrace began to weaken. Once he let go of her, Katie went into the huge kitchen beyond the entrance hall. Just like all the other rooms in the house, the kitchen was large and extravagant. In the centre was a large oak table with six chairs placed neatly around it. On the edges of the kitchen were numerous leather seats and sofas which were crammed with miscellaneous items like school bags and shoes. Katie sighed to herself at seeing the mess.

There was a loud clunk from behind her, which made her turn quickly. She found herself gazing into the eyes of her mother, Daisy. 'How was your day, sweetie?' Daisy asked. Katie sighed and told her mother the edited version of the day, skipping the various experiences she'd had with Zach. 'Sounds like you had a good time then,' Daisy probed. She took a genuine interest in her daughter's activities, not out of overprotection but of general interest.

'Yeah, it was OK.'

'Good,' her mother replied. 'Your father is upstairs.'

'Waiting to interrogate me, is he?' Katie joked.

'Most likely. Just give him the edited version like you gave me and you'll be fine.'

Katie blushed at the comment and looked into her mother's eyes.

'You have never been a good liar,' Daisy pointed out. 'You get that from me.'

Katie smiled, headed out of the kitchen, and began to climb the stairs in search of her father.

The rest of the house was in disarray just like the kitchen. Clothes, toys, and other assortments of objects clogged the corridors. Having lived here for many years, Katie was used to it. Once she reached the top of the first flight, she turned right and knocked on the small white door.

'Enter,' a deep voice eventually answered from the other side.

Katie obeyed and stepped through the door, where a heavyset man sat bolt upright on a computer chair. His concentration was not on his daughter at first; it was on the computer screen where he read emails. Seeing the reflection of his daughter in the screen, he turned on his chair so that his body completely blocked the now black screen.

'Hi, Dad,' Katie eventually said. 'How was your day?'

'It was OK,' he replied. 'How was school?'

'It wasn't too bad,' Katie lied. 'People there are very nice.'

After the strangely brief interrogation, Katie ascended yet another flight of stairs, this one coming out onto a landing that was shaped like the others below it. Turning left, Katie opened a door and entered her large, light-filled room. It had a total of three windows, which all had very thin curtains to attempt to block the rays of sunlight that blazed down onto the house. Her room was was untidy as usual, just how she had left it that morning. As she slung her bag onto the floor, she made her way over to the largest of the three windows. The view outside showed a vast area of fields and an intricate network of small rivers that snaked around the various mounds that grew out of the field. She gazed out over the field. Her thoughts drifted to what she had witnessed today. She had never seen or heard of anything like what she had seen today. Turning her thoughts to Zach, she wondered how he lived the way he lived and how he had survived so long in his current state. She had to find out, no matter what the cost was.

...

The ever continuous stream of rain pelted from the sky with force as Zach stepped off the bus after school. Feeling the various pairs of eyes on him, he chose to ignore them as he began gliding to his house. The door opened silently as Zach walked through, the rainwater dripping off his raven-black hair and onto the always dirty floor. A single letter lay on the floor, one that he had been expecting for a while. He picked it up and read it. As he suspected, it was a note from the council. His reposition was imminent. There was nothing else he could sell now. He would have to go. But where to? He had no family, no friends, no home, and nowhere to go. Still, he was used to being alone. What seemed like a lifetime of people avoiding him had accustomed him to loneliness. He did not dread leaving, as the house brought back far too many bad memories. Instead, he lived in dread that those memories would never leave him.

Leaving the opened letter on the floor where he'd found it, Zach walked to his room. He dumped his soaked bag onto the floor and looked around. The room was still charred after the morning. The futon on the floor was the worst, as the ash had solidified. It was still standing, almost like a dormant fire. Zach hated what had happened and what he had become. Although people always said there was a light at the end of the tunnel, he believed there was no light for him. It had been drowned out by an eternal night of misery and anger. He could feel Shangal in him, but for some reason the demon chose not come out. Zach did not feel relief. He didn't feel anything anymore, just pain. He set about packing into his small bag whichever of his things were not charred. So much of what he owned had been destroyed that his bag had enough room for the sabres to fit in.

With his bag hardly packed and nothing else to put inside it, Zach placed it gently on the floor outside his blackened room. He looked around the house, which had once been a place of much noise and activity. It hosted parties and functions that were always of great excitement to the village and its occupants, but now it had nothing but marks where pictures, chairs, and shelves used to be. Zach's eyes turned black with pain as he saw the emptiness of the structure he lived in. But he fought against his demon, barely managing to put him back into his body. It was going to be another long, dark night for Zach Ford.

...

The car pulled up to the heavy doors of the school. It was larger than any other car that had passed that way all day. In his office, Rodger stiffened. He had long thought about whether calling this mysterious David Alexander had been a good idea, but with hearing the car stop by the door, all his thoughts disappeared. He had chosen to call him, and now he would see what the man wanted or what he could do to help. Rodger heard the heavy doors open and slight movement outside. Then there was a single rap at the door.

'Enter,' Rodger said, trying to sound calm.

James was the first to enter. He was not wearing his familiar motorcycle suit but was in a suit and tie, something Rodger had never seen him wear before. Behind James entered three other people, two of whom were dressed like bodyguards, in black suits and trousers with white shirts and black ties. Both had earpieces in their right ears. The final man, however, was different from all of them. He was dressed much like a scientist, wearing a long brown overcoat which hid a thin grey waistcoat with matching trousers and a white shirt. He wore no tie, which Rodger found peculiar, but he did wear thing eyeglasses. In his right hand he carried a leather briefcase. Rodger guessed this was David Alexander.

'David Alexander.' The scientist stretched out his hand.

'Rodger Green.' He accepted the hand and shook it, surprised by how tight the scientist's grip was.

'Please, sit.' Rodger motioned to the leather sofas in the middle of his spacious office.

David Alexander sat. In a flash, his briefcase was open on the table and he began flicking through files. His bodyguards stood at either side of the door, their hands crossed in front of them, and Rodger sat on the single chair behind the computer. After a few quick flicks of his selected file, David Alexander spoke.

'I understand you have a problem here, Mister Green?'

'Please, Rodger will do. Before I give my details, I would be interested to know your profession.'

'An acceptable request,' David Alexander replied, cleaning his glasses. 'I am a neurobiologist, which means that I deal with people who are mentally unstable. When they are past the help of counsellors, then they are referred to me to see if I can find a scientific way of helping them.'

Rodger was perplexed by what had been said. Nevertheless, he tried to keep his expression blank.

'I don't think my problem here is in your skill range,' Rodger explained. 'The boy is not only mentally unstable; he is unstable in every way.'

'Well, from what your associate has told me,' David Alexander continued, with a quick glance at James, 'the situation falls into my field of expertise. The boy shows unparalleled capabilities which far surpass any normal human's, or for that matter any normal animal's, on the planet.'

Rodger listened as David Alexander went on. Confusion was still in him. *There is more to this man than meets the eye*, he thought, *but what is it?*

'From what has been told to me by various people in my employ, the boy is, in the word they like to use, supernatural. I have seen CCTV footage from here and from locations nearby showing what he is capable of. But I know there is more. I will need your help to get the answers I need, before I carry out the operation.'

'How can I help?' Rodger asked, dreading what the answer would mean to him.

'Firstly, we need to establish triggers. I know that anger and sadness can trigger episodes in mentally unstable patients, so I will need to know if that is the case with this boy. Does he have any close friends here whom he cares about?'

'To my knowledge, he has none. Since the accident, it was my request that the students break all bonds with him.'

David Alexander looked up from his pad of paper, on which he had been writing notes. His green eyes scanned Rodger. 'Is there something that I have not been told?' he asked, his eyes darting from Rodger to James.

With a sigh, Rodger replied, 'I am the cause for why the boy is like this. I am his godfather. I arranged for his family to be killed. All of this is my fault.'

David Alexander laughed. 'You make it sound like this is a bad thing. Well, let me assure you, it is not. You may very well have brought the first case of supernatural behaviour to humanity. This is big. Think of what he will be worth.'

Rodger did not quite understand what he was hearing. He had made a confession of murder, but instead of being told it was wrong, he was being told it would lead to a much better outcome. It suddenly hit him: this man truly was a lot more than he was saying. But what could Rodger do now? He had already met him and had made his confession. If he said no to David Alexander, then he would most likely turn Rodger in and take Zach anyway. Rodger had to bite the bullet and do what was asked of him. He looked back at David Alexander whose eyes were gleaming.

'What do you want me to do?' Rodger asked.

'I need you to find someone he cares about and exploit him or her so that we can have evidence of what his triggers are. It will be useful to know this before we act.'

'What will happen then?'

'I have already approached some members of your school. These people know what to do once you have found the boy. This must be done quickly or else we could lose him.'

Rodger nodded in agreement.

'I do believe that we understand each other,' David Alexander spoke, 'in which case I will leave you to your searching. Nothing must appear out of the ordinary to him. Keep everything normal and you will be famous before you know it.'

With those last words, David Alexander rose and left the room, taking with him his now closed briefcase. His two bodyguards followed closely after, leaving only Rodger and James in the office. Rodger motioned for James to go. He did so quickly, knowing his superior needed to think.

With the room to himself, Rodger set about planning for finding Zach's weakness.

…

It was a bright day. The sun was beating down on the school with warmth that was unseasonal. The morning's lessons had been uneventful for Katie, who had been waiting for the break bell all day. She could feel the eyes of Zach on her. Today they were their usual shade of pale blue, which matched the colour of the cloudless sky. After the strange weather of the previous day, everyone was a little on edge on account of his being back, but no one showed it. Katie noticed that Christian was a lot quieter than usual. He kept his conversations between him and his group, whispers which no one else could hear. When the bell rang, everyone put their books and other things away in preparation for making their way to the field for lunch. As Katie stood, she felt far more eyes on her than usual. Usually it was just the eyes of Zach that she felt, but today Christian and his group followed her with their eyes, like a pride of lions staring down an outsider.

She knew Zach would already be outside, so she went to her locker and put her things into it in what could be seen as a panic.

'In some rush, are we?' The familiar voice made her jump. Turning, she saw Christian behind her. He was alone and not with his brood, as she privately called them.

So he can function without them, she thought. *I learn something new every day.*

She chuckled to herself, but she soon realized that she was laughing in front of Christian.

'I'm glad I make you laugh,' he continued. 'It's something I always look for in a girl.'

She stopped laughing. Now knowing the stem of Christian's interest in her, she did not want to do anything to encourage him.

'I simply want to be out in the sun,' she replied. 'Who wouldn't want to be out today?'

She tried to escape, but Christian put his arms on either side of her body and rested them on the lockers behind her. There was no way she was getting out now.

'Why the hurry?' he asked. 'You have an hour and a half to enjoy the sun. I just want a few minutes to chat.'

'I know what you want,' she countered, 'and my answer is no. Now move.'

'A feisty one, aren't you?' he taunted. 'Come on, just a few minutes.' He leaned closer.

'You really do not know the meaning of the word *no*, do you?'

Christian spun round to find Zach standing behind him, blue eyes fixing him with a glare. Christian stood in fear as Zach took a step towards him, forcing Christian to back away from Katie, who then darted behind Zach for safety.

'I suggest you read one of these.' Zach held out a small dictionary and motioned Christian to take it. 'It seems you have a problem with understanding some words. That wouldn't be good for your exams, now, would it?'

...

Christian was red with anger as he took the dictionary. He had been made a fool of again and had had enough. As Zach and Katie walked off, he prepared to throw the dictionary at Zach's head, but as he got in line to do so, the dictionary sparked and caught on fire, soon turning into a small pile of ash and dust before Christian's eyes. Anger festering in him, Christian pulled out his mobile phone and began to type a text message: 'Weakness found. What is the next move?'

After a few minutes of standing by the ash pile, Christian felt his mobile phone vibrate. He read the reply: 'Be certain that it is. When you are sure, call me tonight at precisely 7 p.m. and I will tell you stage two.'

Knowing what he had to do, Christian slipped his phone back into his blazer pocket and strode outside and into the sun.

...

Katie had never felt more relaxed than when she was in the dead part of the field with Zach. They had come there a different way from the one they had taken last time. Instead of crossing the field, they had gone through the thick dead wood that surrounded the dead section of the field. Katie was still trying to figure out what Zach's story was as she sat on a branch that Zach had shaped like a bench. She stared at him. He was again crouched on his perch and looking out over the field at the other pupils, who were soaking up the rays of the sun. After a few minutes of silence, Katie spoke.

'Thank you, for what you did back there.'

'It's OK,' Zach replied, not looking at her. His eyes were darting around the field.

'Can I ask a personal question?' Katie again broke the silence.

Zach now turned to look at her, his blue eyes showing nothing of what he was thinking.

'Of course,' he replied, hopping off his perch and coming to stand in front of her.

Taking a deep breath, Katie spoke, nervous about what might happen. 'Are you a vampire?' she finally asked.

Zach looked at her and smiled, failing to contain a laugh. 'Why do you ask?'

'Well, you're inhumanly fast, you're strong, you speak like you're from a Shakespeare play, your eyes change colour, and you never go into the sunlight.'

Zach gave her a perplexed look. Instead of talking, he took off his blazer and shirt, showing his pale white skin. Katie gasped as she saw the silvery scars that riddled his front and back as he allowed her to look. He turned and walked into the sunlight. Nothing happened. Zach turned and spoke.

'I'm sorry to disappoint,' he said, still in the sunlight. 'No turning to ash, no sparkling, no screams of pain, and no disintegration.'

Satisfied that Katie now knew the answer to her question, Zach put on his white shirt and blazer and stood in front of Katie once again, who was visibly shocked at what she saw. After the shock came the confusion.

'Then what are you?' she blurted out.

Zach looked at her. 'Why must you know?' he responded, climbing back up to his perch.

'You're not normal,' she explained. 'Not everyone can do what you do. In fact, I think you are the only one who can do what you do. I need to know.'

Zach's eyes did not leave hers as she spoke.

'Why do you need to know?' he asked. 'Can't you accept the fact I am not normal?'

'No, I won't,' she replied with determination. 'You have a gift. You are different, unique. Think about what you could give to others.'

Zach looked back at the field. After a few moments of silence, he looked back at her.

'I will make you a deal,' he said. 'If you find a book in the library and bring it to me, I will show you. Is that acceptable?'

'What book?' she asked.

'First you have to ask Misses Cotton to translate this.'

Katie was stunned as he wrote something down and handed her the scrap of paper on which was printed words in a language she had never seen before.

'Do I have a time limit?' she asked, very confused about what she had been given.

'No, just don't leave it too long,' Zach replied. 'Who knows what may happen.' As he spoke, his pale blue eyes changed to a darker shade of blue. She could feel him become tense. 'I think it's time to get inside now,' he told Katie.

She looked at Zach with confusion, but then she complied. She had not earned his complete trust, but she was slowly getting there. As she walked away from the dead part of the field, the heat of the sun warmed her and made her eyes squint. Zach's area was having an effect on her. She started to look back towards the dead zone, but before her eyes got there, they caught sight of Christian. Something was different about him. He was not his arrogant, overconfident self. He was looking pensively at the dead zone as if planning an attack.

Soon after the bell sounded, everyone began to file back inside. It was time for the last of the new lessons that Katie had to be introduced to, and unfortunately for her it also happened to be the worst. It was not just that the lesson was physics and was unanimously boring but also that the teacher, Mrs Bates, was as boring as the class she ran – and a terrible teacher to boot. Katie had spent much of her time walking to the laboratory hearing from everyone how bad the class was. Soon she was there, in the middle most laboratory, which happened to be the largest. As everyone reluctantly filed into the room, she soon understood and agreed with everyone's comments.

Her first experience of the lesson was Mrs Bates slamming down four textbooks, a writing book, and two sheets of A4 paper, stating all the work that Katie had to catch up on and the date on which it all had to be done. Katie felt overwhelmed already and the lesson hadn't even started.

'Right. Settle down, everyone,' Mrs Bates said in her annoying croaky voice.

Everyone took their time getting to their seats. Once there, they slowly pulled out their menagerie of books and pieces of paper.

'Oh God,' Katie said to herself. 'I swear, this class has more crap given out than any other in the whole school.'

'You'd be right there.'

She jumped as Zach glided past her without a sound. He was running late as he always did. None of the teachers minded, except Mrs Bates, who seemed to have an unnatural hatred of Zach.

'Late again, Ford.' She made a note on a scrap of paper, but still her lens-covered eyes were fixed on him. Zach took a seat by himself at the back of the room as he usually did and seemed to have ignored Bates' comment.

'What do you have to say for yourself?' she asked.

Again, Zach ignored her and stared back into her eyes.

This is obviously usual, Katie thought. After what seemed like an eternity of undisturbed eye contact, Mrs Bates turned to her board and began her lesson.

At the end of the period, the bell rang for the last time of the day. Quickly everyone in the physics laboratory jumped up and left before Bates could give them any more work. As if Katie needed anymore. She struggled to put her many books into her bag. As she walked out of the room, she knew her night would be filled with work. Her feeling of being overwhelmed changed to one of near desperation. She wondered how she was going to do everything Bates had asked her to do, but she knew she had to try. Then, remembering the book that Zach had asked her to get, she swore to herself.

At that moment, Zach appeared in front of her. 'Don't worry too much about the work,' he said. 'It's easier than it looks.' He ran his hands over her bag of books and then, with a smile, disappeared down the corridor and out of sight. Katie took time to come back to the room. Zach always made her feel giddy and different. As she zipped up her bag, she noticed that her new books had been written on. She opened the bag and found that all the work she had to do was in there. Looking down the corridor, she didn't see Zach, she hefted her bag, left the school building, and started her journey home.

...

Christian had shadowed Zach and Katie as best as he could for the whole day. He had written down everything he could and had also told his henchmen the vague plan. He saw Zach talk to Katie before he left and knew that this was the weakness David Alexander was looking for. He had already informed his brood. Things would happen as his new employer had ordered, at 7 p.m. precisely.

CHAPTER 6

THE PHONE VIBRATED ON THE smooth oak table. David Alexander had been waiting for this call all day. He picked up the phone and read the message: 'Definite weakness confirmed. Name: Katie Oldman.' David Alexander opened his private search program on his computer and found Katie. Her full name, her address, and everything else about her was there. He copied the file onto the phone, as well as the instructions: 'Saturday, Methodist Church Hall, 8 p.m. Make sure she is there.' With the message sent, David relaxed and sipped his whisky. Many years of research would finally amount to something. He was pleased that everything was falling into place as planned. The order would be pleased too.

...

Katie awoke suddenly. It was still early. She was thankful that it was the beginning of the weekend. When she had returned home the previous night, she flicked through the work that had appeared in her books. Everything was there and completed to a good standard. Zach had obviously given her a helping hand, but why and how were the questions filling her head. She had also found a book reference, neatly written down on a scrap of paper. This was most likely the book that Zach wanted her to find. It was a day at the library for her. She had to find that book.

After she had eaten breakfast, she began her walk to the town centre. It was not a long walk, but it was very picturesque. Her stroll took her through a public park and past the impressive Salisbury Cathedral. The scaffolding was still up, as the cathedral was being renovated to make the spire less crooked. The sun was again out, and what seemed like the entire populace was out in the parks soaking up the sun and swimming in the river. But Katie was not bound to do that. Her mission was to find the book and find out what Zach was.

After a short walk past shops and more public parks, she found the library. It was a large modern building, nothing like the cliché libraries that she hated. She entered the doors and went immediately to the help desk, where she was directed to the fifth floor. She complied, got into the nearest lift, and ascended the levels of the huge building. Thoughts and visions continued to spiral in her mind. *What is he? How does he live? Where does he live?* So many questions, so little time.

The metal doors slid open with a creak, revealing a large floor filled with shelves upon shelves of books. There was hardly anyone on that floor, apart from a middle-aged man at the help desk. He did not seem to be very interested in anything apart from his book in which he seemed to be engrossed. Katie looked at the piece of paper she had been given. The book reference led her to the religious section. Scanning the shelf, she found the book: *The Purple Star*. It was in immaculate condition. Obviously no one had checked it out in a while. Having found what she was searching for, she went to the desk and checked it out.

As she turned, she saw a familiar face: Christian Jones. Panicking, she hid behind the nearest shelf. He was the last person she wanted to see. It was strange to see him by himself, and of all places in the library. Peering around the shelf, she saw he was by the help desk. She heard him ask the woman at the help desk if any she had seen her. The woman glanced in the direction of Katie and smiled to herself.

'She is on the fifth floor, young man, in the religious section.'

With a nod, Christian flew to the lift. Slowly, Katie emerged. 'Thanks,' she said to the lady at the desk.

'Ex-boyfriend?' she asked.

'Something like that.'

With another smile and a nod, Katie was out and headed home, walking a lot quicker than usual. She felt so much safer when she crossed the bridge opposite the library. It was then that she turned to look at the library. Her heart stopped in fear. Christian saw her. She saw his face turn red as he flew away from the window. Katie did not wait; she ran.

Why is he chasing me? she thought. She did not want to know why. Her house was not that far, but Christian was fast. By the time she was on the other side of the bridge, Christian was out of the library and running towards her. She would have to lose him. Behind her was a multistorey car park, one that Katie knew well. She would lose him in there. She vaulted the wall and crouched down behind a car. And then she waited.

She did not have to wait long before she heard the slowing footsteps over by the exit. Christian came to a stop and scanned the car park. He knew she was in there. She did not have to speed to outrun him. He slowly walked forward, his footsteps echoing around the car park. Katie peered under the car she was hiding behind. All she could see was his feet. Clutching the book, she waited until he passed before creeping to the next row. She made it. Trying to hold back the urge to pant, she lay down and looked under the cars to see where Christian was. She could hear but not see the heavy, echoing footsteps. She began to panic. *What if he knows where I am?* she thought. She remained where she was, motionless.

Christian was getting impatient. He knew she was in there, as he had not heard her run. He did not hear anything. He resisted the urge to call out her name. *I would just be broadcasting my whereabouts,* he thought. He continued to walk. If he did not get Katie, then he would be in a lot of trouble. 'We only have one chance at this,' the voice in his head had said, 'so don't balls it up!'

He would find her. Suddenly he stopped. There was something he had not tried yet. He crouched down and scanned under the cars. It did not him take long to spot his target, who stared fearfully back at him. 'Got ya,' he said, smiling.

Katie leapt up. Christian had found her. There was only one thing she could think of to do: run. Clutching *The Purple Star*, she ran from her hiding place. She could not outrun him or hide from him. Her only hope was to get home by losing him in the ever-growing Saturday crowds. Jumping over a wall, she was soon by the river. Follow the river home: she always remembered that. She ran as fast as she could through the crowds, Christian keeping pace behind her. She was nearly there. Running through one of the public parks, she noticed that no one offered her help, probably thinking it was just teenaged silliness, even though in reality it was far more. Christian was gaining. She was now able to see her house. *Not much farther.*

Christian was very close now, so close he could hear her panting. Stretching out his hand, he tried to grab Katie on the shoulder. With a yank, he had her. Katie let out a terrified scream.

'Shut up,' he said, placing a hand over her mouth. 'Shut up.' But she continued to scream. With nothing working, Christian wrapped his right arm around her neck. Slowly her screams and struggling ceased and she lay limp in his arms. *Good old sleeper hold,* he thought, content with himself. He pulled out his phone and began to text: 'Got the girl. Come and ...' The text was never finished.

He had watched the chase and timed it perfectly. Grabbing Christian's shoulder, he hauled him and his unconscious charge towards the abandoned house. He was so powerful that Christian dropped his phone, which shattered into pieces on the concrete pavement. Before Christian could react, Katie was taken off his shoulder. He was now staring into the angry blue eyes of Zach. Zach, having laid Katie on the ground nearby, glared at Christian. His eyes turned black. He wanted so much to kill Christian then and there, but he was not a monster – not yet. Holding Christian by the shoulders, Zach head butted him in the temple. Christian was now as limp as Katie. With a thud, Zach flung Christian to the ground and walked over to Katie. She was still alive with no permanent damage. Bruises began to show on her neck. Zach moved a gloved hand over her forehead. The bruises disappeared and Katie began to stir.

Slowly Katie's eyes opened. Everything was fuzzy and out of focus, but she could make out the form of someone in front of her.

'Katie?' she heard a familiar voice ask.

'Zach?' she responded. 'Where am I? How did you get here? Where is Christian?'

'Too many questions to ask when you're in this state,' Zach answered with a smile. 'Let's get you home.'

Zach bent over and picked up Katie in both his arms. Her vision was now back. She could see the unconscious form of Christian slumped on the ground by a tree stump. She then turned to look at Zach. His eyes were blue and looking forward. He knew where he was going, which surprised Katie. They were a matter of metres from her house. Zach ascended the stairs in front of the door and rang the doorbell. The loud defensive barking of Rosie began. Katie whistled softly, at which point the barking stopped. Soon the door opened. A young, tall form looked back at Zach, who holding Katie in her fragile state.

'Mum!' Tyler called.

Daisy Oldman poked her head around the door of the kitchen and saw what Tyler saw. She stopped and put down everything she had been holding, shock filling her face.

'Let them in, Tyler,' she said quickly.

She cleared the large oak table in the kitchen and watched as Zach carefully laid Katie on it, not making one sound.

'What happened to her?' Daisy asked, looking from Zach to Katie.

'Just heatstroke,' Zach lied. 'I found her in the park. She is fine now.'

Daisy filled up a glass of water and grabbed a damp cloth.

'Drink this, dear.' Daisy held out the glass. Katie sat up, took the glass, and sipped the water, the whole time not taking her eyes off Zach. Katie had never lied to her mother, but here she was playing along with a lie that someone else had told. She smiled to herself. *He obviously cares,* she thought.

'Sorry, I didn't catch your name,' Daisy said to the young man who had brought her daughter home.

'I'm Zach,' he answered.

'I am Daisy,' she spoke, 'and the boy behind you is Tyler.'

Zach turned round and looked at the tall form of Tyler. 'You're a big lad, aren't you?' Zach asked, smiling at Tyler.

Tyler looked at the floor shyly and then disappeared up the stairs. Zach turned to Katie. Her eyes were still on him. He could feel the affection she showed him, but images of Laura were still in his mind, scarring him mentally.

There was a long silence as Daisy tended to her daughter. Soon she was done. Katie was still very weak.

'I'm sorry, Zach,' Daisy said, turning around, 'but could you carry her up to her room? She needs rest.'

'Of course,' Zach replied. He carefully and silently picked her up and followed Daisy, accompanied by Rosie, who was frantically trying to get a sense of who this strange new person was. The house was huge, three vast floors all with different designs and odours. The top floor was his destination. Daisy opened a door to a large room. A queen-sized bed filled the centre, and all along the walls were pictures of friends and various drawers and cupboards. The left wall was home to a large walk-in wardrobe and sink area. Daisy pulled back the duvet on the large bed. Zach laid Katie gently on the bed and pulled the duvet to cover her. Soon she was asleep. The last thing she had seen that day was Zach. Rosie jumped up on the bed next to Katie, obviously wanting to guard her. Zach patted Rosie, who laid her head down and began her guard duty.

Silently, Zach and Daisy walked out of the room and shut the door.

'Oh, dear me,' Daisy spoke. 'I am a rubbish host, aren't I? Would you like a drink or something to eat?'

'No, thank you,' Zach replied with a smile. 'I must be getting home anyway.'

'Nonsense,' Daisy insisted. 'You brought my daughter home for me. The least I can do is get you a drink.'

'If it pleases you.' Zach sighed. 'Some water, please.'

With a smile, Daisy hurried down to the kitchen, Zach followed, taking in the house as much as he could. Entering the kitchen, he saw four cats sitting outside the door.

'Oh, silly cats,' Daisy remarked, opening the door to let them in. All the cats bounced in and then stopped in front of Zach. They stood there taking him in, and then they all hissed at him.

'Oi!' Daisy shouted at them, letting out a huge clap. They all dispersed and fled upstairs to safety.

'Daft things,' Daisy offered by way of apology, handing Zach a large glass of water. 'We have too many of them.'

Zach accepted the water with a nod in thanks.

'How many do you have?' Zach asked after sipping the water.

'Twenty,' Daisy replied. 'All of those cats have litters of five each, and the odds are the kittens will stay here too.'

'Wow.' Zach was surprised by the sheer number of the animals in that one space.

There was a rumble. The form of another girl appeared in the doorway. She had the same features as Katie but was a few years older, possibly eighteen or nineteen. She looked at Zach and then at her mother.

'What's happened?' she asked, worry filling her voice. 'Tyler told me Katie was carried in just now.'

'It's OK, Becky,' Daisy reassured her anxious daughter. 'This charming young man brought her back. She collapsed in the park from heatstroke, but she is in bed asleep with Rosie.'

Rebecca let out a sigh of relief and turned to Zach.

'Sorry,' she said. 'I just worry about my sister. I am Becky.' She extended her hand. Zach took it and shook it.

As soon as Becky touched Zach's gloved hands, she saw something, a glimpse of something, of the future. She saw a powerful storm raging over the cathedral, heard the clanging of metal on metal, and saw fire erupting from the spire and falling to the ground – all this within a split second. Releasing the hand of Zach, she stared at him. He had seen what she had seen. Fear filled his eyes.

'I best be going,' he said. After finishing off his water, he told them, 'Goodbye.' With that, he flew out the door and was gone. Rebecca watched him leave. Never had she had a vision that potent, that detailed. There was more to Zach than met the eyes. *Now I know why Katie likes him,* she thought.

CHAPTER 7

Z ACH PICKED UP HIS PACE. He had no idea what just happened, but what he had seen sent a chill down his spine. 'What the hell was that?' he asked himself.

He could feel Shangal wanting to break free. Zach had spent much of his energy trying to contain the demon. His long, powerful strides took him back through the crowded town centre and to the familiar scene of the bus station. It was nearly empty, with only groups of friends gathered around the few benches talking about this and that, nothing that Zach cared for. He had only one thing on his mind, and that was getting home and away from the crowds. A creaky bus bearing the number 29 eventually pulled up into its slot. The driver was a thin, bald man who knew the form of Zach well. Even before Zach boarded, the driver had his ticket ready. It was a routine that they were both used to. The journey was silent and uneventful as the creaky bus stopped outside Zach's house. As usual, it was raining heavily as Zach descended the stairs and walked up the slope to the odd L-shaped house.

The floor was once again home to another threatening letter. It was happening; Zach was being evicted. His face contorted with anger as he crushed the paper in his hand. He could feel heat rising within him. Soon enough, the letter burst into flames. Then the demonic voice of Shangal began to chuckle in his head.

'What will the poor boy do without a home, I wonder?' Shangal taunted.

Zach tried not to listen as he checked the packed hiking bag in his room. He had known that he would soon be evicted. He had a week to find a place to live. If he found none, then he would live in a field or a forest somewhere.

'Are those really the best places to go?' Shangal asked.

'It keeps me away from people,' Zach replied angrily, 'people you can't hurt.'

Zach looked up and saw the demon in his mirror, its blood-red eyes looking into the eyes of its host. Shangal had been growing worried about and impatient with Zach. All he wanted was to come onto the human plane and assert his dominance. But Zach was not a host. Rather, he was a prison. His strong mind prevented Shangal from escaping.

'Strictly speaking, it would not be me hurting them, now, would it?' Shangal smiled, showing his silver teeth. 'What self-respecting court would find you innocent?'

'If I go down, you go down with me,' Zach replied, watching the smile immediately disappear from Shangal's face. Zach was then taken off his feet and pinned against the ceiling, Shangal's left hand grasping his throat.

'Perhaps you forget who controls who here, boy,' Shangal said, rage sounding in his demonic voice.

Zach smiled, used his right hand to remove Shangal's left hand from his throat, and kicked away from the ceiling. He landed with a thud on his hands but with no pain. Standing, he looked at the mirror and grinned. 'No, demon,' he said, triumphant, 'I know who controls who.' With that, Zach struck the mirror. It shattered and broke into millions of little pieces, which seemed to melt into the floor.

The rest of the day was quiet and undisturbed for Zach as he sat still and silent in his room, knowing that soon he would have to leave.

...

Katie opened her eyes slowly. Her vision was out of focus, but she knew she was in her room. Rosie looked up and began to wag her tail.

'Hey, Rosie,' Katie said. Her voice was croaky. She remembered only snippets from yesterday's events. She remembered being chased and caught by someone, but more important than that, she remembered being saved by Zach. Leaning forward slowly, she found that her back was aching, probably from being put on the table in the kitchen. Slowly she got out of her huge bed, Rosie following behind her. The house was quiet, which was surprising for a Sunday morning. It took Katie a while, but eventually she made it down to the kitchen. Rosie was still following, making sure that Katie did not fall or do anything that would cause her further harm.

The smell of toast and butter filled Katie's nose as she opened the door. Rosie padded in and then went out the door into the garden, leaving Katie and the busy Daisy in the kitchen.

'Oh!' Daisy jumped upon seeing her daughter behind her. 'I didn't hear you come in. How are you feeling today, sweetie?'

'Umm, I'm not too sure,' Katie answered, 'but at least I'm home.'

'That is very true,' Daisy spoke, handing Katie a plate with two slices of toast with butter, 'and all because of that very nice boy Zach.' Katie blushed. It was the only thing she properly remembered about yesterday, being saved and carried back by Zach.

'You like him, don't you?'

Katie snapped out of her trance and looked up at her sister.

'Maybe I do, maybe I don't,' Katie replied with a smile.

'That's such a Dad answer,' Rebecca said, walking into the kitchen, followed by a menagerie of cats, which had all been enjoying the morning sun.

'Where did he go?'

'He left shortly after meeting Becky,' Daisy replied, still fretting with the cooking, 'which was a very odd way of meeting.'

Katie looked to her sister, who said nothing, although her eyes spoke volumes. She had seen something. Rebecca moved quickly out of the kitchen and went upstairs, out of sight. Katie finished her toast and went back to her room. It was time to read *The Purple Star*.

Her room was a lot different with the curtains open, which transformed it into a room of light. The sun's rays seemed to reflect off the white doors of her wardrobe and light up the whole room. Katie sat cross-legged on her bed. She laid the still immaculate book in front of her, not knowing whether she was feeling excited or nervous about reading it. Slowly and carefully, she opened to the title page: *The Purple Star – The Definite Guide to the Spirit World*. Katie was intrigued already. She could throw away her theories about vampires, werewolves, and Marvel superheroes. This book was about something much more in depth. She continued to flick through the pages. Chapters on the spirit world and the types of spirits passed in front of her eyes, but she did not know what she was looking for. After about an hour, she gave up. All she had gained was a slight amount of knowledge about the spirit world. Whether or not that slight knowledge would benefit her, she did not know.

Confused about the book, Katie got up, crossed the corridor, and went into Rebecca's room. Her sister was lying on her bed quite literally surrounded by cats. Even though each litter had their own box and room, they all chose to stay in Rebecca's room. No one understood why, but they let it happen. Neither the cats nor Rebecca really cared as long as they were somewhere. Katie walked closer and closer until her sister noticed.

'Oh, hey.' Rebecca was busy reading a book about the police. She had been training to be an armed response officer and would soon have her exam. 'How are you feeling?'

Katie walked over and sat on her bed. All the cats looked at her but then went back to what they had been doing before she arrived.

'Still a bit dazed, but I'm getting there,' Katie lied. She knew that her sister would be open if she played the sympathy card. 'So, what did you think of Zach?'

'He seemed to be a nice person,' Rebecca replied, her eyes still reading her book. 'Not many people would carry their friends home after they passed out, so that shows he's a good friend.'

'That's the thing,' Katie said. 'He doesn't have any friends, just me.'

'Well, everyone else doesn't know what they are missing. You have a good friend there.' Rebecca did not dare look her sister in the eye. Katie always had the ability of looking deeper into her sister than she had wanted. It was infuriating, especially when she discovered thoughts and truths that were private. Seeing that she was not going to get anything from her studying sister, Katie left the room and set about reading more from *The Purple Star*. Hopefully more answers would come.

...

Christian awoke with a thump. Looking up, he realized he was being carried by each elbow by two very large and angry-looking men. He had an idea where he was, so he just went with it. After a few minutes of being dragged though long dusty corridors, he eventually was slung into a large room. As the door creaked shut, Christian stood and looked around. The room was huge; a big fire was burning in the fireplace along the left wall. A large elegant wooden table with thirty-two chairs took up the centre, and all along the other three walls hung pictures of famous historic and religious events. At the far end of the room stood the angry and impatient figure of David Alexander.

'Here. Now,' David Alexander said, clicking his fingers.

Christian did not wait to be told again. He hurried towards the other end of the room. David Alexander motioned for him to sit. Slowly he complied, and then watched as David Alexander did the same at the head of the table. After a while of David Alexander shuffling through some papers, he spoke again. 'I suggest you make the answer to this question phenomenally good.' Christian began to shake with fear as David Alexander continued. 'How did you fail at such a simple task?'

Christian could not speak through his fear and instead babbled meaninglessly.

'Let me make the question easier for you,' David Alexander interrupted. 'How did I come to find you lying unconscious by a tree stump and not with the girl as you had promised?'

'It was Zach,' Christian eventually mustered. 'He came out of nowhere and did that. If you had let me take my friends, it would not have happened.'

As quick as lightning, David Alexander flew over to Christian and punched him in the face, sending him off his chair and to the floor. 'The whole point of our operation is that it is secret!' he shouted at Christian. 'We don't need more people like you threatening it!' Christian cowered in fear as bruises began to build around his eyes and nose.

'Now let's try it again, shall we, Mister Jones?' Christian nodded frantically. 'And so help me God, if you don't deliver this time, you shall become target practice for my men.'

Christian remained on the floor as David Alexander walked over to an intercom system and spoke into the speaker. Within seconds, the two men who had dragged him in appeared.

'Please escort Mister Jones home.' With that, the two men picked him up, put a bag over his head, and dragged him out of the room. David Alexander sat again and opened two files. One was on Zach, and the other was on Katie. Smiling, he poured a glass of whisky and sat back in his chair. He would have his prize, one way or the other.

CHAPTER 8

I<small>T WAS ANOTHER</small> M<small>ONDAY BACK</small> at school. The weekend had brought such joy to the students, but now there was none left to see as they filed through the various entrances. As usual, the day started with rain. The staff and students were so used to it by now that none of them showed concern. Instead, they scuttled from dry spot to dry spot, all except Zach, who was marching up the slope at the back of the school, the rain not bothering him as he moved swiftly and silently up the slope, passing fellow pupils who had jackets pulled over their heads or were hiding under umbrellas.

The day started out normally except for one thing: Christian Jones was being a lot quieter and far less unbearable than he usually was. His bruised face was far more prominent. He claimed that he had fallen down his stairs and been sent face first into a wall. But Zach could see the outline of the knuckles on his face. Someone had been unhappy with Christian Jones. As far as Zach was aware, Katie was still in the dark about what Christian had tried to do that weekend. Zach could see her make long gazes at him. It was obvious that she wanted his attention. He could feel it in her demeanour. He had known that she would be back with more questions.

The morning's lessons went on with little excitement from any of the students. Everyone was just waiting for lunch and the long-deserved break that came with it. By the time the bell sounded for lunch, the sun had broken through the clouds, lighting up the town. All the students had taken off their layers and were now desperately soaking up the sun's rays, like they always did. Katie was once again walking towards the dead zone. Zach was there waiting for her. As Katie entered, she saw that Zach had prepared for her company. It was not much, but he had managed to find two wooden chairs and a medium-sized desk and moved them there.

Once Katie made it to where Zach was, she smiled as she sat, watching as Zach sat too.

'I never did thank you for Saturday,' Katie began, her heart fluttering. 'My mum and brother really like you.'

'Do you remember what happened at all?' Zach asked with concern.

'Umm, no.' Katie thought. 'Not at all. I just remember me passing out and you carrying me home.' Her face broke into a smile as she recalled the events of Saturday. Zach saw it and smiled back, the first time he had smiled in a very long time. Breaking out of her daze, Katie reached into her bag and laid *The Purple Star* on the desk.

'I do have a lot to questions to ask you,' she said, looking at Zach. Zach sat back and waited for her to continue. 'I have read this cover to cover and I don't know what I am looking for. I thought you could give me a chapter to read.'

Zach smiled in his reclining position. 'I take it your theories of vampires and whatnot have gone then?'

'Oh yes,' she said, her heart fluttering more. 'I just want to know what you are and what happened to you.'

Zach contemplated his answer. After a long pause, he leant forward. 'Chapter 6, sixth page in.' He leant back again and watched Katie's actions.

Katie opened the book to Chapter 6 and flicked through until she was six pages in, a page with what was apparently a quotation:

> A boy without a family will become lost. But even the lost can be found again.
>
> A boy without guidance will lose hope. But hope can always be restored.
>
> A boy who becomes trapped becomes an animal. But even animals can be trained.
>
> An animal boy who becomes a man becomes a monster. But even a monster can be tamed.
>
> A monster left to fester becomes possessed. But even the possessed can be cured.

A possessed man who has no love has a demon within him. Demons can only be expelled by fire and storm.

But if the possessed man chooses between the demon and love, the answer will be unpredictable.

All that is certain is death.

By fire and storm.

Katie finished reading and looked at Zach with fear in her eyes.

'What stage are you at?' she asked.

'Near the end,' he answered, 'but not at the expelling bit yet.'

Katie was shocked. Her entire perspective of everything was turned on its head.

'So you're being used like a puppet?' she asked, continuing to pry for answers.

Zach stood and walked to the dead tree. 'Yes and no,' he answered after a pause. 'He can control me, but I can also control him and use his powers if I need to.'

'So you are effectively a prison for him?'

'Essentially, yes,' Zach answered. 'He can't escape from me like he could other people, and I can tap into his powers. But if I use them too much, he can break free.'

Katie stood and walked over near Zach. She could feel the heat from him even from a distance.

'So that storm was you?'

'That was me controlling him and tapping into his powers for the first time,' he answered. 'That was the day I got these.' Zach removed his black fingerless gloves to reveal the two marks on his hands branding him as possessed. Katie took his hands gently and looked at them. They almost seemed to glow like embers and were hot to the touch.

'Doesn't your family know about this?' she asked, still holding his hands.

'What family?' Zach retorted. 'They are all dead. I am all that is left.'

'You live by yourself?' Katie was shocked even more.

'Yes.' Zach nodded. 'For the moment. The house is being foreclosed on at the end of this week.'

Katie looked into his eyes. Zach was not lying. She was looking at someone who had lost everything but was somehow still trying to get on with life with a terrible secret.

'What will you do?' she asked, concerned. 'Where will you go?'

'I don't know,' Zach replied. 'Somewhere away from people.'

'Well, that will not do,' Katie spoke, taking charge. 'I'm coming back to your house tonight. I will find somewhere for you to go.'

Zach smiled at this promised act of generosity.

'If that is what you want, then you may come back home with me.'

Katie smiled back and got caught in his eyes. There she remained until she thought of something.

'Maybe you can stay with me and my family,' she said, expressing her thoughts out loud. 'Mum likes you already and has been thinking of a way to thank you properly for Saturday. I'm sure she will say yes if I ask her.'

Zach continued to smile as was he was listening to Katie. 'Ask her if you must,' he said.

With that, Katie pulled out her phone and frantically typed a text message. After a long wait, her phone vibrated with the reply. She smiled and turned her face towards Zach.

'Mum said I may come to your house tonight. I will ask her about you tomorrow and see what she says.'

Zach smiled and embraced Katie lightly in thanks. Her heart began to beat faster as she accepted and returned the embrace. This day may have revealed some very dark and dangerous things, but she did not care. She now knew what Zach was and what had happened. And now he had a friend, which was all that he needed, she was sure.

...

Like a soaring hawk, Christian had watched Zach and Katie talk. Anger was building within him, not only because of last night's encounter with David Alexander, but also because Zach was taking the girl Christian wanted for himself. Christian had always gone after the people Zach liked. He just wanted Zach to suffer, as it gave him such joy to cause pain to

Zach. But he always got paid back for it. It was not a very efficient way of causing pain, but it was all that Christian could do. Soon he would have the opportunity to try again. This time, he knew, he would not fail. He had no intention of being filled with holes. He continued to watch as Zach and Katie talked more, and then he watched as they walked back inside, very close to each other.

The rest of the day was uneventful for everyone, just the usual sights and the sounds of lessons, but with one difference: Katie sat with Zach at all times. Students and teachers alike were confused about what they were seeing. Was this the beginning of a new era?

As the bell sounded for the end of the day, Katie was very happy that she was spending more time with Zach. That feeling was not long-lasting, as the speaker system crackled to life.

'Attention, students. Would Katie Oldman please see the headmaster immediately?' Katie sighed as she packed her bag. Zach appeared behind her as he usually did.

'Don't worry about it,' he said. 'I will be waiting by the overpass.' With that he glided out of sight.

Katie began to walk to the headmaster's office. Zach had told her that this would happen. But she knew what she would say to Mr Green. She knocked on the white door and entered. Rodger Green was sitting on his chair as she entered. His face was neutral, but Katie could see his frustration.

'Ah, Miss Oldman,' he said. 'Please take a seat.'

Katie complied and sat opposite him on a small chair.

'So,' Rodger began, 'how are you finding things here?'

'Very good, thank you,' Katie answered. 'Everyone is very welcoming.'

'Good,' Rodger spoke, 'very good. And I understand you have made many friends here as well. That is encouraging.'

'I have,' Katie said, seeing where the conversation was going.

'Including Zach Ford,' Rodger stated. 'In fact, since you have been here, you have spent a lot of time with him.'

Katie nodded, not wanting to speak yet.

'Katie.' Rodger leant forward. 'Zach has changed a lot over the past few months and is prone to do so again. I suggest you try distancing yourself from him.'

'No,' Katie retorted defiantly. 'It is because people have done that that he is the way he is now! I will not abandon him like you have told everyone else to. I would much rather have only him as a friend than everyone else here.'

Rodger sat back in his chair, his face reddening. 'I take it you know what happened to his family then?' he asked slowly.

'Yes,' she answered, still defiant.

'And there is nothing I can do to persuade you to keep your distance from him?'

'Nothing in this whole universe.'

Seeing that he had failed, Rodger sent Katie away and returned to his work.

She was near furious by the time she made it to the overpass behind the school. But she managed to calm herself when she laid eyes on the form of Zach. He was leaning on the rails watching the endless stream of cars pass underneath him. Katie was relieved to see him. As she approached, he slowly turned and smiled. The walk to the bus station was silent. Neither one of them wanted to speak about anything for fear of destroying the feelings they both had. Katie was silently shocked at seeing what Zach had to cope with every day. The bus station was full of teenagers who struggled to string together a simple sentence without swearing or grunting. Katie did not know how to take all this in. But when Zach walked under the creaky cover of the station, the kids all scattered at the sight of him. *He obviously has a reputation,* Katie thought. Zach looked at her, his eyes saying that he did.

As with the walk, the bus journey was silent for them. Katie again was shocked at what she saw. There was a buffer zone of three rows between where they sat at the back and where everyone else sat. Katie was confused about and concerned for Zach and wondered how he could have lived like this for the length of time he had.

Soon they entered the village. Katie saw Zach's house and the surrounding area. Zach looked back at her. The rain was still falling, as it had done every day. Katie pulled her blazer over her head and followed Zach up the hill to his house. The shock did not leave her until she entered the house, at which point it was replaced with sorrow. He lived with basically nothing. Every room he showed her had nothing in it, apart from the small kitchen and the bathroom. But when Katie was led into another room, her perspective changed, as it was a fully furnished large bedroom with a king-size bed taking up most of the space along the far wall. An elegant wardrobe filled a corner, where there was also a chair and a small desk. It had been Zach's parents' room, the only room that was still intact. All the other rooms had been taken apart and their contents sold so that Zach could get the money to keep living there, but he hadn't had the heart to take this one apart.

'You can sleep here,' Zach said. Katie felt honoured that he would entrust this last piece of normality to her, be it only for a night. She nodded and smiled as Zach left the room and went to find some food in the garage. When she looked around, she saw pictures of the family. They looked recent, although Zach's hair was blond, as opposed to the jet-black it was now. She saw pictures of him and his sister holding animals, in smart clothing for a special occasion, and with what looked like to be a family dog. And then she saw his parents. His father was tall and broad much like Zach, and his mother had long blonde hair like Zach's and the mesmerizing blue eyes that he had evidently inherited. Katie felt that she had just met his whole family even though they were all dead. She was overwhelmed by what she was seeing.

She carefully placed her bag and things down on the floor next to the bed and then went to find Zach, who was in the kitchen. He had changed into jeans and a tattered grey shirt. He was busy cooking for her. She lingered at the door, hoping he would not hear her. Looking at his form, she saw a scar on a part of his exposed neck. It looked like a burn, but she was not certain.

'It's a burn,' Zach said, making her jump, 'from the accident. I picked up a few that day. Now, are you hungry?'

'Umm, yeah,' Katie answered, trying to catch her breath. 'Do they hurt?'

'All the time,' Zach replied, serving up lamb chops with potato wedges and peas, 'but it's what I live with.'

Katie looked once more at him and then began to eat.

'Aren't you going to eat?' she asked, noticing there was nothing for him.

'I'm not hungry,' he answered. 'Don't worry about me. I'm going to clean up.'

With that, Zach disappeared from the room and walked down the hall. It was a few minutes after that Katie heard the boiler kick into life and the noise of a running shower.

Katie finished her food and went to unpack a bit. She walked through the empty living room. It was very eerie walking through a room that would have once been the venue for social evenings or in which the whole family would have gathered most evenings to play games or do what families did. Instead of filled with people and activity, though, it was empty, which was not natural at all.

The shower was still hissing down the corridor. Katie had already seen Zach's scars, but she felt intrigued and wanted to see more. There was a part of her that wanted to get to know him better, but another part of her wanted to run from him like the headmaster had told her to. Yet she knew she would stay to the end.

She went into the bedroom, took out her clothes and everything else she needed, and changed into loose-fitting trousers and a shirt. The house was abnormally hot despite the fact that none of the heaters were on. She picked up her phone so she could call home, but there was no signal.

'It's the valley.' Zach had again scared her. 'No signal on any network here.' Katie had not heard the water switch off, the boiler stop humming, or Zach walk past her room and get dressed. But she managed to get control of her heart and breathing.

Zach's hair seemed to be much longer than it was at school. The back fell down well beyond his shoulders, and at the sides, his hair hid his ears. But his fringe never went over his eyes, like a true hunter. She could not see any more scars, as Zach had changed his shirt, covering his trunk.

'If you want a shower, then let me know.' Zach broke Katie's scanning and glided back to the living room, leaving his guest alone once again.

The rest of the evening passed quickly. Katie was desperately trying to learn what had happened and how Zach had lived this way for so long. The image of the scars and burns on his body filled her mind. He had suffered a lot during what was a short life, and he continued to suffer in a way no one could ever imagine. Before she knew it, Katie was asleep. Zach carried her to her bed and awaited the dawn of another day.

CHAPTER 9

T HE MORNING STARTED QUIETLY. KATIE was first awakened by the sound of birds chirping in the nearby trees. She had not seen them properly when she arrived on account of the failing light. But now that she did catch sight of them through the window, she saw that they were burnt and singed on one side, as if they had been caught in a fire. As she sat up, she heard the gliding movement of Zach. He was quietly trying to find food for her.

Katie found Zach once again in the kitchen. The frying pan was hissing and spitting as Zach cooked near enough to a feast: bacon, sausages, eggs, tomatoes, mushrooms, hash browns, and beans – just for the two of them. Katie once again saw the burn on his neck. But now she could see more of it. It went farther down his back and front. Another burn of equal length ran down his side. Zach must have been in intense pain to have suffered through that and now to live with it. Her heart grew heavy with sorrow as she saw the many scars and burns that littered his body. She did not dare move in case he saw her looking at him, as he would likely disappear to cover up. Some of his scars looked more recent than others. Silvery lines scattered his body along with the bigger burn marks. The oil from the various pans spat onto his body, but he did not flinch or curse. He just continued as if it had never happened. It perplexed Katie how he could live like this, by himself in a house with next to nothing and with so much physical and emotional pain residing within him.

'You know it is rude to spy on your host,' Zach joked, 'especially when he is cooking your breakfast.'

'Sorry,' Katie replied, her heart thumping in fear. 'What happened to you?'

Zach turned to look at Katie, at which point she saw that he had scars and burns all over his chest and stomach. She dreaded to think what the rest of his body was like.

'There was a car crash,' Zach answered slowly. 'Seems like such a long time ago now. The bulk of the scars are from that.'

'And the others?' Katie dared.

'Are we going to stand here all morning, or shall we eat?' Zach said, quickly changing the subject.

'Of course. How silly of me. I'm sorry,' Katie said. 'It's just … how can you live with those scars?'

'Not easily,' Zach answered, 'but this is hardly a decent conversation to have whilst eating.'

Zach laid the food out on the windowsill of what was the dining room and found his guest a chair. After fussing for a few minutes, he once again disappeared, leaving Katie to eat and continue to wonder. It felt strange for him, as he had never entertained before by himself. He was used to keeping the littler children happy with his many games and stories. But now he was by himself with someone of equal age, which made him feel peculiar.

Zach entered his room and quietly closed the door.

'Is the little one falling in love?' the patronizing voice of Shangal spoke in his mind. 'The soppy thoughts going through your mind and her mind are infuriating. They sound like fingernails on a chalkboard.'

'You can scan my mind all you want,' Zach replied, feeling his anger build, 'but stay out of hers!'

'How dare you tell me what I can and can't do, mortal!' Shangal boomed. 'I own you.'

'Or do I contain you?' Zach retorted. 'As long as you're in me, you're going nowhere, and that's how it is going to stay. So get comfortable.'

Zach heard nothing more as Shangal retreated deeper into his mind. With a sigh, he got dressed and went to find Katie.

Zach knew that the demon was right. How could he fall in love when he had something so strong and terrible residing within him? It did not matter anyway, as soon he would be gone from his home and maybe even the area. Plus, visions and memories of Laura still plagued his mind and haunted his thoughts.

He turned sharply and shuddered as he saw Katie at his door. She had seen and heard everything; her understanding was now complete. She had seen Shangal in the window and saw Zach talking to him. She was pale white in fear, but she stood her ground. Her thoughts and feelings for Zach had not changed at all.

When Katie looked at Zach's body again, she saw that the scars were almost glowing. The same was so of the brands on his hands. The demon was there. Katie stood silent and shocked, trying to think of what to say to break the long silence.

'That was him, wasn't it?' she eventually mustered.

Zach nodded, almost in shame. Previously, no one but he had ever seen Shangal. Katie rushed towards him and hugged him. Zach, confused, hugged back. Tears rolled down Katie's face as she cried for Zach. No one in the world knew what he was going through or what would happen in the next few days and weeks. Katie moved away from Zach's chest and looked at him through teary eyes. His pale blue eyes also held sadness, but he could not cry. Katie gazed a moment longer and, without any hint of warning, softly and quickly kissed his lips. Zach was stunned as Katie moved away, but not so stunned that he couldn't smile and kiss her back. Neither of them knew or even cared how the rest of the day would go. They had each other, and that's all that mattered to each of them.

...

Christian had seen them both that day. Zach wore a smile for more than a millisecond and Katie's eyes never left his face or gaze. The circumstances were perfect, and Christian knew it. All he needed to do was pick his moment. Half-term was approaching, giving him two weeks to plan, snatch, and trap. He felt better that David Alexander had given him resources he needed. Christian knew that Zach would give chase and that he would fall for the trap. His only fear and concern was whether or not Zach could and would fight his way out. Christian watched and planned silently. The time would come soon.

...

The lunch break again found Zach and Katie in the dead zone. Katie had been frantically talking to Daisy on the phone, trying to convince her to let Zach stay with them. From what Zach could hear, Daisy was apprehensive at first, but then she warmed to the idea, seeing as Zach had brought her daughter home after Christian had tried to abduct her and also that he had helped with Katie's transition to a new home and school. Katie clicked her phone shut and looked at Zach, happiness filling her eyes.

'She said you can stay with us for as long as you need,' she nearly screamed in joy, launching herself into Zach's arms. 'And she said she would even help you get your stuff from your old house.'

Zach did not know how to feel. This day had not exactly gone the way he wanted. In one aspect it had, in that now he did not have to run but he could stay near enough where he was. But in the other, he would still be near a large population of potential victims for Shangal. He could feel the demon swell inside of him, still trying to break through his host and onto this plane.

'We can get your things tonight, if you are up to it,' Katie said, not seeing that Zach was in deep thought.

'Yeah,' he replied, 'that would be good, thank you. There's not too much to get.'

'What's wrong?' Katie asked, concern filling her face.

'I don't know,' Zach mustered after a few seconds of thought. 'It's just a feeling I'm having.'

'What kind of feeling?'

'Just that something is going to happen – to me, to you, to your family, and to everyone in this town.'

'It's probably just the shock of going somewhere new on such short notice,' Katie said, looking into his eyes and putting her arms around his neck. 'Think of it as a new beginning. I'll do anything I can to help you.'

...

Seeing Zach put his arms around her and draw her in for another kiss was all that Christian needed. He had managed to get all of his friends, or 'grunts', together to spread the word about David Alexander and what he could offer those who helped him. Support was growing as he continued to talk about the plan. He soon had many supporters and people willing to help. With a smile and a nod, he sent off his 'followers', opened his phone, and dialled the number for David Alexander. After a few dial tones, there was an answer.

'This had better be good, Jones,' the angered voice of David Alexander spoke. 'What have you got for me?'

'I have got more supporters for you here and a huge leap in Zach and Katie's relationship …'

'Will Zach come after her, Jones?' David Alexander interrupted. 'That's all I want to know.'

'Yes, he will,' Christian said, smiling as he spoke. 'And in two weeks we will have a prime opportunity to take him.'

'I will leave it to you, Jones. But remember, fail me again and you will find yourself on the end of a gun line.'

With the threat lingering in his mind, Christian clicked his phone shut and began executing his plans.

David Alexander sat back in his chair, satisfied that Christian would do well. 'James,' he called to the end of his huge office. Within seconds, James came striding into the room.

'Yes, sir?'

'Call together the order,' he said with a cruel smile. 'I think it is time for me to put my plan into action.'

With a nod, James strode out of the office, intent on gathering together the necessary people.

'Finally,' David Alexander said to himself, 'centuries of planning will soon come to an end and I will be the most powerful man on the planet.'

'You mean us.'

'Of course,' he said, turning towards a huge full-body mirror and smiling at the black form within. 'There is no me without you.'

CHAPTER 10

H ALF-TERM CAME QUICKLY TO ALL the students – just over two weeks of 'freedom'. Those few days before for Zach had been busy and eye-opening. He had seen first-hand the generosity of humanity. The Oldman house had welcomed him with open arms and as one of their own. Daisy had cleared out a small box room for Zach. It was not much, and in fact it was smaller than his room in his own house, but it was a room in a house, which was all he needed. His room was sandwiched between Katie's and Rebecca's, making it easy to see his new love. However, Rebecca had been very hesitant about Zach. He remembered first meeting her. She was still unnerved by him, but did his best to put her at ease. Zach's old house had been emptied of everything remaining, and the city council had repossessed it and prepared it for auction. Zach was sad to leave the house he had grown up in, but it had to be done. And now that he had a new home with a new family, it was time to move on. But Shangal had no intention of making that easy. Every so often, Zach disappeared into the tiered garden behind the Oldman house, where Shangal tried to break through and test Zach's strength and resistance. So far Zach had won, but his strength would not last forever – and Shangal knew it.

The day was abnormally hot. The sun's rays pelted down onto the earth. As usual, people turned into sunflowers, desperately trying to soak up each and every ray of the sun before it ducked behind a tree or cloud. Zach and Katie were walking through the busy market town hand in hand, as if they had been together for years. Katie wore a huge smile on her face; Zach could see her glowing in happiness. Zach too wore a smile, but he was also tense as they walked through the streets. He knew that they were being followed. Christian's issued grunts had been keeping an eye on them all day. Zach had seen, heard, and smelt them multiple times throughout the day. Even Shangal was nervous. He too had been watching the trackers, wondering what was to happen. Although Katie could not see it, Zach knew she was in danger.

The town square's market was bustling like it usually was. Anything you could imagine was sold, legal and illegal. Katie had been given a list from her mother for various fruits and vegetables from the stalls. She busied herself with selecting items and bartering with the stallholders as Zach scanned the crowd. He hoped to have lost the grunts in the market so that he and Katie could slip out the other side unnoticed. He had lost most of them, but he saw that two of them had made it into the maze of the market. One had apparently given up and was looking in awe at the items at one of the stalls. The other was still trying to find the couple in the mass of people. Zach went up behind Katie, placed his hand on her shoulder, and whispered, 'I'll be back in a minute. Wait here.' With a nod and a kiss on her cheek, Zach disappeared into the throng to hunt the hunter.

It did not take him long. With Zach using the unguarded Katie as bait, the grunt soon emerged. Zach grabbed him by the throat and marched him to the outskirts of the market. Still with his hand around his throat, Zach slammed the unsuspecting grunt against the wall of the town hall and glared at him with red eyes.

'You have ten seconds to give me a reasonable explanation for why you are following us, or I will bring out someone you really won't want to see.' Shangal was burning with anticipation at the prospect of being summoned, but he knew deep down that it was an idle threat.

'We were sent to follow you,' the grunt replied, in fear of his life.

'By who?' Zach asked, his grip tightening around the grunt's throat.

'Someone worse than you,' he responded with a cruel smile.

Zach released the grip on his throat long enough to punch the grunt in the stomach, forcing him to keel over, and then he kneed him in the temple. Checking to make sure the coast was clear, Zach returned to Katie.

...

Katie was beginning to get worried. Zach had been gone for quite a while and she had finished getting all the things that she needed. There were whispers travelling down the stalls that there was an unconscious man by the town hall. Katie did not know whether to believe the report or not. All thoughts were gone when Zach appeared. She ran to him and jumped into his arms. Once he caught her, they shared a brief embrace before returning home. The sun was still high, and everyone was still out enjoying it. Many people from school saw the two gliding through the mass of people. It struck them as strange that Katie had completely gone against the rules. They all wondered if what the headmaster had told about Zach them could be true.

Zach and Katie made good time back to the house. They were greeted, as usual, by an excited Rosie and a fretting Daisy, the latter of whom got busy sorting over what appeared to be an elaborate lunch consisting of French bread, a selection of meats, cheeses, spreads, and the fruits and vegetables that Katie had brought from the market. Tyler and Rebecca busied themselves with setting up a huge glass table outside, under an equally large parasol. Philip was, as usual, out with his various businesses.

The family had gotten adjusted to Zach very quickly. Even his unexplained night terrors did not cause them to waver them in their decision to let him stay. He had brought a lot to the family even though he had been there for only a few weeks. Tyler liked him because of Zach's ability to tell stories and help him with his work. Daisy liked him because of his general helpfulness and the fact that he made her daughter happy. Philip liked having another man in the house to help him with the various jobs requiring lifting and fixing. And of course Katie loved him and would not bear to see him suffer anymore.

It was strange for Zach to leave his old home to live in a new one. He had spent much of his life there. The memories and experiences of the house and the place would and could never leave him. He was never one for the busy towns and cities, but his choices were limited. In the end, his new love for a new person was the main factor in his agreeing to stay with the Oldmans. Katie's face would have fallen if he had said no. Even as he was now, the feelings and preferences of others continued to come before his own. Shangal had also changed in the past few weeks. Whereas previously he had always tried to niggle at Zach, forcing him to get angry, now he was working with Zach, almost sensing that he too was in danger from some unknown but familiar force. Zach and Shangal had come to an impasse.

The only way for either of them to survive was to work together to make Katie safe and find out who killed Zach's family. Once those two things were done, then they could work to free Shangal from his prison, which would not be easy or simple. They both knew how difficult it would be.

Everyone in the house except for Rebecca was convinced that Zach was a kind and normal person. Rebecca had not forgotten what she had seen when she shook Zach's hand. There was something about him that she did not fully trust. But as long as Katie was happy, Rebecca would not do anything to interfere. With her interview and assessment for the armed response unit coming up soon, she had not had much time to think about what her vision truly meant. She always kept Zach in her sights in case something did happen, though. Despite her lack of trust in him, the two of them did get on to an extent. Zach was always willing to help her revise and test her.

CHAPTER 11

THE DAYS WERE PASSING QUICKLY. Soon half-term would be over and the multitudes of once happy school pupils would be going back for another term. It was the last two precious days of freedom. Compared to the rest of the half-term break, the day was hugely different. The sky was thick with clouds – not rain clouds, but dark and threatening ones – even though it was plain to see that it would not rain. It was a strange and uncomfortable day for Zach, as he had spent the majority of the day without Katie. She was away with her guide troop, but Zach was planning to surprise her by turning up at the Methodist church, where they would meet and he would walk her back. Until then, he occupied himself by helping the Oldman family. They always appreciated his help, especially with Rebecca moving away to the college for her final exams and training. If all went well, she would be an officer with the armed response unit by the end of the month.

As the day went on, Zach helped with the shopping, went through some of Tyler's schoolwork with him, and helped Daisy cook lunch for not only the family but also the animals. Zach's eyes never strayed far from a clock. As the hours clicked by, he readied himself for Katie's surprise.

...

Christian had watched and followed Katie all day. Finally he knew why David Alexander had chosen the Methodist church. She would already be there. Throughout the day, the rest of the group formed up in the park near to the church. They had already been met, briefed, and equipped by one of

David Alexander's scientists, and now it was up to them. As the hour was nearly upon them, Christian's mobile phone buzzed in his pocket.

'Yes?' he answered, remembering the last words David Alexander had spoken to him.

'This has been handed to you on a plate, Jones,' David's voice growled at him. 'The cameras are in place, and the CCTV network is under our control. Remember, provoke but do not attack – unless you need to. I need a clear picture before we can move on. Don't fail me again.'

With that, the phone went dead. The group moved into position. Christian had been more tactical this time. He had scouted the church to find all the entrances and exits. He made sure that at least one member of his group was covering each doorway before the mass of screaming girl guides erupted from the main doors of the church. As the last of them filtered out, Christian moved in.

…

Behind the traditional worship area of the church was a large hall, where the guides met. The long basic hall had chairs stacked up neatly on one side and a hatch leading to a kitchen on the other. With a goodbye and a hug from the senior leader, Katie was left by herself to gather up the rest of the paperwork and the rubbish from the hall to make sure it was tidy for next week. As she was finishing, she heard a noise from one of the fire exits. With her heart in her throat and her knees weak, she crept over to the door and placed her ear against it. She could hear someone whispering something. And then she heard the words that made her run: 'Moving in.'

It all happened at once. The fire exit doors and the doors to the hall burst open. Multiple figures dressed in black descended on her. Before she could let out a scream, a hand blocked her mouth and she was wrestled to the floor. Then she heard a familiar voice, which made her fear deepen.

'Get the rope and a chair and lash her to it,' the cruel voice of Christian spoke. 'Let's see how he will come for her.' Turning to Katie, he smiled a cruel smile and drew his flick knife. Katie began to weep, hoping that Zach both would and would not come.

…

Zach moved through the streets with speed and grace. He was excited to see Katie again after a day without her and was imagining what her face might look like once she saw him there waiting for her. By now he knew the guides would have left and she would be cleaning the hall. He also knew he still had time to make it there. As he arrived, he saw the hall lights on in the back of the church, so he hid in the shadows and waited. Minutes went by and no movement was seen. Zach's expression of happiness turned to worry and then to panic. Something was not right.

He went down an alley that led to the hall's main fire exit, pressed his ear against the door, and then looked though the keyhole. His eyes turned red as he saw Katie tied to a chair crying and Christian looming over her, all his evil on show. He felt Shangal wanting to break free, but he forced him back.

'No,' he told the demon, 'let's give them a show.'

Agreed was the only word the demon spoke as they both readied themselves.

Christian's mobile phone buzzed again, making him jump as it broke the silence.

'Yes?'

'You have had over an hour since you caught her and still nothing?!' David Alexander bellowed.

'I don't know what has happened. He should be here ...'

Those were the last words spoken over the phone.

Zach burst through the fire exit doors at the other end of the hall, with one of the grunts in his left hand and his right landing punch after punch to the helpless man's face. As Zach dropped him, another grunt flew in from the side, knife in hand. Everything went out of control, as no one was supposed to attack. Zach blocked the clumsy stab, threw the attacker into the ceiling, and watched as he crashed to the floor, unmoving. The third came from behind, but Zach sensed the motion. He turned, grabbed the grunt's throat, and looked into his attacker's fearful eyes as his own went night-dark.

'Ford!' Christian said, trying to contain his fear. 'Drop him!'

Zach turned to see Katie being held in front of Christian, his knife to her throat as her tears fell from her eyes like rain. Zach released the choking attacker only to uppercut his chin, and then marched straight towards Christian.

'This has gone on for too long now, Christian,' Zach hissed, still striding towards him. 'You have crossed the line.'

'You did that first when you changed,' Christian desperately replied. 'I'm only following orders. Stop walking or she gets a permanent necklace.'

Zach stopped dead in his tracks. Christian was desperate enough to mean it. Zach would not risk Katie's life.

'Whose orders?' Zach questioned.

'That, you don't need to know.' Christian smiled cruelly. 'All you need to know is that you will suffer and I will have everything that you have.'

Zach looked at Katie. Her tear-filled eyes met his blood-red ones. 'Crush his foot with yours and strike his nose with your head when the opportunity comes.' She looked confused, but then she understood. In that split second, her tears stopped and she waited.

'Now you will show me and my generous partner what you are, Ford,' Christian spoke, his voice ripe with overconfidence. More grunts appeared from the door, each armed with knives like Christian's. Zach turned to face them, preparing to give them a show. Two charged at him, one on the left and the other on the right. Zach caught the lunge from one, and slammed the blade into the shoulder of the other. As the other grunt swiped and howled in pain, Zach broke the first one's wrist and then kicked the stabbed one to the floor. Both fell in pain, defeated. As Zach dispatched each assailant, Katie prepared herself. It was as Zach was finishing off the last grunt that she struck. Summoning all of her strength, she slammed her foot onto Christian's. As he leant forward in pain, she wrenched her head back to connect with his nose. His grip and balance failed at once. She elbowed his ribs for good measure, and then she escaped his grasp, sprinting to Zach.

Zach turned and embraced her, feeling her relax and cry. But it was not over. Zach drew her behind him and told her to take cover as he made ready for his finale. Christian and a handful of grunts remained and made ready for a desperate charge, but Zach had something more terrible in mind.

'You ready?' he spoke to Shangal.

'Draw blood and it will happen.'

Picking up one of the many knives on the floor, Zach ran the blade over one of his burnt palms. The pain was excruciating as the blood ran thick down his hand, but it was needed to end the night once and for all.

Thunder boomed in the distance as the clouds turned threatening. The lights in the hall flickered, and the wind smashed against the windows like waves. Zach held out against Shangal for a few seconds before letting the demon take control. It was a painful and vicious transformation as Shangal took form. Zach's eyes went completely red, his skin went black, his nails turned into claws, and his teeth turned into fangs of silver. The ground shook beneath him as he let the raw power build up. The wooden floor splintered and the walls cracked. Christian and his grunts stood in amazement as everything around them began to smash.

Katie watched in horror as the transformation neared its end. Out of nowhere, Zach roared like a beast, sending all the grunts running in fear. Tendrils of fire leapt from his hands, and the wooden floor cracked and broke, sending small and large splinters around the room. Christian fell to the floor both out of fear and because he was seeking protection from the flames, which out of control. The storm outside raged as lightning of all colours lit up the night sky. Zach's roar was loud and long, lasting until the wound on his hand had healed, at which point Shangal retreated back inside, leaving Zach burnt and even more scarred but still standing and glaring at Christian. It did not take long before Zach's enemy ran, leaving everything behind.

As Shangal left him, Zach fell to his knees. The pain was too much to bear. Katie, seeing his pain, ran to him. His body felt like it was on fire. More scars formed on his back, but he still managed to pick himself up and check that Katie was unhurt. Just as they were about to leave, Zach heard something, a buzzing coming from where Christian had been standing. Striding over the splintered floor, he found Christian's mobile phone vibrating. His anger still with him, Zach snatched the phone up and answered.

'Jones, what happened? All the cameras went down. We saw nothing!'

'Christian is gone,' Zach's demonic voice spoke, 'and you will be too.'

'Ah, Master Ford,' David Alexander said after a long pause, 'how nice to finally hear your voice after all these months. I am such a fan of yours and what you are carrying.'

'You have corrupted teenage boys to do your dirty work, Mister Alexander,' Zach replied. 'Know that you will pay for your so-called scientific work.'

'You know my name?' David Alexander asked, confused. 'How is that possible?'

'Because I know what you are, David Alexander,' Shangal growled. 'Or should I call you Azrael?'

There was another long pause. The voice that replied was as demonic as Shangal's. 'Know this, Shangal,' it said, 'I am the only demon that will rule this plane. Neither you nor our lord himself can stop me. Either exit the body you hold or else I will hunt you both down and consume you.'

'I have a different offer,' Shangal continued through Zach's mouth. 'How about a meeting? Face-to-face. No henchmen, no order, and no weapons. You can only bring Christian with you. We shall discuss terms.'

'Agreed,' Azrael responded after some thought. 'Where and when?'

'Contact me in three weeks. Seeing as you are apparently an intelligent man, you should be able to find me.'

With that, Zach crushed and burnt the phone in his hand. Then he carried Katie home.

That night he did not sleep. He had made the greatest of mistakes: trusting Shangal. Zach had spilt his own blood at the demon's request, which was the worst possible thing he could have done – and sooner than he had hoped. Things would only get worse. Much worse.

CHAPTER 12

EVERYTHING WAS A BLUR TO Katie. One minute she was in the Methodist church watching her boyfriend turn into something monstrous, and the next she was waking up in bed. She did not remember walking back or falling asleep, but there she was lying in her bed. Rolling over, she checked her clock. It was four o'clock in the morning, five hours since the incident at the Methodist church. Slowly and quietly, so not to wake her Rosie, she went to her mirror. She had no visible injuries or marks. Zach had saved her from that. But she could not rid herself of Christian's cruel smile and voice as she was lashed to a chair and jeered at. Throwing on her dressing gown, she went onto the landing to find Zach.

She did not find him in his small box room or in any other part of the house. Instead, she found him down at the end of the garden with his feet in the river. She did not know if it was her imagination or not, but as she got closer, it almost looked like Zach's feet and legs were steaming as they were submerged in the fast-flowing current of the river. As she came even closer, Zach turned to her.

'Are you OK?' she asked after a moment of silence.

'I'm not so sure now,' Zach replied. 'I thought I was after yesterday evening, but now I feel like something much worse is on the way.'

'Why do you say that? What could possibly be worse?'

'I will soon be what I always was, a monster.' Zach quivered as he spoke those words. The steam from his feet and legs grew thicker.

'You're not a monster,' Katie responded, throwing her arms around his neck. 'How could you be? You've saved my life more than once, and you have helped protect other people from the cruelty of Christian – even though they abandoned you when you needed them most.'

Zach smiled and put his arms around her waist. He shed a single tear as he replied. 'Soon none of that will matter. What is about to happen will change everything: me, you, the whole world, and the road that humanity will take.'

'Well, I won't let that happen,' Katie said stubbornly, looking at him. 'You've lost and suffered too much in your life. You won't lose me. Not at all.'

They kissed and stared at the stars seen through the gaps of the thick cloud that remained above the market town. After a while, they went back up to the house to go to sleep. Soon it would be back to school and all the problems that would bring. But for Zach it would be the upcoming event that would bring him even more sleepless nights.

David Alexander paced angrily up and down his office. Everything had gone wrong, and now he had been called out. He changed from David to Azrael almost every second. His anger was visible, but he did not know whom to be angry at. Maybe Christian, who had delayed the test time and time again with his incompetence. Or was it Rodger, for not letting him take action sooner? Or was it James, for not simply killing the boy at the beginning so that the whole hunting and consumption process would have been avoided.

'How could he have survived that inferno?' he yelled to no one as he slumped into his chair 'Unless,' he replied to himself, 'unless the crash was not the trigger.'

'Shangal has been missing for decades, since the inferno he tried to orchestrate. As for the child, I cannot be sure how long he has contained the commander,' Azrael spoke in his mind.

'No, he can't have had him in for that long,' David Alexander responded, bewildered. 'He can barely control him now, so how could he have controlled him when he was younger?'

'What makes you think he is mortal? I have heard whispers of another incident eight years ago at that educational place owned by Rodger Green.'

'Then let's go and pay him a visit.' David Alexander rose, throwing on his coat and pressing a button on the intercom. 'Get me to Salisbury immediately.'

As David Alexander and his entourage flew down the halls of the laboratory, he came across Christian, who was slumped in a chair, looking both tired and terrified. David picked him up by the scruff and dragged him to the convoy of people-carriers. With one of the doors wide open, David Alexander slung Christian inside and sat next to him.

'Come, Jones,' David Alexander spoke, struggling to contain his demonic voice. 'We are going to see your headmaster. There are some things neither of you has told or shown me.'

Fear gripped Christian as the convoy moved out. He had tried to forget that day for many years. That day had terrified him more than the Methodist church incident and every other time he had confronted Zach – and for very good reason.

...

Rodger Green was working late in his study, as he usually did. But for once he was not on the school grounds. He had decided this time to go back to his home with Carl to work. His son had long since gone to bed and left him to his nearly endless supply of paperwork. Some of the papers were accounts for the school, some were bills from builders, but most were complaints and questions. Nearly every parent of every pupil had written to him complaining about the bullies or asking questions about why there had been so many injuries to students around the school. But some had been even more daring, venturing to ask about Zach. It seemed that the pupils had been speaking about his god-son. Soon he would not be able to control them as he had. It was obvious that he was losing his battle to control the school. Ever since David Alexander had sauntered into his school and demanded access to Zach, the school had gone into a downward spiral.

It was late. Rodger could feel himself begin to tire. Tomorrow he would see the pupils return to school and begin another term. For some, it was the final term before their exams. Zach would be gone and out of Rodger's mind. Rodger packed the sheets of paper into his briefcase and set about readying himself for a new term and new troubles.

All he heard next were two loud bangs. The first was his front door being blown off its hinges, and the second was his bedroom door being slammed open. Figures dressed in black body armour dragged him from his bed and yanked him to his feet. Carl was pulled into his room in the same fashion. After a few moments of confusion, everything became clear, as David Alexander stepped into the room smiling.

'You have no right to do this in my house,' Rodger screamed. 'Get out now and I will not take this further!'

'Shut up, Green,' David Alexander spat. 'I have the authority to go where I need to get the answers I seek. There is something you have not told me, isn't there? Something about Zach.'

'You know all you need to,' Rodger pleaded. 'I know nothing else.'

'Liar.' David Alexander punched him in the stomach. 'For the sake of your son, do not lie to me again.'

Rodger gasped for breath as he was pulled up by David Alexander's henchmen.

'You will not hurt my boy?' Rodger begged.

'Not if I don't need to. Take the boy away, and take Mister Green to the car.'

Rodger was again yanked to his feet. He struggled as more henchmen took Carl out of his sight. Another punch was thrown into his stomach, and then a rag was put to his face. He did not remember anything else as he drifted into unconsciousness.

CHAPTER 13

RODGER AWOKE WITH A JOLT and found himself in an oddly familiar place, the district hospital. He ached all over as he pulled himself off the bed he was lying on. His senses were blurred as he became accustomed to his surroundings. All he could think about was his son and the fear in his eyes as he was dragged off to an unknown place awaiting the order to be either released or killed.

That bastard will pay for what he has done to me and my son, Rodger thought.

'I would not bet highly on that, Mister Green,' a dark voice responded.

Whirling around, Rodger saw David Alexander sat in front of a huge table. It was piled high with both medical and police report folders. Judging by the way they were arranged on the table, it seemed to Rodger that David Alexander had already read and organized them to his liking and was merely waiting on Rodger to wake up.

'What do you mean?' Rodger tried to hide his fear, but it was useless.

'Well, firstly, you could receive a severe prison sentence or even life for suspicion to commit murder or being highly connected to a murder, which was originally filed as an accident – as well as being sacked from your job as a headmaster and teacher on account of this being covered up.' David Alexander waved a large red file in front of him. 'You know exactly what this is, don't you, Mister Green?'

Rodger did not even have to respond. He just nodded in shame.

'Now I am going to ask this question as simply as I can,' David Alexander continued. 'Where is the footage?'

'Release my son and swear never to take him again and I will take you to it – and to the rest of the evidence you need.'

'And what evidence is that?' David Alexander asked.

'I know exactly what you are looking for and what you want answers to. This is not the first time Zach has done this and, I suspect, not the last. But his parents, who had too much power in the order, waved it off as gossip and said that I faked it. Why do you think I had them killed?' Rodger was shaking with anger and shame, but he knew he was defeated and had nothing more to lose.

Smiling, David Alexander stood and strode towards Rodger.

'Lead me to everything that you have on Ford and you and your family will never hear of or see me again without cause or prior notice.'

Nodding in agreement, Rodger shook David Alexander's hand, sealing the arrangement. Just as they were about to leave the room, there was a rap at the door. A man dressed as a doctor stepped in. His white robe and gloves were covered in blood, and he was visibly sweating as if he had just finished a major surgery.

'Sir.' The doctor bowed. 'Everything is finished. They await your pleasure.'

David Alexander turned, looking at Rodger, and motioned to his henchmen outside to escort him out. That was the last that Rodger Green saw of David Alexander before he was bundled into another car, which sped off towards Rodger's office.

David Alexander turned to the doctor, grinning.

'Show them to me,' he commanded. The doctor bowed again and led David Alexander down a long maze of corridors and passages, before finally stopping in front of a large heavy door. The doctor took out a huge iron key and turned the lock. There were very many clicks and cracks as the various locks loosened and slid out of the way, until the door creaked open, showing a huge dark room. Both men stepped inside. The door closed with a boom. Lights slowly flicked on, revealing four large forms covered in a mix of robes and clothes.

'Are they ready? Will they respond to my voice and commands alone?' David Alexander's demonic voice spoke, with Azrael's red eyes gleaming through.

'Yes, my lord.' The doctor bowed again.

'Good. See to it that they are armed and ready to be moved at a moment's notice,' Azrael said, walking past each of the beings that were strapped and chained to the wall. He could hear the animalistic primal grunts and groans from each of them. Listening to them filled the demon with satisfaction.

'Everything is prepared and ready, my lord,' the doctor continued. 'They will be ready when you command.'

'Good.' Azrael came though completely. His black and red form glided towards the doctor. 'You have done well, servant, and you will be rewarded as promised.'

The doctor smiled and thanked his overlord, but before he could finish, Azrael picked him up by his neck and held him in the air. The doctor struggled for breath and balance, but all was futile. Before he lost consciousness, he saw his death approach. Azrael open his mouth and inhaled deeply, sucking the life force and all energy from the weakened doctor. The terrified doctor tried one last time to escape, but he weakened visibly as his life force, energy, and very being were consumed and absorbed by Azrael. All that was left when the demon was done were the bones of his loyal servant. As the demon finished his feast, he sank back into his host, letting David Alexander come back. David looked a lot younger and physically fitter.

'I'll be needing more of that before I see Ford again.' David Alexander licked his lips sadistically.

Once I consume both the loyal foot soldiers and our new foot soldiers, the boy and the renegade won't stand a chance.

David smiled at the demon's thoughts and left the room, leaving a group of visibly scared henchmen and doctors to transport the new creations to his headquarters, where they would await his command. All he had to do now was wait.

...

All the Oldman household were gathered around the television watching the weather report, all of them stunned and shocked by what they were seeing.

'As you can see, this storm hanging over Wiltshire, in particular the Salisbury area, has come up without warning and has baffled all experts looking into it. As you can see from these satellite pictures, this huge, black, almost storm-like cloud has hung over the area for the past week now but has produced no rain or storms that we know of. All that experts do know is that it has built and seems to continue to build in intensity as each day passes. No weather warnings have been released as of yet, but be prepared for strong winds, rain, and storms should this unknown and strange weather system decide to break,' the visibly nervous and confused weather reporter said.

All of the family looked at each other and the screen in awe. The storm had come out of nowhere and had built in size and intensity every day that it remained. But no rain, strong winds, or other signs of storm could be seen. Instead, it just blocked out the sunlight and cast a gloomy and sinister black shadow over the whole town. Katie could see that Zach looked pensive, as if he knew something about the storm, but either he would not share his knowledge or was not completely sure of its origins. He had been unusually quiet even for Zach. He barely ate or slept. Every time Katie checked on him during the night, he was not in his room. Usually he stood out in the cold night looking up into the sky at the only other thing that inhabited the black: the moon. As the storm grew in power and intensity, so did the moon's light and, strangely enough, the heat.

As the weather report finished and the last of the evening's news began, Zach quietly left the room. After a few seconds, Katie followed, her intuition beating her caution as always. As usual she found him on the roof, bathing in the surprisingly warm moonlight.

'What is it?' she asked, softly holding his arm.

'It doesn't matter,' he responded.

'It does to me. Since that night at the church, I don't know whether to love you or fear you. But I cannot do both. I know that there is something about to happen. On account of these past few weeks, I no longer believe in coincidences. This storm above us is not natural, much like what you have inside of you. Now if there is something much darker that I don't know about, then just tell me. Nothing can be worse than this silence.'

A tear rolled down her face and dropped from her chin. As it plummeted to the ground, Zach's hand flashed out and caught it. As he passed it from finger to finger, his eyes went red and Shangal spoke through him.

'He fears our death. The storm signals the start of a duel, a duel between immortals and, more importantly, between two highly ranked

99

demon commanders. The storm is meant to cover the battle from mortals. Two step onto the field of combat, and one leaves, only after feeding on the other and consuming his strength. Azrael is the highest-ranked, most ruthless, and most dangerous demon commanders that exists. My power alone will not best him. Nor will your mortal partners. But if he allows me to become one with him, then we stand a chance – a slim one, granted, but better than what we have alone.'

Katie did not know how to take in what she heard. Not only was it the first time she had spoken to a demon, but also she detected actual fear from a being that caused terror and dread in all humans. As the red eyes became blue, Zach nodded in agreement with the demon. Then he picked up where Shangal had left off.

'The problem is that I will not allow the blend between me and him. As co-operative as he has been recently with me in saving you and aiding my fight, I still don't overly trust him. After all, he is a demon, a being of evil, lies, and corruption. If I were to trust him, it could be the end of me and the beginning of him. Only through an empty body or vessel can a demon ascend to our realm.'

'So what you are saying is, it is a fight to the death as him, as you, or as both of you together? And if you lose, he loses, or both of you lose, then Azrael gets more powerful?' Katie asked hopefully.

'Basically, yes.'

'Then whatever you need of me,' she continued, taking Zach's hand, 'you can have it. As long as you do whatever you can to stop that from happening.'

That was the last thing they spoke to each other as they sat under the heat and the light of the moon, embracing as they always did when they were together.

CHAPTER 14

Dᴀᴠɪᴅ Aʟᴇxᴀɴᴅᴇʀ ᴅɪᴅ ɴᴏᴛ ᴋɴᴏᴡ whether to happy or petrified as he scanned through everything that Rodger Green had given him. Journals, files, and audio and video recordings were strewn over the huge table in his office. Like Rodger had told him, this was not the first time that Shangal had surfaced, but the incidents were far more in number than David Alexander had realized. Overall, excluding the current situation, Shangal had visibly surfaced and dealt damage five times since inhabiting Zach. Even though only two situations had been caught on film, they were brutal and worrying to David's and Azrael's plans.

Snapping out of his fearful daydream, David Alexander typed a code into the intercom system and spoke only two words: 'Bring him.' Within minutes, Rodger Green was being dragged into his office again. The man was weak and broken, just how Azrael liked his future slaves to be. As Rodger was flung onto a chair and meekly took a drink of water, David Alexander began.

'This is utterly amazing,' he spoke, flicking through his notes. 'The fact that this was concealed from every level astounds me. This boy has nearly killed, and it was just washed aside like sand on a beach. No questions, no protests: just gone like it had never happened. And you did not even think to tell anyone about it.' Before Rodger could shake his head, David Alexander broke the silence.

'Do you have just any idea how valuable this boy is? He is the next step in the superhuman chain. Think of what the governments, military organizations, and secret institutions will pay for the opportunity to create super-soldiers from the DNA of this boy. All we need to do is find him and bring him to us.'

Rodger Green looked blankly at the glass of water in his hand. He had failed at every attempt to be the legal guardian of Zach. The worst part was that that did not bother him. Looking up at David Alexander, he sighed and spoke. 'What more do you want to know?'

'Talk me though these two pieces of footage,' David Alexander answered, holding two tapes in his hand.

'Well, the oldest one, as you know, is indeed the most violent and most horrific thing I have ever seen,' Rodger started. 'To see someone so young commit those acts in a school was simply appalling.'

'But it did not come from nowhere, am I right, Mister Green?' David Alexander asked sadistically.

'No, it didn't. Zach was a frequent target for the bullies, who treated him worse than nothing.'

'You did not see it all, did you? Just the watered-down version, so to speak?'

Rodger nodded, sipping his water.

'And what about the more recent hospital footage? Not as violent as the other episode, but still reason to worry, would you agree?' David Alexander probed.

Rodger nodded again, his will utterly broken.

With a smile and a flick of David Alexander's hand, Rodger was dragged out of the office, leaving just David Alexander in the room. Turning, he switched on the television set and placed the older of the tapes into the VCR to play it.

'Let's see just how much we can use this.' He smiled as he pressed play on his piece of equipment, anxious to see his own bit of torturous entertainment.

CHAPTER 15

EIGHT YEARS PRIOR

The sun shone that day. Every member of the school was out enjoying the sunshine. It was a day in which to forget everything wrong and bad about school and the world and to just enjoy the heat and light. All of the students but Zach, as usual, were enjoying themselves. It started as ordinary name-calling about his growing blond hair, names like 'girlie' and 'queer boy', but he could let these go and carry on walking. But then out of the blue, those who taunted him became violent. Jumping on him as he sat on his own in the changing room, they bound him with cable ties from the art room and took great delight in dunking his head into a toilet. As usual, the prime bully, Christian, was there. Zach's would-be friend had turned into a bully so he himself would not get picked on. Zach knew that if he just relaxed, it would all be over, but something deep inside of him began to awaken. Even as his head was fully submerged and his arms held by two others, he felt hot and powerful. His last thought that was his own was, *No more.*

Almost at once, he exploded out of his imprisonment, causing two of his attackers to lose footing and fall. In seconds, he had broken the cable ties and had kicked another boy out of the toilets and into the changing room. Hearing a satisfying crunch of young bones hit the far wall only propelled him on. Some had already run for it, but others stood and tried to intimidate him as they normally did. With his red eyes blazing with raw anger and hate, he threw them down to the ground like they were rag dolls and then gave chase.

The next one he caught in the conservatory area connecting the changing area with the outdoor playground. Catching him by the scruff of the neck, he spun his bully target around so fast that he lost consciousness before Zach hurled him through a classroom window to his right. The next tried to stand and fight but received a vicious punch to the face, followed by a stamp to the chest. Then he lay shocked on the floor. Zach's next two victims tried to hide behind the outside doors of the conservatory, but to no avail. They ended up being crushed by the very objects they thought would protect them.

By now, panicked pupils and teachers alike were running for cover as Zach's murderous vengeance continued and escalated. Another bully was caught, thrown to the floor, and then hurled at a nearby fence, over which he lay limp like a market fish. The next two who stood guard over Christian were paralyzed with fear as Zach strode towards them, no mercy in his blood-red eyes. Their appearing to be weak and petrified did not spare them. He grabbed them both by the throat and dangled them in the air, before crashing their heads into each other's and tossing their limp bodies to the floor with a sickening thump. It was just Christian left, eyes wide, sweat falling like tears from his face. Dropping to his knees, he begged to be spared, offering as many apologies as he could think of. But Christian was the worst of them all. Zach answered with a kick to the chest that sent Christian flying into a wooden fence behind him. Before Christian's feet touched the ground, Zach grabbed him by his light blond hair and smashed his head repeatedly against the same fence, each hit making Christian more limp and less conscious. With strength and viciousness well beyond that of his age, Zach flung Christian face first into the sharp, hard concrete of the playground. There he lay, barely conscious, barely aware of what was happening. His face and body were bloodied and bruised all because he wanted to be the big boy. Now Zach was teaching him and his other bully friends what they had never known or seen or felt: how it was to lose and suffer.

It still was not enough for Zach, as he flipped Christian onto his back and held him in the air by the neck, watching the breath seep out of him. But that was when it hit him. An ear-screeching pain in his head forced Zach to toss Christian aside as he fell to his knees, wailing in agony. Voices, memories, and pains that were and were not his flooded into him all at once. It was too much to bear. What seemed like a lifetime passed before it all stopped. There standing before him was a creature from his nightmares, red eyes glowing like rubies in its obsidian skin, claws and fangs like fine steel catching the light of the sun. But as frightened as Zach should have been by the demon, he stood tall and unafraid.

'See and fear true power!' the beast roared, as much to Zach as to the plane he had arrived. He flung his very being and life force into Zach for absorption. As the painful and arduous battle of will and mind happened within Zach, Christian and the rest of the lower school looked on in horror. A seemingly normal Zach eventually stood from his weakened state. They did not know how wrong they were until he roared like a beast and struck the huge oak tree – the symbol of the school – down with one swing of his hand. With a creek, a crack, and an almost groan of pain, the tree crashed to the ground, its echo heard on the other side of the city. The last image most people remember from that day was not the limp and lifeless bodies of schoolchildren littering the area. It was not the tree laying on the ground, as still and motionless as it was in life. It was the power and volume of Zach's demonic roar as he leapt from the tree and disappeared from sight.

Most would not remember that day. Some would say it was a myth. Others would undergo years of therapy to help them cope. But Christian never forgot, not even when he was interviewed later that day by a man called David Alexander.

CHAPTER 16

REBECCA'S MIND WAS IN A blur. It was the last thing that she needed, with her final exam the next day and her dream that much closer to becoming reality. She would be a member of the South-West Armed Response Unit if she passed her final exams, both physical and written. But lately all she had in her mind was a storm, not the one that was brewing beyond the safety of her window, but another one, one that was infinitely more powerful and disastrous. Still, the one outside was growing and slowing with each day. *Maybe, just maybe, the two storms are the same,* she had once thought in a brief moment when her concentration lagged. She had been trying to worry about nothing other than her exam.

However, as much as she tried to forget it, her thought of Zach lingered. There was something off about him, no matter how kind and generous he was to her and the Oldman family. There was a minute aspect of him that did not sit well with her. And lately she had noticed strange things about him. His lack of sleep was one of those things. A person of his age should have slept longer than he did, but every time she had seen him at night, he was wide awake and staring out at the sky as if in a daydream. His lack of appetite was another of those things. Given his build, he should have been eating a good deal of food, but instead he opted for either nothing or – more the case when her mother pushed the matter – a tiny portion of a meal. The last thing that disturbed her, and this more than anything else, were his recent bouts of unconsciousness and his fits.

Most days Rebecca would come home to see Katie and Daisy in a state of worry and panic, as Zach was writhing in agony on the floor, clutching the side of his head as if it was about to explode. And then he would go as limp as one of the cats would when it had been caught, and all would return to normal. During his last fit, she almost swore she heard him say words, but in a different voice. They were words she did not understand. The deep booming voice that said them scared her and her mother. Katie was unfazed as she helped him up and cared for him.

'No, you fool, focus!' Rebecca shouted to herself, realizing another break in concentration. Pushing those crazy thoughts from her mind, she carried on with her revision.

...

Zach awoke with a gasp, clutching at his throat and breathing fast and deep as if he had been drowning. His head pounded with the noise and visions of days past, days he tried to forget.

'You must not forget them, human,' Shangal hissed from within. 'You must harness and unleash them at the right moment. Only then can we claim victory – and soon.'

'I will not allow myself to lose control,' Zach replied. 'You will be used as a last resort and as nothing more. You and I have a deal: I survive and you leave. We both help each other to achieve this.'

'As you wish, mortal. But do not act like or believe that you did not enjoy every last morsel of power that I gave you.'

With that, Shangal violently retreated back into Zach, causing him to stumble. Bracing himself against a wall, Zach heard familiar footsteps approach.

'Are you OK?' the soft voice spoke, pushing the door open. 'Was he talking again?'

Her words made him instantly calm, but the pain was still there: the constant reminder of what he was and what he had done.

'It's nothing. Just popping in to check on his prison.' Zach smiled as he responded. It seemed strange to joke about it, but he knew it was true.

'That's good. Mum and Dad said that because of your fits, you are allowed to sleep in my room, so I can keep an eye on you and make sure you don't hurt yourself.' Even though she was unhappy about the fits, she seemed happy that he could share a bed with her. Zach inclined his head and followed her.

...

It was already darker than normal on account of the storm, but judging by the lights slowly flicking off, both Zach and Katie knew they were the only ones awake. Katie's heart was a drum, beating hard and fast at the anticipation of her and Zach sharing a bed together. She did not know what it would lead to or if anything good or bad would happen, but at last she would get the opportunity to try. Already prepared for bed, she climbed in and watched Zach as he partly changed for bed. Like at his house, he slept in just his undershorts, as otherwise he would get too warm and become restless. The scars on his back and torso caught the light as they usually did, but there were newer ones. In the dim light, these looked almost like burns and faint scratch marks. With Katie slowly shuffling closer to see better, Zach turned, as if reading her mind.

'They hurt, but not that bad,' he said, his voice soft as a breeze as he lay next to her on top of the duvet. Propping herself up on her elbow, she ran a finger across his chest, softly feeling the burns. They were warm as a smouldering ember, but the scratch marks were ice-cold. None of it made sense. But tonight she did not care.

'That's good,' she said, laying her hand on his chest. 'I hate to think of you in pain. If I could protect you from all pain and harm in the world, I would.'

'I believe you would try your best.' Zach smiled, taking her hand in his and placing the lightest kiss on her knuckles. 'But I'm afraid to say that the pain has already been inflicted.'

Katie did not hear what he said, as the sound of his voice and the touch of his lips sent her heart and head spiralling out of control. Before she knew it, her lips were on his. She kissed him, and he replied in kind. Her hands went around his neck pulling him closer, as his went around her waist. Everything was perfect and as it should be. How she wished it could be like this forever.

Then everything changed. Zach's lips went cold and unmoving as he lay almost lifeless on the bed. His eyes rolled up so only the bloodshot scleras were visible. Small twitches began to break out on his body. This was something she had not seen before. The twitches increased in power. Soon his whole body was writhing like a landed fish searching for water. He gasped for air but could say nothing. As the fit built in intensity, Katie stared in amazement as Zach collapsed lifeless on the untidy bed. Seconds felt like months as he lay there lifeless. Katie reached forward and shook him lightly. Nothing happened. Moving round to see his face, she whispered his name and kissed his lips. Still nothing.

Rising to get help, she leapt in fright as his hand lashed out to grab her. Looking back at him, she gasped in alarm. One eye was his normal sky blue, but the other was blood red. And when he spoke, both his voice and the demon's voice spoke as one, saying, 'I have to return home.'

CHAPTER 17

AZRAEL HAD FED WELL OVER the past few days, and it was beginning to show in his host. David Alexander was supple and powerful, as he had been in his youth, and had the looks to match. He had gotten tough on his fellow staff and brotherhood members. Any hint of disobedience or negativity in any of them, regardless of rank, was punishable with consumption. The stench of fear was ripe in the headquarters, but David Alexander did not care. For once, the demon inside of him had given him something in return for his years of service. It was not long before he picked up a sword again, practised with the trainers, and bested them. He even had one of his 'test subjects' duel against him, with a surprising outcome. It took all of his and Azrael's strength and experience to best the subject. But he found out two very important things that day. Firstly, he discovered that the newly dubbed titans were completely, utterly, and solely under his command. No one else could give them orders or commands, because they would not obey. Secondly, he found that during his digging of the other events, and using his demon's connections, they had begun to terrorize Zach from a distance, giving him painful visions and memories of days gone by. It had become a very useful tactic and weapon, as they could almost feel and taste Zach's pain and misery from the headquarters.

'It will make them attack without thought and with carelessness, and that will be their downfall and our rising.' Azrael's arrogant phrase began to annoy the increasingly youthful David Alexander, but he was inclined to agree. However, if that plan did not work out, then they had their fallbacks. Four of them, to be precise.

...

The Oldman family's mood had completely changed, which opened up something Zach never thought he would see at such a time of scepticism and concern. What it opened up was a period of celebration and joy. Not only had Rebecca passed both her exams with flying colours, but also, because she had scored higher than anyone else, she had been offered on that very day an officer's post, which, naturally, in the shock she must have been feeling, she accepted. She had left that morning a lowly cadet and had returned a sergeant of the armed response unit in Salisbury and Wiltshire County.

No one could quite believe it, but they did not care, as what was close to a feast was prepared in the Oldman household and everyone was there congratulating Rebecca. The phone almost never ceased ringing, with friends and other relatives all shouting and squealing to her in happiness and joy. Zach could see the happiness in Rebecca's face. All her dreams had come true. Even when she caught his eye, she smiled, which was something rare enough in itself. Even Shangal had agreed to a truce and willingly went deep into the recesses of Zach's mind, where he could not hear or act upon what was going on. It was a nice gesture from the demon, one that Zach thanked him for.

...

Katie was so happy for her sister that she did not know what to say or do at first. Initially she jumped with joy, and then she hugged Rebecca. Finally, tears rolled down her face. All of this was to show how happy she was that her older sister had accomplished all that she wanted.

As the food was whittled down bit by bit, most of it going to the ever growing Tyler, Rebecca stood up to make an announcement.

'Thank you all so much,' she started. 'It has been a hard few weeks for all of us, but finally I have done it. It will be sad to leave you all tomorrow in my new outfitted car.' She stopped so everyone could express their jealousy and sadness. 'But I hope you all know that I will visit as often as I can.' She raised her glass. Everyone joined her in a toast. Then the meal continued with a mixture of merriment, comic jealousy, and sadness.

The evening wore on. After most everyone had gone up to bed, Zach and Katie stayed below to help Rebecca finish off what was left of the food. As the door clicked shut, Rebecca carried on their secret conversation.

'I know you have said you are sorry because of the timing, but you can't expect me to drive the both of you to the middle of nowhere in the middle of the night, wait for God knows how long by myself, and then drive you both back with no explanation as to why we are going or why it must be a secret.'

'Please, Becky,' Katie pleaded, 'it's really important. Zach needs to go back to his old house to collect something he left behind.'

'That's all very well, but why does it have to be tonight? And why can't Mum or Dad do it? I'm sorry, but neither of you is giving me enough to go on. Now that I am what I am, I have to be careful of what I do.' Rebecca was fitting into her role perfectly as a sergeant.

Zach knew there was only one way around this. 'Rebecca,' he started, knowing that he and not his demon was in full control, 'what is happening outside and to this city will come to an end soon, and not the good kind of end. I know you see things in me when you are near to me, and I know you do not trust me completely. But, please, if I do not go back and collect what I need, then we could all be in grave danger. I think you know of what I speak.' His eyes locked with Rebecca's, and then they both shared the vision of the powerful storm engulfing the cathedral, the sheer power of it knocking the gargoyles to the ground and sending tiles and bricks spiralling into the air.

'I'll give you an hour once we get there. Anything over and I will leave you both,' Rebecca answered after a long, pensive pause.

'That's all I will need,' Zach replied with a smile.

They were in the village before any of them knew what had happened. Rebecca pulled up into the gap opposite the house. Zach sighed with grief upon seeing all the lights off and the vines starting to reclaim the walls and pipes. As he climbed out of the car, he kissed Katie and nodded to Rebecca in thanks.

'Remember,' she whispered to him just before he stalked off, 'no more than an hour or we are gone.' With those words ringing in his ears, he disappeared into the night.

Softly and stealthily climbing the vastly overgrown bank, he looked over the house and felt the sting of anger build up inside him. The home of him and his late family was not as empty as it looked. He saw shadows moving within, and outside in the garden. These were not the vague wanderings of squatters but the professional and predictable patrolling of guards. Even though Shangal was not there with him, his anger built. Taking a silent deep breath, he planned his route and made for it.

...

Katie sat with her sister in the cold dark of the latter's car. As much as she did not want to believe it, she knew her sister would leave if Zach did not come back in time. Rebecca was sitting nervously at the wheel. It was the last journey she was giving the car, before letting it gather dust in the garage and taking her new, outfitted car out for its first drive in the morning. The minutes felt like years as the two sat alone, neither one speaking for fear of losing track of time.

'Do you love him, little sister?' Rebecca finally broke the silence.

'I do,' Katie replied as naturally as breathing, 'with all my heart.'

'I hope so. If you don't and something does happen like he says and you can't deal with it, I think it will be the end of him.'

'Don't worry, Becks. He will look after me, and I will look after him.'

'I *do* worry because – what is that?' All of Rebecca's thoughts of their conversation were destroyed as she saw the light of fire take and build within the house.

Before they could even open their doors, Zach appeared in front of the car, his face tense but bloodless, his hands clutching what seemed to be another old tattered book and pictures. As he climbed in, he spoke with deep authority. 'Drive. Drive now. Don't look back, and don't stop.'

That was all Rebecca needed. She brought her car to life and sped away from the clearing and out of the village. She did not care that she was going the wrong way; she just needed to be away from what was going to happen.

A single tear rolled down Zach's face as the night sky erupted in flame and smoke. His home, the last refuge of his happy memories, was destroyed. Everything positive and good about Zach faded into the night. The sky was bright as if the sun had risen early, only instead of the promise of morning, it was the promise of death, destruction, and vengeance. For all of his wrongdoings and grievances against Zach, Christian Jones, his old would-be friend, had now gone too far. Zach would see to it that he knew it.

CHAPTER 18

Z ACH'S FURY AND ANGER FESTERED within him for days, like an unmoving, unyielding sickness. It was borderline pure, unbridled rage. Through his descending weakness, his demon had been a constant voice in his ear, thinking his influence was growing. However, since the night when his home was taken by flame, Zach had learnt what must be done. He knew what had to happen and what must not happen. As much as it pained him, he knew what he had to do and what that would mean. The tattered book he had salvaged had told him everything he needed to hear. The apparent truce Shangal had made with him was a true godsend, as it meant he could put his plan into motion without the demon becoming aware.

It had become apparent to the both of them where the duel would take place. The centre of the storm had come to rest over the cathedral. The fact that it was covered in scaffolding and exterior walkways made it an interesting and treacherous battleground, even more so because many people visited it daily, despite the storm cloud slowly circling overhead. But something else had also become apparent. David Alexander and Azrael were becoming more powerful with each day. The overwhelming feeling of unease and betrayal swamped both Zach and Shangal. There was a strategy behind it all.

Try as he might, Zach could not concentrate on anything. He should have been focusing on the storm and the possibility of his death, but in reality he could not focus on any one thing. This was what Shangal wanted. This was the opening he had craved for, for so many years.

...

'The cathedral? How interesting. A highly public and religious place to do battle, don't you think?' a youthful David Alexander questioned his demonic reflection.

'This is true, but it can be used as a staging point for our strike against humanity. What a message it would send by levelling such a building. The message that would send to our human cattle would truly be inspiring to see,' Azrael arrogantly said, eagerly waiting for the day to arrive.

'Soon we will both have what we want.' David smiled, stepping over more drained and consumed bodies. 'We get this realm to rule, and we utterly destroy the one best chance of stopping us, who just happens to be a boy whom I have hunted and an old comrade you want to execute. What more of a sign do we need that our cause is the winnable one?'

The demon chuckled in David Alexander's head as the latter finished speaking his words with a smile. It had all gone according to plan. His titans were battle-ready, he was in the form and had the youthfulness that he wanted, and the demon within him was already readying his shock troops for invasion. All that was left was the boy, the mongrel from that demon-hunting Inquisitional family that had hunted him to near death. The irony now was that they had not seen their own child and heir as one until it was far too late. Soon David Alexander would have that pleasure, before his demon consumed them both.

...

Rebecca's mind was ablaze and her head ached like she had been out drinking every night since she had taken Zach and Katie to his old house. It was unnatural and broke her focus. Her mentor kept saying it was the shock of being where she was, but she was not so sure. It had been a fast-paced day. She had met the unit that she would command and saw how they all worked and operated in a practice test environment. She was pleased with them all. It seemed to her that her unit were not as trigger-happy as she had thought. They rather seemed to talk first, even if that did include loud, thuggish profanities, before shooting. She was proud of that.

She was then taken around the staging area, where those in her unit would store their weapons and leave their vehicles when they were on duty, and the sleeping quarters. This happened much sooner than she had expected. After her various introductions and tours, she was shown to her room, where she unpacked everything she would need and tried to find some quiet and solace in her head. Flying around in her mind was the lightning storm over the cathedral, but she also saw more than that. She saw figures dancing a vicious dance in and around the spire. With each flash of lightning, they moved to a different spot, until one fell as if dead and another looked up at the sky and screamed a scream she had never heard and could not quite gauge. The scream ended when a near atomic boom erupted from the sky with a flash of purple light illuminating the sky as if hell itself had come to earth. After her vision, she collapsed onto her bed, her thoughts and head ablaze with images that could not and should not be true. Only when her phone rang by her ear did she wake up as if from a yearlong nightmare. All she needed to see was the name of her sister on the screen to know that something was wrong.

CHAPTER 19

THE FIRST TIME ZACH HAD slept in months, he had a nightmare, a nightmare that changed everything that he had planned and spurred him to action. The dream was a mixture of memories stretching back to the day of his true possession, not the false one of a few months ago when Shangal wanted to remind him who was 'in control', but the day when he, as a child, was nearly killed. The dream made him angry at Christian for betraying him, but he also felt powerful for doing what he did. He had memories of his family dead around him in smoke and fire, but the most potent image was the last memory he had before he woke: the memory of the hospital.

Hours after the lorry had slammed into his family convoy and left all for dead, Zach's eyes flickered open to behold the overly white ceiling of an emergency hospital ward. He had tubes in his arms and sensors on his blistered head and chest. Everything ought to have terrified him, but it did not. Summoning strength he did not know existed, he hauled himself from his bed and fell with a bone-shattering thud onto the floor. He was weak but he willed himself to stand. Just when he thought he could not, his muscles awoke as if controlled by another and he leapt to his feet. Everything felt warm to him as if he was on fire, but he did not care. He padded over to the door and tried the handle. It was locked.

Just before trying to break it down, he heard voices. Calming himself for a moment, he pressed his ear to the thick wood and listened.

'How is he, Nurse?'

'I'm not sure, Doctor. He was unconscious when he came in, likely caused by shock and exhaustion, but he should have come out of that by now.'

'We shall see if we can bring him out of it. The police want to ask him questions when he is able to answer. What of the others in the cars?'

'None of them survived.' Zach could almost hear the tears in the nurse's eyes as she spoke. 'They were either crushed or incinerated. Their bodies are being taken down to the morgue now for examination.'

'Such a waste of life, but we have a chance to save another one now.'

'Doctor, is it really wise to wake him now? It could have severe repercussions to his mental stability.'

'We have to try, Nurse, or else we could lose another person today.'

Zach heard the conversation finish as the doctor's and nurse's footsteps walked away. He then heard another set of footsteps, these coming towards his door. With no thought or hesitation, he set up the ambush. As the lock gave and the handle opened, the doctor stepped in, his coat as white as the ceiling, his tired face filled with sadness. He did not even have time to react before Zach leapt at him, hands wrapping around his neck.

'The morgue,' Zach demanded, squeezing the doctor's neck. 'How do I get to it?'

'Out the door, turn right, level 4 in the lift,' the doctor replied, struggling for breath.

Zach thanked the helpless doctor before knocking him unconscious and leaving his limp body on the floor. He knew he had to be quick, as the nurse could return at any moment. Moving at a fast creep, Zach went straight for the lifts, but he did not get that far before he saw her. They were bringing her covered body to the morgue. He did not even need to see her face. He knew it was Laura. Changing to a sprint, he charged straight at the porters, who were oblivious to him until the last minute. He bowled one over before he could scream, and then he threw the other against the wall, tears stinging his eyes and blinding his sight. Slowly, and with the respect and love he had for Laura, he raised the cover and looked at her.

She looked so peaceful lying there with no life, her face neutral and blank, her skin cold. She was dead. Zach could contain his emotion any longer as he sobbed and cried over her. He did not even hear the shouts of the security guards as they closed in on him. Sadness, pain, anger, and fury coursed through him like fuel as he sent the guards flying. No one would take her away from him again. But it was all in vain, as two more guards came from behind and pinned him against the wall. In anger and sadness, he pleaded with both of them to let him go, but all he got was a needle in the neck. The world slowly blurred. The last thing he saw before the blackness was Laura's face being covered over again. But as he drifted into the black, he heard a voice. It did not belong to anyone around him. It spoke with a deep boom, even though it said only four words: 'And so it begins.'

…

Since having that nightmare, Zach had changed his plan. Now he had to air it. The whole Oldman family had gathered in the kitchen, including Rebecca, fresh back from the academy, her face filled with worry. Zach stepped into the room. Silence fell as they all waited in anticipation.

'Thank you all for coming,' Zach began, sorrow filling his voice. 'I only have one thing to say, and it is something you are not going to like. I know there may be questions, but know that I cannot answer them all or answer them truthfully.' The Oldman family looked at each other with confusion as Zach took a deep breath and continued. 'Today I must leave you. This may very well be the last time we see each other.'

After a momentary silence of shock and amazement, the kitchen erupted with questions and objections from everyone. Everyone but Katie spoke. She knew what this was about, but she still could not stop herself from weeping. Holding up his hand for silence, Zach spoke again.

'I know this is hard for all of you. It was difficult for me to come to this decision, but it is for your protection. If I am not here, you will all be safe.'

'What are you talking about, Zach?' Daisy asked. 'We all see you as a family member now. Whatever has happened or will happen, we will face it together as a family.'

Zach was touched by what Daisy had said, but it could not change his mind.

'I wish I could tell you why, but that would put you in even more danger.'

It was then that Philip stood and spoke, forcing the other to quieten.

'I know I am not the easiest person to get along with, Zach, and we have had our differences in the past. But you have to give us a hell of a good reason for all of this before I even consider letting you go. Because in allowing you to go, I will be hurting my daughter. And nothing is more important to me than the happiness and safety of my family.'

Zach glanced at Katie with a look of love, but also as if asking a question. Katie nodded as her silent answer.

'All right, Philip.' Zach stood, regret filling him. 'This will mean putting you in grave danger. But at least I can tell you all the truth.' Zach undid the Velcro on his fingerless gloves and pulled them off. Tossing them onto the table, he took a deep breath and opened both his hands to them. Everyone jumped back in shock as they saw his orange brands throbbing with power and glowing like the fires of hell.

'Even if you do not know what these are or what they mean,' Zach said to the shocked family, 'you know that this is not normal. Plus, there are people who want these for themselves. They will kill if they have to so they can get them. In leaving you, I protect you.' The family looked at each other and confided in each other before walking over to Zach. They took turns embracing him, as if they were bidding goodbye to a son. They all left, except Katie, who stood and held Zach close.

'Know that I love you,' Zach said, tears in his eyes, 'and that if I survive, I will come back.'

'If you do,' she replied, 'come back quickly.'

Those were the last words they spoke to each other. Zach kissed her and left the Oldman house. He would return either alive and demon-less or not at all, the latter being the most likely.

...

As the door clicked shut and Zach disappeared off into the night, Katie turned and wiped the false tears from her face, now wearing a broad smile. After she climbed the stairs and entered her room, she pulled out her mobile phone and dialled a number. It was answered in seconds.

'Hey, you,' Katie spoke like a giddy schoolgirl, 'he's left now. Tell your friend that he is broken and ready. When will I see you next?'

'I'll let him know now. Oh, I am sure we can see each other soon,' the happy voice of Christian replied from the other end. 'After all, we have to celebrate, don't we?'

With a giggle, Katie agreed. They made their plans as the night drew in around the city.

CHAPTER 20

Dᴀᴠɪᴅ Aʟᴇxᴀɴᴅᴇʀ ᴡᴀs ᴀʙᴜɴᴅᴀɴᴛʟʏ ʜᴀᴘᴘʏ with himself. No one in the order's headquarters had ever seen him as happy as he was now. It was almost unnerving, but no one questioned it because anyone who would have done so would have been consumed. But David Alexander had good reason to be happy. Everything had come full circle and according to plan. From the subtle manipulation of Rodger Green and the decimation of the Ford family, to the secret inserting of the trigger in the form of Katie, Zach was now lost, alone, and vulnerable. All this came together the day before the duel would happen. The odds were with Zach. They would see to it that the chance would not go to waste.

Nearly skipping around his office with glee, David Alexander pressed the intercom button and spoke to his acting assistant. 'Ready the titans for battle and travel. And prepare my things for tomorrow.'

'Yes, my lord,' his assistant replied. 'I have an audience request from Rodger Green. Response?'

'I had almost forgotten about Green.' David Alexander chuckled with his demon. 'Yes. Why not? Bring him to me.'

Uncorking a fresh bottle of wine, David Alexander prepared two crystal glasses and waited for his captive to arrive. Unlike the previous times, Rodger walked into his office with the aid of a cane, his legs having become nearly useless because of his imprisonment. With a smile, David Alexander stood with his arms open as if to embrace his captive.

'Ah, Mister Green,' he called as Rodger meekly sat down close to him. 'I feel I must apologize because I have not seen as much of you as I had hoped. With all the preparations being made and things being filed, I'm sure as a former head teacher you can understand?'

'It's fine,' Rodger replied, taken aback by how happy David Alexander was. 'I just wanted to ask one thing.'

'Really?' David Alexander said, all happiness draining from his face. 'And what is that?'

'Now that I have done all you asked,' Rodger began, fear taking him, 'and I can no longer see my use to you or this operation, I was hoping that you would let me see my son again before you release him.'

'Is that all?' David Alexander laughed. 'Well, I think you are ready to see him before he goes. Follow me if you can, Mister Green.'

It was painfully slow-going for Rodger as he tried to keep up with the surprisingly youthful David Alexander, but he just about managed it. The maze of walkways and corridors never ceased to amaze him. Wherever it was, it must have been completely hidden from view of the people around it. After what seemed like an age, David Alexander opened a door to a huge hall and ushered Rodger in, asking the guard to bring Carl.

Nervousness and fear hit Rodger as they waited in the vast empty hall. All he could hear was the breathing of his captor behind him.

'How have you been treating him?' Rodger asked boldly, wanting to break the silence.

David Alexander was completely stunned by the question. He smiled after a sizeable pause of thought before replying. 'He has been treated like a god amongst men,' he said with a sadistic smile.

Rodger was confused by the answer. As he tried to think about what those words meant, he felt and heard something else coming from the other end of the hall. It was distant at first. Then he heard what sounded like a thud and felt the ground tremble under his feet. The noise and tremble grew louder and felt harder as another door at the end of the hall burst open and three forms stepped in. The thudding, Rodger quickly understood, belonged to the footsteps of a huge being, which shook the floor each time his foot made contact with it. The being's face was covered as it was led into the centre of the hall. Its handlers moved away after removing the cover from its face.

Rodger fell to his knees with a sob as he beheld his son, but not as he once knew him. Carl stood taller and more muscular than anything Rodger had ever seen. But it was the lack of symmetry that shocked the father more. Carl's right arm was as round as a tree trunk with veins and arteries literally bursting from the skin, whereas the his left arm was normal but deformed. The same was true of the lad's chest, face, and legs. Rodger's son was a monster.

'What have you done to him, you bastard?' Rodger cried, swinging his cane in the direction of David Alexander.

'I have given him a gift,' David Alexander replied, catching the cane with his left hand. 'He is a god amongst men. He will never tire, never weaken, and never betray me. He is more than a human. He is a titan.'

Seeing Rodger broken, David Alexander took the advantage. He kicked Rodger towards his son whilst ridding him of his cane. As Rodger landed with a thud, David Alexander spoke in a demonic voice.

'Titan, cripple the human who would assault your lord.'

With that, Carl roared and stomped towards Rodger.

Seeing his son coming with a building rage, Rodger tried to pick himself up, but he had no strength left. Before he knew it, he was hoisted into the air by the huge arm of Carl and tossed into the air. He crashed into the ceiling, screaming in pain as his back broke and his body hurtled towards the ground. Before he hit the floor, he was caught again in Carl's huge dominant arm and hurled at a wall. The impact nearly killed him. The crater where he made contact was where he stayed. As Carl made to charge him, Rodger spoke again with a demonic voice of authority.

'Titan, cease and stand down.'

With a nod of acknowledgement, Carl stopped and stood in place, watching his broken father.

Rodger could not move. His spine was broken. *He* was utterly broken, both physically and mentally. He had nothing left and now hoped against hope that David Alexander would put an end to his miserable life. Managing to open his eyes, he saw that same form in front of him smiling, like he knew exactly what Rodger wanted.

'You see, Green,' said David Alexander, picking up Rodger by the throat, 'your son is better than anything and everything the world has ever seen. And soon everyone, everywhere, will be the same, or they will be slaves like you, tired, broken, and weak. Look upon your son one last time, Rodger Green.'

Unable to feel or speak, Rodger looked at his deformed beast of a son for the last time. Sadness and regret filled him as he remembered his real son. He also remembered the child he should have helped instead of abandoned. He kept those thoughts ripe in his mind as he felt his life force being drained from him, until he was utterly consumed by David Alexander and his demon.

...

Since Zach had left the Oldman house, Rebecca had not felt right. She had thought that once he was gone for good, she would feel better and less tormented by her dreams and visions. Instead, an overwhelming feeling of dread and despair pounded at her like waves against a sea wall. This began after she'd talked to Katie on the phone. Instead of hearing sadness in her sister's voice, she detected the smallest hint of happiness so subtle that an untrained ear would not have heard it. But to Rebecca it was as obvious as a slap in the face. Katie had lied to her and to Zach. The question was, why? And for what reason?

Rebecca spent that night at the academy with her team, as their call duty started the next morning. All of them were positive that it would be a quiet day with the storm overhead. They even joked about having a lie-in after the morning alarm bell sounded. But she knew they would be ready for whatever was or was not thrown at them in the coming days. Rebecca was not as positive as they were. Her visions and dreams were clear on one thing: when the storm started, the battle would begin.

Slowly walking to her room, she made ready her equipment for tomorrow and readied herself for sleep. For once, her mind did not bestow on her dreams or nightmares, but rather remained quiet and promised to allow her to sleep. Just as she was about to surrender to sleep, she heard it. It was not far away or soft, as it usually was when it happened, but rather close and explosive like nothing she had never seen. There were no flashes of light, just the booming of thunder.

This is it, she thought. *This is the start of my visions. And so it begins.*

CHAPTER 21

THE BOOM OF THE THUNDER woke Zach, who had been sleeping in the hiding place he had chosen. It sounded like the bowels of hell rumbling in anticipation of a hard-earned meal. Both Zach and his demon were nervous but not scared. They had both been through enough to feel fear. It had been a while since he last slept. Unlike the other few times, this time he slept out of necessity rather than an actual need for rest. It calmed his mind, almost as much as sharpening his long hidden sabres did. Today would be their last battle too. That was his hope, anyway.

Rising, he stretched and surveyed his surroundings. He had chosen the spot near the river and close to the cathedral. With the weather the way it was, Zach did not expect anyone to venture too near. He was close enough to leave when he wanted. He knew that David Alexander and Azrael would already be waiting for him on the cathedral grounds. The question was where. Pulling on his long salvaged coat, which kept his sabres nicely hidden beneath, he stretched and clicked his aching bones and muscles one last time. Everything was in place, ready for his enemies. It was now down to pure skill and hopeful co-operation from Shangal. This is what would see him live, nothing more and nothing less.

As he stalked the town, he was happily surprised to discover that it was abandoned. The storm cloud had cast every inch of the town in darkness, as if it were perpetual midnight in winter. Not even the street lights were on. No one and nothing walked the streets with him. The town was near enough a ghost town. Zach did not slow down. He could not afford to be late. If he did not show up on time, there would be dire consequences. Turning right, he walked under the archway that led into the grounds.

Stopping momentarily, he removed a brick from the wall and placed his hand inside, checking to see if his deposit was still there.

After lightly grasping the thick wool and being satisfied that it was unmoved, Zach replaced the brick and marched on to his destination.

'What was that you were checking?' Shangal questioned from within Zach's head.

'Nothing to worry you,' Zach replied out loud. 'Just focus on what we need to get done.'

'Do not worry about that, human.' The demon sneered. 'I know what I need to do.'

Knowing what that meant and satisfied that all arrangements were made, Zach approached the cathedral.

It was in a sorry-looking state. The scaffolding was wrapped around it like vines and had been there for as long as Zach could remember. Nearly the whole structure was covered top to bottom with rickety wooden walkways and rusty metal scaffold poles. All of these just made the spire appear straighter. Zach paid little attention to that now as he scanned the doors he walked past. All were sealed shut, which was unusual, as nearly every day without fail the doors would be open for worshippers and tourists. Looking up and down every inch of the aging monastery, Zach did not understand where he should go. Even Shangal was confused. He was also agitated, not liking the blatant trickery.

Another boom of thunder rolled across the sky. That was when Zach felt it: another presence, a presence like him, not quite normal. Zach did not even know he was running as Shangal took physical control, sending him sprinting towards the cloister door. Seeing that it was sealed shut, Shangal sent out Zach's fist to strike the door down, but to no effect. Zach, not liking being a puppet, tried in vain to regain control. Eventually he settled for half control as he leapt onto the roof and moved down into the enclosed cloisters. As he landed, he knew that all exits were sealed, all but the one leading into the worship area of the cathedral. It quickly became apparent that he and Shangal were not alone. Zach's hands instinctively lowered to the hidden hilts of his sabres as a form crept from the shadows and came to stand in front of him.

'And so it begins,' the harrowingly familiar demonic voice spoke, 'the clash of two immortals trapped in the body of mortals. One will rise and ascend to rule, whilst the other will fall and be consumed.' It was the overly youthful form of David Alexander that had strode from the shadows to stand in front of Zach, his eyes the red eyes of Azrael. Zach knew that David Alexander was standing before him in form but not mind. Azrael was in complete control.

'Let me take control, human,' Shangal spoke in agitation. 'It is the only way now.'

'Stay with the plan, demon, or we both die.'

'No matter what plan you have,' Azrael roared in arrogance, 'I will not be beaten this day. Titans, destroy the demon usurper who would kill your lord.'

It was then that Zach realized the trap. Three huge forms dragged themselves out of the gloom and stood next to Azrael, who promptly retreated, a huge demon smile on his face. Zach padded backwards as the titans closed in, growling and groaning in either agony or pleasure – Zach was not sure. Then one charged unprovoked at him. Summoning Shangal's speed and strength, but still keeping the demon at bay, Zach drew his sabres together, sending the arcs at the titan's face and stomach. It howled with pain as Zach darted around it, sending it to floor, one of its eyes sliced in half and its abdomen spilling black blood onto the floor. Zach did not have time to finish him off as the others ran at him, roaring.

Ducking under the oversized arm swing of one beast, Zach hamstrung it with one quick slice from one sabre and stabbed the tip of the other into its head. It twitched for an instant and dropped down dead. The death fuelled Shangal, but Zach kept him back as he dodged and struck the other charging titan. As Zach dodged, blocked, and attacked his opponent, he noticed the wounded one pick itself up and limp back into the fray. No matter how much pain it was in, it would do its master's bidding. Seeing the opening in his current aggressor's clumsy attacks, Zach took the advantage. Rolling under the titan's opening legs, Zach sliced off both of its feet with surprising ease, thanks to the aid of Shangal and his strength. As the beast wailed and fell, Zach leapt onto its back and then its head. The titan was fell right at his wounded brethren.

Timing it perfectly, Zach waited for the thud of impact before jamming one sabre into the back of the falling titan and vaulting into the air. Landing on the shoulder of the other, he pushed its head towards the already dead titan, connecting again and again, which resulting in the satisfying sound of crunching bone. As the wounded titan whimpered in pain, Zach put it out of its apparent misery by deeply slicing its neck. More black blood poured from the creature as it died. Yanking the blood-soaked sabre from the back of the titan's head, Zach strode towards Azrael, letting Shangal have a bit more control.

Zach could see visible fear in the red eyes of the demon. As Azrael turned and fled the cloister ground, Zach was hard on his feet. The storm was building in power as Zach gave chase up the tower of the old cathedral. No matter how fast Azrael ran, Zach and Shangal were right behind him, sabres ready. Rapidly ascending the spiral staircase leading higher up the tower, Zach heard Azrael stop. Slowing, Zach and Shangal made ready as they turned into the bell-ringer's room. The ropes swung slowly in the gathering wind from the storm, but Zach did not give them a second thought as he approached Azrael. The fear left Azrael's eyes as a shape fell from the ceiling right at Zach. Rolling away just in time, the titan crashed onto the floor, breaking and cracking the old bricks as it landed. Readying himself for another foray, Zach noticed something different about this beast. It was Carl Green, but not anymore. Laughing, Azrael summoned demon-fire to his hands and fashioned it into a cruel-looking blade as Carl attacked.

Carl was not like the others. They were slow and predictable, whereas Carl was powerful one moment but fast the next. Each attack was different. Zach struggled to gain the upper hand. Soon Azrael had joined the fight too, whirling the sword around his body, sending searing-hot strikes at Zach's body. Then it dawned on Zach, as sudden as flash of lightning. He knew what he needed to do. Leaping into the air, Zach set his own blades ablaze with demon-fire, his being purple, as opposed to the red of Azrael's sword. Keeping away from the other demon as much as he could, he struck out for Carl's weak spots. Soon the titan was covered in flames as Zach seized the advantages he needed. Then the titan erupted in flame and fell to the floor, shrieking as it burned.

'You pathetic excuse for a soldier,' Azrael boomed, taking off Carl's head with a swing of his sword, 'must I do it all myself?'

'Where is Jones, Azrael?' Zach demanded. 'He was also part of the agreement.'

'Well, seeing as you asked,' Azrael replied, chuckling, 'why don't I show you?'

Casting aside his sword, Azrael summoned more demon-fire, but this time it appeared in a circle between the two of them. The circle gradually turned into a ball and then into a half circle, and then an image appeared, subtly at first – but then it grew into something that made Zach's eyes red with rage. Christian was with Katie. She was not fighting him or pushing him away like last time. Instead, she was lying next to him and planting light kisses on his cheek whilst he smiled. With a hiss, the ball disappeared. Zach looked upon the smug form of Azrael.

'It was all a lie, boy,' he began. 'Did you really think that anyone would love or want a mongrel like you? Your own filthy parents bred you for one purpose alone, to imprison a demon that they could later exorcise, killing you in the process. You are of no use to anyone. Why not just give up now? I will kill you quickly.'

'I have one use,' Zach spoke, rage building within him as Shangal came through more, changing his voice. 'Killing you.'

Azrael roared as he re-summoned his sword and leapt at Zach. Zach now knew it was time. He surrendered himself to his demon.

Shangal took control with ease and caught his old comrade in the air, sending him to the floor with a thud. Both demons had flaming swords, but Shangal had two – and he knew how to best use them. With blinding speed and ferocity, he unleashed a flurry of flaming strikes at Azrael, their sheer power and speed sending the older, more experienced demon backwards. Knowing that he had Azrael where he wanted him, Shangal began the execution. Sending a blast of pure power around the room, Shangal willed the ropes to come alive. They became animated like snakes, moving to wrap around Azrael like he was their prey. He managed to cut and burn a few before retreating out of their range, but foolishly moving within Shangal's. Slamming the sword from Azrael's hand, Shangal began a series of swift, brutal strikes at his foe's body. Each slice opened up a red gash on the demon until he was backed against a wall. Summoning every ounce of strength, Shangal plunged a sabre straight through his old comrade's shoulder, pinning him high against the cold grey stone.

Once Azrael was stuck there, Shangal sent the ropes at him again until one got a tight hold around his neck. Clenching his fist until it was as hard as stone, Shangal struck the floor underneath Azrael with enough force to make a near endless drop into the black of the cathedral. Azrael was stunned at his defeat but also at the apparent mercy his adversary was granting him. He watched in nervousness as Zach regained control and walked towards him.

'You have taken everything from me,' Zach started, every negative emotion possible fuelling him. 'Why should I not let you hang like the criminal you are? Do you even have a reason?'

Azrael could not speak with the rope around his neck, so he shook his head.

'I did not think so.' This time it was Shangal who spoke. 'But fear not, demon brother. You have left this realm in fine hands.'

Shangal willed the sword to life. The blade flew out from Azrael's shoulder, after which the demon fell into the darkness, leaving nothing but the snap and creak of the rope to confirm his death. Gasping, Zach tried to sit, but Shangal stopped him.

'What are you doing?' Zach questioned, already knowing the answer.

'Taking this realm for myself.'

Shangal burst through Zach's defences and took full control for a moment before the storm burst into life and sent purple lightning across the sky. With the battle of trapped immortals won, the battle of will and mind began with a streak of purple lightning.

CHAPTER 22

REBECCA WAS ROUSED FROM HER daydream by the sound of the alarm. The storm had broken and lightning was striking all over the town, but another call had come in, this one regarding apparent gunshot-sounding noises coming from the cathedral. Her team was ready in an instant. Gone were the thoughts of a relaxing day as they had hoped. Their minds were now solely focused on the task at hand. They arrived at the cathedral in minutes. In an orderly fashion, they disembarked their vehicles and then moved in hasty formation to the cathedral doors. The storm was growing in power and intensity like a sleeping dragon that had been suddenly wakened to find its treasure horde gone. Now it was getting violent and destructive. Police officers had already cordoned off the whole area around the cathedral and were trying in vain to keep the public out. The sight of the armed response unit made the crowd part and fall quiet, but not for long. After a pause to collect her thoughts, Rebecca readied her pistol and gave the order to enter.

It was haunting to see the cathedral so deserted and dark. The whole building was without power, and no one was willing to risk trying to make it to the substation with the storm raging overhead. Only the lights of their torches guided the team through the black. It was not long before they realized something was wrong. It was the odour. The stench of rotting flesh was nauseating, mixed with what could only be described as stagnant blood. The origin of the odours was the cloisters. Rebecca gasped and gagged with shock when she beheld three bodies, their hideous faces and deformed bodies going against everything she knew. She ordered that section to be guarded and sealed until a specialist team arrived. Then she ordered the remainder of her unit up to the bell tower, her vision slowly coming true.

The offensive odour hit them again as they reached the bell-ringing area. Another monstrosity lay charred on the floor, the smell of burnt dead flesh not helping the already pungent aroma. It was then that Rebecca saw the rope and the hole in the floor. She paced slowly towards it, her weapon raised. When she was at the edge of the black hole, she leant forward and shined her light down. She saw the makeshift noose at the end but no corpse there or on the ground under it. She could faintly make out some black marks on the rope, but all thoughts of those left her mind when she heard the roar and scream from above, mixed with the noise of thunder. Her unit were already prepared and continued upwards.

With each step she took, her heart beat faster. Everything was coming true, but how and why? Reaching the top of the stairs, her unit climbed onto the scaffolding and slowly ascended the stairs leading to the very top of the spire. She could hear growling and whimpering as she crept to the top, where she gasped again at what she saw. It was Zach, but it was not Zach.

...

Zach did not remember climbing the tower or making his way onto the spire, but he remembered the pain of the battle he was fighting now: the battle to regain himself. He knew that the fight with Azrael would give Shangal enough rage to break through, but he did not know that it was enough for him to break through into this realm. Zach was using every ounce of his strength to stave off the demon, but he knew he was losing and that he would most likely bring about the destruction of his world. He had almost surrendered to that thought when he saw Rebecca standing before him, fear and shock filling her face as her unit took up their positions.

'Brought some friends, did you?' Shangal spoke from inside Zach, hungry for more death

Zach knew what was coming before the demon did. With Zach screaming at Rebecca to take cover, Shangal sent a purple ball of fire at her. She heard the warning just in time. The ball sailed inches past her and disappeared out of sight. Just as Shangal prepared another, Zach took control of that hand and held it in front of his face. Laughing in amusement, Shangal sent more energy against Zach defences, hoping to push what was left of the boy out. Zach almost lost his grasp on the fireball as Rebecca's unit opened fire. Bullets flew at them, but Shangal deflected them all with the sabres, his concentration lost on Zach. Angered, he sent a blast of energy at the officers, forcing their weapons out of their hands. Zach knew it was now or never as he sent the message to Rebecca and briefly took control.

Taking control of both hands, Zach plunged one sabre into his own chest and pointed the other skyward. Shangal howled with pain as the sword went deeper into his chest, but he did not for a second anticipate the lightning. As if reacting to a command, a bolt of purple lightning struck Shangal and Zach together, the excruciating pain affecting them both. Using the break in the demon's control, Zach shied away from the pain for a split second and sent them both over the edge of the spire, hurtling them towards the ground. Everything in his miserable life had led him to this. Even though his demon still struggled for control, Zach was ready for death, ready for the long rest that he craved. He heard the crash as they went through the roof and higher floors of the cathedral, but he felt nothing. He did not even feel the impact as the demon's body was impaled on the font.

...

Rebecca could not stop the tears from falling. She was crying not only in sadness but also in sheer disbelief of what she had seen. Zach, the boy who loved her sister, was not a boy but something far more vicious. But instead of letting that other thing win, he chose to fling his body from the highest point in the town. He did this rather than harm Rebecca. She was the older sister who hated him for no reason. She did not remember running down the flights of stairs or barging through the various doors to get to the font. But she remembered the body. It was Zach's, but again it was not Zach's. The face was his, but the eyes were red, the nails were claws, the teeth were fangs, and the skin was ash grey. How could Zach be that? She sat on the ground by the body, utterly shocked and in disbelief.

Soon the teams were inside, clearing the bodies away. Zach's was the last. As Rebecca stood, she looked at the people slowly removing his broken body from the font. It was then that it hit her. She recognized none of them. Before she protested, a dart hit her in the neck and she was falling. The last thing she heard was Zach's voice in her head saying, 'What begins now ends, but what ends can never be forgotten. It can only come back as a different beginning.'

EPILOGUE TO PART I

SIX MONTHS LATER

'It has been half a year since the unnatural and hellish storm struck. People are now just coming to terms with it,' the news reporter on the old pub television screen said. 'But there are still questions to ask and answers to be found. Some people are happy to forget, but most now want the most important thing, the truth. Police and other official enforcement bodies are still desperately searching for the one person who could have the answers. He has been named as sixteen-year-old Zach Ford. He is still marked as violent and extremely dangerous. If you encounter him, do not attempt to restrain him. Either call the police or the number below.' The news report ended with one picture of the dark-haired Zach and another of him on a Salisbury CCTV camera.

'What a charmer,' a drunken patron blurted to his friend sitting across from him. 'Strolls into a cathedral cool as a cucumber, murders those people, and nearly has a go at the fuzz before flinging himself off the spire and damaging the place beyond easy repair.'

'Hear, hear,' his equally drunken friend replied, lifting his pint. 'If he were here, I would show him what real violence is. I'd make him wish he weren't alive.' Shouting at a young lad who was silently tidying other tables, he asked, 'Isn't that right?' Not knowing how to reply or how to take the patron, the lad quickly scampered out of sight.

'What's with the new lad, Jim?' the patron called. 'Seems a bit skittish.'

'Ah, don't mind him,' Jim, the heavyset landlord, replied, filling both pints to the brim. 'Doesn't speak a word of English. Got him cheap from Germany – but on the hush now, lads.' Understanding why their pints were now full, both patrons smiled, nodded, and drank.

As the evening drew into night, Jim saw that his patrons were up and away. He locked and bolted the main doors and set about cleaning and tidying.

'Gunter,' he called. Within seconds, the blond boy was back again, meekly looking at the floor as if he had done something wrong. 'Have you done all your jobs and tasks?' Jim asked in flawless German but with an atrocious accent.

'Yes,' Gunter replied heavily in the accent of his home country, 'everything is clean and ready for tomorrow.'

'Very good.' Jim nodded happily. 'You can go now if you want.'

'Thank you,' Gunter said, collecting his coat and fastening it up tight as Jim opened the heavy door to the harsh sea breeze. Bidding his employer goodbye, Gunter set off into the dark, shuffling away as meek as a mouse.

The walk was pleasant enough for Gunter. It was that time of night when people were readying to go out on the town, so the streets were free of people for the moment. Rounding a bend, Gunter changed his shuffle to a stride as he walked up a sudden and long steep hill. It always took longer than he expected as he turned again into a gate which opened to show a block of flats high above the little sea town. Walking to the end flat, Gunter took out his keys and let himself in. He was instantly greeted by the happy barks of a black Labrador, no more than a year old. Greeting his four-legged friend with a pat and its evening meal, Gunter took off his coat and padded to the bathroom. Preparing himself for another long night, Gunter changed from day-to-day Gunter to actual Gunter.

Facing the square mirror, Gunter flexed all his muscles and joints one after the other until they were supple and light again, not tense and useless as they were in the pub. His light blond hair slowly darkened into a night-black, and his eyes went from field green to ice-blue. To confirm that all was as it should be, Gunter looked down at his hands to see the crusting-over brand marks still on his palms. Smiling, he knew it was complete. Gunter was gone for the night. Now it was only Zach alone in a tiny flat with no one but a dog and the constant pain of the lightning burns for company. He knew it was not much of a life, but it was something. And it had its positives. It entailed a paying job that did not require much interaction with people. Also, he had a companion in his Labrador, Ebony.

And most important of all, his mind and body belonged to him alone. The demon was dead, although its essence was not fully gone.

However, there was one thing that he was absolutely certain of: this was not the end but the beginning. Seeing the report in the pub made him afraid once again. For months he had been living quietly, using his new abilities to impersonate whomever he needed to be in order to survive. But now there were others in on the hunt, others who would not give up. And there was another overwhelming thought that hit him every night. If he was able to survive what had happened, then what had happened to David Alexander? Only time would tell. Either way, Zach had no more tricks or strategies to play. If events spiralled again, then he did not know what would happen. The embers he had created and fanned for all those long painful years were now sparking into a fire, a fire that looked set to ignite the country in a blaze of anger and aggression, as people flocked to a group that made Zach shudder every time he heard its name. People flocked to the New Inquisition.

PART 2

SPARK AND IGNITION

PROLOGUE TO PART 2

ONE YEAR LATER
Rebecca awoke with a jolt, like she always had since she had been in captivity. She had forgotten how long she had been in her overly white padded cell. It had been too long. The last clear memory she had was imprinted on her mind: the day on the cathedral spire. After that, it was a haze of thoughts all mingled into one. The one thing she was absolutely sure of was that she had not been questioned since she arrived at wherever she was. Every so often she was wakened, showered with ice-cold water, fed what could only be described as weak gruel, weighed, physically checked for injury or disease, and then flung back into her cell. None of it made any sense. At least she had not been darted for a long time. That was the only positive that she could find in her current situation.

Eventually she heard footsteps approach. Then the lock of her cell door gave and opened. Two forms in white coats and masks entered. They picked her up carefully, seeing that she was weak and had lost a lot of weight, placed her down onto a wheeled bed, and pushed her out of her cell, taking great care as they wheeled her this way and that down the long corridors and walkways. Her eyes would not focus no matter how much she tried, so she listened instead. She could hear the voices of the masked people who were pushing her along, but she could not manage to make out the words they spoke. There were other voices from people who walked past her or as she was wheeled past an open door. Again she could not make out the words. Knowing she would get no information from her ears, Rebecca gave up and surrendered to unconsciousness.

She did not know how much time had passed before she was wakened again, this to the feeling of a cold liquid applied to her face. Weakly opening her eyes, she let them adjust to another small overly white room. But this time there was another in it. The person was sitting on the other side of a plain metal table with a folder in front of them. The person spoke, but Rebecca could only hear the changes in the tone of voice, not the actual words. Another quick shot of water to the face made her rapidly adjust to where she was. Sitting before her was a middle-aged man. He looked like he had had a few sleepless nights judging by the bags underneath his overused grey eyes. His face was a maze of wrinkles and worry lines, and his greying hair was visibly receding. He was clothed much like the other people she could remember, in a white lab coat and white trousers, but sewn into his coat above where his heart would be was a peculiar emblem. Seeing that Rebecca was more focused, the man spoke again.

'Miss Rebecca Oldman?' the man questioned.

Rebecca nodded in reply.

'Good. My name is Doctor Jarvis.' He spoke slowly so she would understand every word. 'I am sorry that a long time has passed before I could see you, but we had to make sure you were not in any way contaminated.'

'Where am I?' Rebecca's voice was weak and croaky as she feebly questioned the strange doctor.

'That, I cannot answer, Miss Oldman,' he responded, handing Rebecca a clear cup of water. She took a small sip and sighed in relief as it trickled down her throat, soothing, healing, and casting out the dryness.

'What then can you answer?' she asked with more determination as her voice came back to her.

'What do you want to know? Bear in mind that I only have time for one question.'

'How long have I been here?' Rebecca asked after a long pause for consideration. Jarvis opened up the folder in front of him and flicked through the pages. Once he found the answer, his eyebrow twitched with surprise before he closed the folder and looked her in the eye.

'You have been here for precisely eighteen months, seven weeks, and two days, Miss Oldman.'

Rebecca was shocked. Nearly two birthdays had past and she has remained unaware. What had her family been told? What had anyone who knew her been told? Why was she even here? The questions spiralled around her head like a tornado.

'I know this must be difficult for you,' Jarvis continued, instantly dissipating her mind tornado, 'but it was and still is necessary. You are here because you came into direct contact with a person possessed by a demon. These abominations are known to be highly contagious. We do not want an epidemic on our hands. But now that we know you are clear, we can begin to question you.'

'What information could I possibly have for you?' Rebecca asked, noting that Jarvis had used the word *abomination*.

'You knew Zach Ford, did you not?'

'Not very well. He was in love with my younger sister, who was equally infatuated with him.'

'Well, it is unfortunate that I am the one to tell you this, Miss Oldman,' Jarvis said with a sigh after flicking through his folder once again, 'but that was not the case with your sister, Katie Oldman. She was under the employ and possible corruption of another person possessed by a demon, whom we currently cannot trace.'

'How do you know this?' Rebecca blurted with anger. 'Where is my sister? What have you done to her?'

'Unlike you,' Jarvis answered with an icy-cool calm, 'your sister and other members of your family did not pass the contamination tests. They were hastily questioned and then disposed of before they could infect other members of my staff.'

'You mean you killed them?' Rebecca had fully replaced her strength with anger as she threw herself over the table to attack Jarvis.

She had not even cleared the table before an unknown force propelled her backwards, pinning her to the wall. Before she could locate the source, she was flung to the floor, damaging her knee as she landed. As she looked up, her anger waning, Jarvis stood and picked up his folder. Almost on cue, the two masked men entered, having heard the disturbance and restrained Rebecca before she could launch another attack. As they brought her under control, Jarvis stepped forward, a neutral expression commanding his face.

'Your families were abominations,' he started, his voice filled with venom. 'God will not stand for filth roaming the mortal word unchecked.

Unless you give me the answers I need, I fear you too will be found to be contaminated.' Before she could even look at her captor, he struck her across the temple. There was nothing now but black and the voice of Jarvis circulating in her mind.

CHAPTER 23

ZACH WAS GETTING USED TO his remedial day-to-day life: wake up, walk Ebony around the cliffs, breathing in the salt air as he did so, go back to the flat, change into Gunter in both clothes and physical appearance, work at the pub until the late evening, return to the flat, eat, change, sleep, and repeat. It was the only thing that kept him sane. That and Ebony. He had found her wandering the streets when he limped weakly into the once familiar seaside town. Not only had she followed him all the way to the old family flat, but also she had even pushed him up the hill with her nose when he fell. For that he gave her food, a home, and companionship. Zach was happy for that, especially since the days had been getting tense down at the pub.

The locals were becoming restless as news from Salisbury filtered all over the country. The people had been happy thinking that there was nothing else to the world but them. Now that 'unconfirmed' reports were drifting around of demons and the possessed, the locals were scared and were grasping for anyone who could give them guidance and answers. Luckily they were contented with believing that it was all a farce. But for how long, Zach did not know. He heard whispers of the Inquisition from the drunken and frightened locals in the pub where he worked. Usually before they could do something stupid, like organize a lynching mob, Jim would come over and refill their drinks. Then all would be forgotten.

As happy as Zach was that he had a job, he was still unsure about his employer. Jim could speak German better than Zach did sometimes, but whilst being his Gunter persona, Zach could get around it with his confused expression, claiming he did not understand. But there was something else. Jim neither indulged the patrons with their talk of the

Inquisition nor dissuaded them from speaking of it. It was as if he knew of the Inquisition's existence and was just gauging his patrons and others in the town. Whether that was part of Zach's growing paranoia or whether it was his gut feeling telling him the truth, he could not say. But Zach had to play his part and play it well enough to remain undetected and alive. That was all he cared about now. He had lost too much to care about answers or reasons.

The evening was passing with ease as Zach flitted about doing his duties whilst the patrons drank away their woes or ate until they exploded. It was all going as an ordinary evening should, until a patron called to Jim.

'Oi, Jim, turn up the TV, would you?'

With a sigh, he did as he was asked and turned up the volume on what appeared to be a breaking news story.

'Good evening,' the reporter began. 'We apologize for the break in this evening's broadcasting schedule. News has just reached us of a second person for whom police and relevant authorities are searching in connection with the incident at Salisbury Cathedral over eighteen months ago. David Alexander, a neurobiologist and doctor living in the Salisbury area, has been named as the second person after Zach Ford. Unlike Ford, David Alexander is not considered to be dangerous. Police and other relevant authorities want to question him about the events of that day, as he was caught on CCTV entering the cathedral shortly before Ford. If anyone has any idea of his whereabouts, please either contact the police or call the number on the screen now. Thank you for your attention. We return you now to the evening's scheduled program.'

Jim turned the volume down again. The pub began to simmer with group conversations. The word *conspiracy* was thrown around as people resumed drinking and began to talk about what they'd just heard. Zach had not realized it, but he had been stone still throughout the news broadcast. Shaking himself from his stillness, he continued with his duties, hoping that no one had noticed. Jim did notice, however. His eyes had been pinned on Zach more than on the broadcast.

Soon it was closing time. Jim shuffled his drunken, concerned patrons into the street and bolted the doors tight. After a few minutes, Zach readied himself for a quick leave.

'Is everything OK?' Jim asked in near perfect German.

'Yes,' Zach said, speaking as Gunter. 'I am just tired. It has been busy tonight.'

'Did you understand much of that news broadcast?' Jim probed, unhappy with Gunter's answer.

'A little bit,' he replied after a pause. 'Some words did not make sense.'

'They are looking for those two men, Gunter,' Jim said with meaning. 'If you do see them, you will tell me, won't you?'

Gunter nodded, hoping that he would be allowed to go. Seeing the truth in his German assistant's eyes, Jim unbolted the door and let him out.

Zach walked faster than he ever had back to the flat, in case he was followed. His mind was racing. David Alexander, the man who destroyed everything he knew, was still out there somewhere. It made sense. After all, Zach had survived, but only through sheer luck and a small amount of planning. Did David Alexander know? Did he, like Zach, have powers without his demon? Or did Azrael not leave him when they 'died'? So many questions. Zach did not know where to start. Opening the door, he was nearly thrown to the floor by the excited Labrador. He fed her and walked her again for being good, after which time he began to settle down for the night. Tomorrow he had a day off and he would investigate as much as he could without getting noticed. He would need a new, new face, something that he always found hard and painful to do. But it was necessary, as somewhere out there in the world, David Alexander was preparing for another conflict.

CHAPTER 24

REBECCA WAS BROUGHT BACK TO an unwilling conscious state with another jet of ice water to her face. She was battered and bruised, but she still kept her wits about her. She only spoke words that were truth, not what Doctor Jarvis wanted to hear.

'Come on now, Miss Oldman,' Jarvis said in his cruel but neutral voice, 'you can't keep going unconscious on me every time you refuse to answer. Where is Zach?'

'I don't know,' Rebecca said as she had done before. 'The place he used to live, the only place to my knowledge where he would go again, he destroyed. I gave you the address. Go and look for yourself!'

'A team has investigated the site you claim to be his, but it has no residue of evil. You are lying to me, Miss Oldman.'

She had almost gotten used to the clunk of the handle, but not to the pain that came with it. The electricity coursed through her entire body, her muscles twitched uncontrollably, and her sense dulled to the point of blackout before it stopped and she dangled, limp as a caught fish.

'Where is Ford, Miss Oldman?' Jarvis asked again.

'Burn in hell.' Rebecca spat in his face, which took the last of her summoned strength.

'I do God's work, child,' Jarvis said, wiping his face. 'He will not stand for this. Tell me the truth or your life will be a very short and painful one.' He awaited her answer, his hand resting on the power handle. Rebecca said nothing. There was no point. This man was not interested in the truth; he just wanted his own private version of the truth.

Losing his patience, Jarvis prepared to lower the handle again. As he neared the point of release, a knock came from the door and another white-clad, emblem-wearing man walked in.

'Doctor Jarvis, there is someone waiting for you in the entrance hall. They say that they have some useful information for you.'

'Take Miss Oldman back to her cell,' Jarvis growled in annoyance, 'so she can thank God for sparing her life for one more day.'

With that, Jarvis strode out of the room, leaving Rebecca dangling from her restraints.

She did not feel it when she was let down or wheeled back to her cell. Her body was broken again. She could just about see through her eyes and hear faint noises, but that was it. Near to surrendering to the blackness of unconsciousness again, she was yanked from it at the last moment. She awoke to a young man, barely older than she, holding smelling salts to her nose and holding open her eyes.

'Come on, Becky,' the echoing voice said. 'Come back now.'

Her vision returned after a few moments, and her hearing returned a few seconds after that. She was back in her cell again. She tried to move, but everything hurt. It hurt even to breathe.

'Easy now,' the voice spoke again. 'Everything will hurt, but this will help.'

Slowly he pushed the needle into her arm and eased down the plunger. Everything then relaxed. Rebecca felt no pain. All she felt was her heart beating and her lungs taking in air. Laying her down softly onto her bed, the young man made to leave. Just as he stood from her bedside, Rebecca shot out a hand to grab him.

'Help me,' she said, the only two words she could muster in her weakened state.

'You have people who are helping you, Becky,' the man said softly, moving his hand over her head. 'You just have to hang in there, OK? Zach needs you.' Those were the last words she heard as she drifted into a heavy, dreamless sleep.

...

Doctor Jarvis was annoyed. He carried that energy with him as he stomped through the various white corridors to the entrance hall. He had been so close to breaking that girl when he was interrupted. He just needed that one last bit of information to complete his puzzle and then he would be ready for the next stage – and all the rewards that would come with it. His thoughts now turned to the apparent informant that had surfaced. Hoping that it would be something useful, he set himself up in one of the many side rooms away from the entrance hall and ordered the person to be brought to him. Within a few moments, the door clicked open and a young girl, barely nine years old, was ushered in. She was in a state. Her tattered red dress was stained with mud and other substances that Jarvis could not make out. Her shoes barely covered her feet, and her face and hands were grubby and dirty. Pushing back his disgust for the child, he spoke in his soft voice.

'Hello there. And who might you be, little one?'

'My name is Mary, sir,' she said in a well-mannered and proper tone. 'Am I safe now?'

'Yes, you are, my dear,' Jarvis continued, starting to feel sorry for his prejudgement. 'No one can get you whilst you are here.'

'That's good.' Mary relaxed into her chair. 'I was worried I would be found.'

'Found by whom, little one?'

'What is your name, sir?' she asked innocently, almost forgetting her train of thought.

'Doctor Jarvis, but you can just call me Jarvis. Who are you afraid of, Mary?'

'David Alexander,' Mary whispered over the table. 'I know where he is.'

The name sent shivers down Jarvis's spine, shivers not of fear but of anticipation. Everything was going ahead of plan.

'Can you take me and some colleagues to him, Mary?' Jarvis asked, snapping out of his daydream.

'I can only take one more person with me, Doctor,' Mary said, fear gripping her. 'Your friends won't fit as well.'

'OK, Mary, I'll make a deal with you. You can eat and sleep here tonight, and tomorrow you can take me to him so I can make sure he won't scare you anymore. Deal?' With a nod and a gentle handshake,

Jarvis ordered a guard to feed and clothe Mary and give her a suitable sleeping cell. All thoughts of Rebecca and Zach were pushed to the back of his mind. With one abomination in his custody, Jarvis could see his promotion. He could almost touch it with his burnt gloved hand.

CHAPTER 25

THE ONE GOOD THING ABOUT his job was that Zach had the day free. But he could not be Zach in his free time. With all the posters and advertisements in the papers and on the television, Zach was finding it harder and harder to be himself. The energy it took to create and sustain another form was draining at the best of times, but now he had to do it more often and for longer periods of time. His only saving grace was that his other forms had sprung from his imagination. When they were real people, that was when it became complicated, much like the day was panning out to be.

For his information-gathering mission to work, Zach changed into the form of his dead grandmother, who had owned the flat. This was especially difficult because not only had Zach not seen much of her when she was alive but also the only point of reference he had was pictures of her face and fading memories of her voice. But it was the only form that would work. Being elderly, he could get answers from people that even Gunter would not get, thanks to the innocence and respect shown to the elderly in the town.

With Ebony asleep on the carpet, Zach examined his changed form. He had caught his grandmother's face and form perfectly, but it was the voice that would let him down. Sighing, he made his voice as much like his grandmother's as he could and then ventured out into the town. As he shuffled around the town from place to place, gathering all he could, Zach could see that his disguise was already paying dividends. People he talked to about the town said that there was a gathering place for people who wanted to join the New Inquisition, but no one knew where. Seeing that that was a dead end, Zach had one more card left to play.

As the sun hit midday, Zach shuffled into the local police station. He knew that when his grandmother was alive, she used to frequent the station. It was a risk, however. If those at the station knew that she had died, then everything would go back to square one. Knowing this, Zach braced himself and pushed the door open. Luckily it was a new officer behind the desk, one who smiled and stood upright as Zach shuffled in as his grandmother.

'You all right there, love?' he said slowly as Zach approached in the form of his grandmother.

Dreading having to speak, Zach took a deep breath and began. 'Oh, I am fine, dearie.' He had her voice down almost perfect. 'I was hoping you could answer a question or two for me.'

'How can I help you then?' The officer leaned on the desk to hear Zach better.

'Well, I have been watching the television recently,' Zach began, growing more confident with the new voice, 'and reports keep coming up with pictures of two dangerous men. I forget their names …'

'Zach Ford and David Alexander?'

'Yes, that might be them.' Zach was taken aback by how quickly the officer said his and David Alexander's names. 'Is there a card or leaflet you have with ways of contacting authorities should I see those two men? I would feel a lot safer if I had something like that close at hand in case I do see them.'

'Give me a second. I think I may have something back here for you.'

As the officer turned and searched the rack behind him, Zach saw that this disguise was very useful to have. But he could feel his energy begin to waver and could feel himself losing control of his grandmother's form.

'There you go, love,' the officer said, handing Zach a well-presented leaflet.

Hastily thanking the young officer, Zach moved as fast as his form would allow him until he was out of sight of the station. He was rapidly losing control over his new form. His energy was almost gone, but he was out in the open amongst the fearful public. Darting into a nearby alleyway, he let his transformation take place. Now he had the problem of walking back to the flat without being seen. And he had only a few hours until he needed to be Gunter back in the pub.

Waiting until it was clear, Zach did the only thing he could think of. He ran, darting this way and that so no one would see his face. He hoped that people would think he was just someone in a hurry and not take any notice of him. It seemed to work as he disappeared down a long thin alley that led nearly all the way to the flat. But it was dark and dank and smelled of a back-alley toilet. Moving with speed, Zach began the climb when he felt a hand on his shoulder.

'You lost, boy?' Zach could smell the alcohol on the man's breath, which nearly made him wince and shrink away. Before he could do so, he saw the flash of a blade from the man's other hand. He caught the strike aimed at his neck and broke the man's wrist. Zach had retained all his training and would use it. Gasping in pain, the man looked at Zach's face and realized who he was.

Before the man could call out, Zach caught the back of his head and smashed it against the wall. The drunkard went limp and slid to the ground. Zach did not know if the man was alive or dead, but he could not take the chance of being discovered. Heaving the man onto his shoulder, Zach stowed the body in an even darker corner and covered it with whatever he could find. Then he moved with more speed to the flat. That was the first man he had attacked since David Alexander, and it felt good. Zach used what was left of his willpower to stop himself from going back and ripping the man apart.

Opening the door of the flat, Zach felt safe. Ebony looked up from her sleeping spot and wagged her tail before falling back asleep. After cleaning himself up and changing his clothes, Zach sat down and read through the leaflet. It was exquisite. It looked like it was printed on parchment with gold inlaid ink. The words were almost too faded to read, but Zach could just about make them out. It was more than he could have hoped. Not only did it have a telephone number, but also it had an address. What shocked him more was that the address was in Salisbury. The Inquisition was already there. Sitting back, Zach now feared for the poor people of the town he had fled and weakened. They would not have a chance to recover before the Inquisition descended with their questions and burnings.

CHAPTER 26

J ARVIS WAS MORE EXCITED THAN he had ever been. Even as a child he had never been this excited, as both he and Mary were transported to the last place where she had seen the abomination David Alexander. All thoughts of caution were gone from his mind. All he wanted was the man himself. If he could capture him alive, then everything would finally be on the up for him. No more scraping the bottom of the barrel for worthless assignments, and no more cowering away from those superior to him. Once he had David Alexander, he would be at the top. He would give the orders, and everyone would obey.

The slowing and screeching of the car's brakes snatched him from his thoughts as it parked up by a huge abandoned dilapidated house. The village it was in was nearly abandoned, but none of the other houses were as bad as this one. It was more vine than brick, with a few windows that were gathering dust, and a huge oak door that was encrusted with leaves and vines. Readying himself, Jarvis ordered his men to remain in the car, pushed open the door, and strode out, the terrified Mary close behind.

Jarvis headed straight for the main door, pressing his hand against the Inquisition emblem on his coat.

'It won't open for strangers,' Mary called to him, 'and he wasn't there. Follow me.'

Mary headed for a small opening in the vast hedgerow that encompassed the building. Jarvis had to crawl to follow her. A few minutes later, they emerged into a huge blackened garden. All the plants were dead or dying. A huge willow tree swayed in the soft breeze, all of its branches black and oozing sap onto the ground. It was near impossible to see anything in the gloom. Jarvis could just about make out the red of Mary's dress in front of him. As he took a step forward, he heard faint sounds of movement ahead.

Mary was frozen in fear, her eyes wide and staring into the darkness ahead of her. A whirling sound started and stopped as if a giant bird was flying around them and periodically stopping to examine its prey.

'Come behind me, child,' Jarvis spoke softly, moving Mary behind him. 'Everything will be all right.' It was then that a deep, unknown, booming voice spoke from the shadows.

'Mary, Mary, quite contrary, how does your garden grow?' The voice laughed as it spoke the rhyme. Jarvis had his left hand on the chest emblem and his right outstretched, ready, as he spoke.

'David Alexander, you are hereby under arrest by order of the New Holy Inquisition. If you come with me peacefully, no harm will come to you.'

'It is rude to interrupt someone who is talking to another,' the voice retorted from behind Jarvis. 'And besides, do I sound like a man to you?'

'I know what you were and are, abomination.' Jarvis did not know where to speak. 'It makes no difference to me or my order.'

'Maybe this man is your little lamb, Mary?' the voice continued, but this time from a different position. 'His coat is as white as snow. Do you offer him to me, like the older peoples offered sacrifices to their gods?'

Mary was on the floor, legs crossed, face hidden, slowly rocking backwards and forwards. Jarvis could pay her no attention as he set his defences.

'I am no sacrifice. I am here to rid the world of your scum and villainy.'

'That is rich coming from you.' The voice laughed from all sides. 'I kill and maim when I need to, but you and your order have killed and destroyed far more than I have. How are the children of the school in Salisbury that was mysteriously closed for no reason? I doubt that many still live or are fit enough to rejoin society. You are far more scum-like than I am, Doctor Jarvis.'

'I do not remember saying my name to you,' Jarvis said, his worry building. 'How is it you know of my name?'

'Your speech is not needed.' The voice was in front of him and close. 'I know you and your kind all too well.'

'Enough of this! I command you, enter the light.'

Jarvis sent out a ball of light from his right hand at the position where the voice was. It hit nothing. But he saw the flash of a shadow moving around the perimeter.

'You think you have power?' The voice laughed. 'This is power.'

Jarvis had no time to defend himself against an unknown force that knocked him into the air and pinned him against the trunk of the willow tree. As he tried to fight against the tree, its branches came alive, like snakes, wrapping around his arms, legs, and body, until he was tied against the trunk and left helpless.

'That is but a taste of it, godly man.'

The branches relaxed and Jarvis was thrown to the ground. He braced and recovered from the fall, not taking much damage. He replaced his left hand over the chest emblem and made ready. Summoning much of his skill and energy, Jarvis cast a light circle around the whole area. Within moments, everywhere in the garden was lit; no shadows or darkness remained. Jarvis scanned everywhere but saw or found nothing but him and Mary. But he still heard the laughing.

'You think that will be enough to find me? Darkness always prevails.'

As the voice spoke, darkness quickly fought back against the light and descended again onto the garden. Jarvis moved forward, blind again to everything. Suddenly he felt fingers at his leg. Snapping around, he saw Mary clinging to his leg. Tears were rolling down her face. She was petrified.

'Mary, Mary, quite contrary, your garden does not to grow,' the voice rhymed again from the shadows. 'The day you left the house where you were never meant to go.'

'Stop this trickery and give yourself up,' Jarvis shouted, being careful not to hurt Mary.

'What did you promise him, Mary? That he would be able to find me and take me back to his precious order?'

'I promised him nothing,' Mary screamed in reply from Jarvis's leg.

'Mary Louise Alexander,' the voice boomed from all sides, 'do not lie to me.' It was then that it clicked for Jarvis.

'You are his daughter, Mary?' he asked. Mary nodded and began to sob. 'Why didn't you say?'

'Because she knows what happens to those who are close to people whom your order wants,' the voice replied for her. 'What would you and your people have done to her to find me? I shudder to think.'

'This is your last chance, David Alexander. Give yourself over to me and you and your daughter will be spared.'

'That is all the proof I needed,' the voice replied cruelly.

Jarvis made ready for the attack, but it never came. There was just silence, an eerie silence. Jarvis looked around as much as he could with the petrified Mary clinging to his leg. Not seeing anything, he guessed that the voice and its owner had gone.

'It's all right, Mary,' he said, holding out his hand to her. 'We are going now.' Mary slowly reached up and took his hand, the tears seeping away. Jarvis was about to walk away when the girl's grip tightened with bone-crushing strength. Turning, he saw Mary smile cruelly as she threw him into the air and then forced him to the ground with a shattering thud. Trying to gain his composure and fight back, he was picked up again by the same force as before and flung repeated against the willow tree. He lost count of how many times his gradually weakening body smacked against the tree. After what seemed like an age of pain and thuds, he was flung to the ground again. His body was broken, but he still tried to flee. When he looked up, he saw Mary again, the same cruel smile on her face.

'Your kind are so predictable,' she spoke, but with the voice from the shadows. 'Offer them an easy way for victory and they will take it rather than work for it. It is a weakness I adore to use.' Jarvis felt her hand wrap around his neck and his body being hoisted into the air slowly. Never taking his eyes away from her, he saw the flawless trick. Standing before him now was David Alexander. Mary was no more. It was just Jarvis and David Alexander.

'And now I take control of your order and do to it what you would have done to me, my family, and the rest of humanity who did not agree with its objectives: burn it.'

Jarvis felt a tug at his skin and at his very being. Looking down, he saw his body begin to flake off and break away as it joined David Alexander's. He fought with all that he had, but it was useless. After a few moments of agonizing pain, Jarvis was gone from David Alexander's grasp but was now standing alone in the garden: another new form for David Alexander to use. Smiling upon seeing that the change was successful, David Alexander as Jarvis strode to the front of the house to begin one of his two missions: destroy the Inquisition.

CHAPTER 27

IT SEEMED LIKE AN AGE since Rebecca had last seen Jarvis or the mysterious man who would free her. The walls of her cramped cell were beginning to feel homely as she resigned herself to the idea that she may never leave unless she was in a body bag. She had given up trying to gauge how much time had passed since her last questioning by Jarvis. She did try to guess using her two daily meals as a signpost, but now she had forgotten which came first out of the two.

You have to hang in there, Becky. The phrase kept circling around her head, the phrase that kept her breathing. It was her hope against hope that the man would do as he had said and free her from wherever she was.

There was movement at her door, sounds that she had not heard in a long time. The door creaked and swung inward. Then the familiar routine of being wheeled down corridors and into rooms began anew. Only this time, after Rebecca's ice wash and physical check, the masked men left her in a well-lit and camera-less room. After a few agonizing minutes, the doors opened and another masked being stepped in. Looking around to make sure he had not been followed, the mysterious man revealed himself and released Rebecca from her restraints.

'We haven't much time,' he spoke in haste. 'Jarvis has returned sooner than expected. We have to go now.'

'Returned? Where did he go? What has happened?' Rebecca was now alert and ready to go as her feet touched the cold floor.

'I don't know, but he is not happy. And when he is in this mood, people like you will suffer.'

Rebecca felt the stab of fear in her gut as the man dressed her in the same style of clothes that he was wearing. When he was satisfied that everything was ready, there was a thud at the door.

'Simmons!' the angered voice of Jarvis boomed. 'Stop what you and your colleague are doing and come with me now.'

'Lower your mask. Keep your eyes down and your mouth closed,' Simmons instructed as he opened the door to Jarvis.

'The High Inquisitors are here and have requested to see me. Escort me to the conference chambers.'

For Rebecca, the walk was painfully slow and filled with terror. She was literally inches away from the man who had imprisoned and tortured her, and he did not seem to know it. In truth, Jarvis seemed completely different to her. His demeanour and very being had changed, almost like Zach's had. She could feel his turbulent energy swirling around. This was not the calm Jarvis from before.

Finally they reached the chambers. Jarvis dismissed the two with a wave of his hand before composing himself and entering the flame-lit chamber. Before Rebecca even had a chance to relax, Simmons grabbed her hand and pulled her away. They walked down more corridors until they came to what appeared to be a dead end.

'Why are you risking everything for me?' Rebecca asked as Simmons ran his hands around the wall. 'You don't even know me.'

'That is precisely where you are wrong, Rebecca Oldman,' he replied, smiling. The wall opened up into a small passageway. 'I know who you are and what you are and how you can help me and this town before it is too late.'

'What are you talking about?' Rebecca asked, in shock from what Simmons was saying as he guided her through the low passageway.

'You are a Voyant,' he replied, not taking his hand from her wrist, 'and you are the only one who can rally us together and help us find the one person who can stop this.'

They stopped. Simmons ran his hand along another wall until it opened up to daylight. The sun greeted Rebecca's pale, cold face like an old friend. As she looked around, she saw other people, who helped them down from the ledge.

'Just what exactly am I supposed to do?' she blurted as her energy returned.

'You have to help us find Zach Ford so he can put an end to this.'

She did not even have time to truly think about what was said to her before she was helped into a car and driven away as fast as the driver could go. It was like she had been freed from one solid prison and then confined to an invisible one instead. Once again, her path would take her to Zach, the enigma.

...

'Doctor Jarvis Richard Peterson,' one of the High Inquisitors spoke, 'level-three Inquisitor and member of the Wiltshire Lodge.'

'That would be me,' David Alexander, in his new form, said. 'Why am I summoned here?' he asked, standing before a group of men and women seated at a table.

'You went on an illegal and unsanctioned hunt for a supposedly possessed being without aid or clearance. And you returned with nothing. This council has come to decide if you are a liability to our cause, given the circumstances that have arisen. How do you answer?'

'I never wished for it to be so.' David Alexander began slowly walking forward in the body of Jarvis. 'I knew that if I hesitated, then the opportunity would be lost. Imagine what could have been if ...'

'Exactly what could have been,' another council member interrupted, 'but I see no sign of this possessed being, this David Alexander, in our midst. Instead you return absent the child who went with you and with no information or anything of use.'

David Alexander kept approaching as he thought how to play the next move. He would not be able to take all their forms, as doing so would be costly and counterproductive. He needed them all.

'I ask your forgiveness, High Inquisitors,' he pleaded, kneeling on the floor. 'I did only what I thought best.' Slowly he formed and guided tendrils of shadow across the blackened floor, two for each High Inquisitor.

'Be that as it may,' another voice spoke, 'you have acted against our best wishes. I think I speak for the whole council when I say ...'

The High Inquisitor could not finish his verdict, as the tendrils attacked together and with strength. One tendril wrapped around each of the Inquisitors' arms, pinning their hands to the table. They were powerless as David Alexander rose and shed his Jarvis form, showing instead his half-demon form.

'You great movers of the world,' he said whilst sneering, his voice demonic, 'you great men and women who are powerless against me. I would not have you so.'

As he spoke, the second wave of tendrils rose behind the Inquisitors, the ends aiming for their heads.

'I would rather have you powerful and in my service, so I will now give you a gift, the gift of true power and of servitude to me.'

With his speech ending, the tendrils swooped down on the Inquisitors. Within seconds the tendrils found their way into each Inquisitor's head, either through mouth, nose, ear, or eye, until each High Inquisitor had stopped twitching and shouting in pain and had come to relax. Satisfied they were paralyzed, David sent dark demon energy down each tendril, infecting every High Inquisitor.

'Rise again.' He chuckled as the bodies took new life and rose from their chairs. 'Rise again, my new soldiers.'

CHAPTER 28

THE TOWN HAD BEEN IN an uproar since Zach's attack. He did not remember killing the man, but apparently when he was found, the man was dead. The local paper even went as far to say that his body looked like it had been mauled by a bear. It was all ridiculous, as Zach knew that the man was alive after the encounter. How was he now dead? It mattered little, as since that time Zach had been more careful. He rarely ventured out in another form, save that of Gunter, as he had to continue to work and focus regardless of other events. Zach felt uneasy every day. Even Ebony sensed it. The Labrador was more alert than usual, as if looking for an invisible, unknown assailant.

As the evening drew in, Zach changed to Gunter and walked with purpose to the pub. The evening was cold and dark for the time of year, as if the weather were reacting to the uneasiness of the seaside town. As Zach entered, he was shocked by the number of people who were there, almost three times more than any other night. And they were all silent as they watched the television, like moths drawing closer to a flame. As Zach padded silently through, he glanced at the screen and then froze as he sensed energy he had not felt in a long time.

'We are the New Holy Inquisition,' a tall man in white and gold robes said to the camera. 'Having been hiding and acting from behind the scenes for far too long now, we have decided to make a public announcement and a stand. Events have transpired in this country that should not have happened. Other government organizations and officials have tried to bury them, but they continue to surface again and again. Now we have stepped into the light to challenge and destroy this threat. We ask every member of the public who is God-fearing and life-loving to step forward with us.

If you are such a person, then make your way to our bastions, which are located in every major church, cathedral, and abbey, and pledge yourselves to God and to the New Holy Inquisition.' Mutters of agreement began to sound from the patrons as the man continued his speech.

'We will not cover these events up, nor will we tiptoe around the ones that will come. We will tackle them head-on with a clear conscience and with the help of Almighty God. We have already found and dealt with one being who has tainted our holy land. Only Zach Ford remains. If you see him or know of his location, or suspect that he is in your area, I charge you now to do what you can to either subdue him or lead our officials to his location. He is extremely dangerous and will do whatever he needs to do in order to escape and live, the coward. Neither we nor God Almighty will tolerate his existence. Already we have sent our trained representatives to various suspected locations to begin the search. But I ask you to help them in any way and to be vigilant and watchful for this abomination of the Lord.'

The pub erupted in applause. Everyone, including Jim, wore a huge smile. Something was wrong, but Zach could do nothing except hope that his Gunter disguise would not be detected as such.

As the announcement ended, the majority of the patrons left, all heading to the church to join the New Holy Inquisition. Only a few remained, those who wanted to think it through or to have another drink. Zach began his flitting, planning not to be stopped or talked to by anyone.

'What do you think about that then, Jimmy?' a drunken patron asked.

'I reckon that the coward is here, judging from the attack that happened. Reckon he was caught by that man and then killed him so he could run. It disgusts me.' Jim spoke with a venom that Zach hadn't heard from his boss before.

'You might be right, but this whole Inquisition that are about seem like a bunch of God-loving wackos to me.'

'It's comments like that that makes my job so much easier.' Both the patron and Jim jumped and turned to see a figure standing in the doorway, his body covered with a long leather coat and his face masked by a wide hat. He moved with grace and silence as he approached the bar.

'People like you are the spreaders of fear and doubt who will send others into sin. I hunt those people and bring them in for questioning usually. But I am here on another, more important mission, so count your blessings, drunkard, and be gone from my sight.'

The patron did not need to be told again. He scampered to the door, along with the rest of the clientele, until it was only the three of them left: Zach, Jim, and the visitor. Zach carried on with his work but listened intently. He did not like the energy coming from the new arrival.

'I am disappointed that a brother would mix with someone like that,' the man began, dropping his belongings and squaring up to Jim, 'but you have your uses as a barman, Jim. And it is good to see you again.'

'Likewise, Marcus,' Jim replied, smiling and shaking Marcus's hand. 'I was wondering if my reports ever made it into hands of note.'

'They did,' Marcus said, sitting down and removing his hat to show his pale skin and emerald eyes, 'and they made for great reading. It is our belief that Ford is here. It is time for him to be brought in. Keep playing your part as you have, and leave the fun work to me.'

'That is fine with me.' Jim smiled, pouring Marcus a drink. 'No one will know a thing but me.'

'What about him?' Marcus pointed right at Zach.

'Don't worry, he doesn't speak a word of English. But I can send him home if you want.'

'Please, there is much more to discuss.'

'Gunter.' Jim switched the German. 'Go home. I will be fine on my own.'

Zach nodded in his disguise and made for home as quickly as possible. Everything was getting bad. Not only had he apparently killed someone, but also now the Inquisition was hunting him. And they already had David Alexander. But something unnerved him more than all of that. The man who spoke on the television and the one who was in the pub with Jim both had the same energy feel. It was dark and shrouded, not like normal human energy, and certainly not light and holy like the Inquisition suggested. It felt dark and powerful. It felt like David Alexander – and like Shangal when he tried to break through to this realm.

Zach did not know what to do or what to think. If he ran, everyone would know it was him who had killed the man and hunt him down. But if he stayed, he would undoubtedly be discovered and more people could be caught in the crossfire. Ebony saw the conflict in him as he returned to the flat. She did her best to calm him, but even she sensed that the next move would be played. No matter how hard Zach had tried to keep things together, everything was failing and turning again. His backup plan would soon fail. There was only one thing left to do: run again, to somewhere more remote and less inhabited.

CHAPTER 29

EVERYTHING WAS GOING ACCORDING TO plan for David Alexander. Since he had infected the High Inquisitors, the whole order turned and bent to his will. He was in complete control, also thanks to his genius move of making the order public, as now more eager volunteers flooded the bastion centres – more minions for his conquering force. Often he asked himself why he even needed or wanted soldiers from the other realm, but the answer was always a simple one: to satisfy his growing need for fear and power. Since he had come forth into his half-demon form, David Alexander's power grew. It grew daily with each infection of and each victory over a person he changed into an overlord. Even his personal minions around the Salisbury bastion called him 'Lord Alexander', a title that he adored beyond measure.

However, not everything was set or easy as he had hoped. Two obstacles blocked his way to total domination of the South-West. First was the pitiful but effective resistance movement that had sprouted up like a weed, constantly harrying and foiling his plans here and there, before disappearing in an instance and without a trace. The second was vastly more serious and worried the new half-demon lord to no end: Zach Ford. The boy had once ended his plans to be a host to a demon lord, and he could easily do it again. But what he feared most was what Zach was. David Alexander did not know if Zach was still possessed or a half-demon like himself. This was a question that would need to be answered soon, assuming that the elusive resistance movement let him have a chance and the resources to do so.

There was a rap at the door to David Alexander's massive private chambers. A robed man hurried through. The two hellhounds at the feet of David Alexander's throne awoke and snarled at the man, blood-red eyes fixing on their target. With a wave of David Alexander's demonic hand, they hushed and sat, but remained ready to pounce.

'Lord Alexander,' the minion spoke, fearful of the hounds, 'your report as ordered.'

'Speak, Inquisitor.'

'The prisoner known as Rebecca Oldman, whom we had held here for some time for questioning and assessment, has disappeared, along with other members of lower- and higher-level staff from this bastion. We can only assume they are in league with or were infiltrators of the resistance movement. Enforcers and searchers are being mobilized to bring her and the other members back, but they are clueless as to where to begin.'

'Continue, worm,' David Alexander hissed as the man hesitated.

'Senior Enforcer Marcus has arrived at his destination, at the suspected home of Zach Ford, and has begun his investigation. Preliminary reports suggest that he could be there and that the town is nearly under your control, my lord. His next report will either confirm or deny the presence of Ford and will provide further details into the search, or his journey to you.'

'So basically, minion,' David Alexander said, his anger building, 'is that you know nothing! You came to me after I ordered a full investigation into what has happened to our bastion and you come back with inconclusive nonsense and knowledge that I already have.'

With a grunt, the hellhounds leapt at the man and dragged him to the feet of David Alexander, ripping flesh as they went. The screams of the man echoed repeatedly around the hall until he came to a stop by his overlord.

'Now you know just what you are worth to me,' David Alexander said cruelly, hoisting the man up by the scruff of the neck. 'You are all a means to an end, an end that I choose. And I choose you to be the hounds' next meal. Everyone in this bastion will hear the price of failure. This will not happen again.'

Before the man could even beg for his life, he was tossed with ease towards the ready hellhounds, who immediately began their meal. The man could only scream for a second before his throat was ripped out and devoured, as was every other part of his body. Hearing the contented sounds of his hounds, David Alexander strode towards his private chambers, anger driving him to do more. His next move would be fast, brutal, and unyielding. It was the only way to drive his prey from the safety of their hideouts.

...

The journey seemed to take an age. It was difficult for Rebecca to keep track of what movements she had made. In the end she gave up and opted for sleep. She awoke when the car stopped and she was moved, under the cover of the blanket, to somewhere else. When she was moving no more, the blanket was taken off of her and she stood in shock and awe. She was in front of her, her sister's, her brother's, and Zach's old school. It was not the same as before; in fact, it was completely different. It looked like it had been invaded and burnt. The energies she got from the place now told her that it had been burnt with no mercy, as had the people who were trapped inside. Simmons moved next to her and led her to one of the gardens away from the main building. Everything was charred and ash-filled, left as a warning to everyone who defied the Inquisition.

She did not remember going into another dark space or going down the lift, but she did remember the second shock. Far under the charred, destroyed place of education were faces she knew, such as the former teachers and students of the school, and others she did not recognize. They all looked at her as if she were a saint. Hope filled all their faces as she was led past them to a huge cavern. Simmons let go of her hand and spoke as much to her as to everyone else.

'Welcome to Sanctuary,' he stated. More people moved closer from unseen tunnels. 'You are now in the headquarters of the resistance against the Inquisition. We have one purpose and one only, to remove and destroy the Inquisition from power so as to stop the same kind of destruction as what happened above you. The only way for that to happen is for you to help us find Zach Ford so he can help us gain retribution. Everyone here will treat you with respect and kindness. You are our only hope in finding him. Members of Sanctuary, after what seems like an age we have found a Voyant who will help us bring an end to our suffering.'

A cheer erupted around the cavern as people, young and old, applauded Rebecca. She did not know what to do or what to think. How was she a Voyant? Was Simmons talking about her ability to sense and read energy, or was there a lot more to it than that? Her thoughts were cut short as Simmons appeared in front of her and raised her hand.

'You are now a member of the resistance of Sanctuary, Rebecca Oldman.'

CHAPTER 30

'FOCUS MORE,' THE OLDEST MEMBER of Sanctuary pleaded to Rebecca. 'See the energy that I project. See its colour. See how it moves around me and interacts with everyone and everything around us.'

Even after the weeks of training and preparation that Rebecca had gone through since entering the cavernous Sanctuary, it felt as if no time had passed and that she had not improved in her Voyant abilities at all. The elder who was with her was only a seer of energies, and was struggling as much as she was to progress. She could see her energy just about, the faint shade of pink resonating from the elder's chest, but that was it. It was difficult with all the pressure and negative vibes she was getting from other members of Sanctuary. Patrollers and ambushers came and went, and each one of them had the same thing to say to Simmons: that Rebecca was a liability and was useless. They said that they would much rather use what they had perfected, which seemed to be ambush attacks on convoys, lower-level and lightly defended bastions, and volunteer centres.

For her part, Rebecca was glad to be shunned, as it meant she could attempt to focus more on her supposed gifts. But there was another, more pressing thought in the back of her mind. When she found Zach, what would happen to her – and why was the energy of Jarvis so different from when she had first met him? Everything was so different. She had no home, no family, and no friends and was never trusted. All she had was Simmons and the elder, who were hoping against hope that she would be the answer to their problems. Whether they wanted to admit it or not, the resistance of Sanctuary were losing their planned war to attrition and demoralization. The Inquisition had raised the bar, and the resistance could not match their tactics, numbers, or mercilessness.

Rebecca was shaken from her concentration with raised voices coming from the main cavern. Instinctively she was on her feet and marching towards them. There were more people in the cavern than she had ever seen. It looked like every person that the resistance had was on recall and no one was happy about it.

'If we are here, we are not doing damage to those arrogant sons of whores,' a hot-headed young woman yelled at Simmons, who stood on a crudely erected stage.

'Face it, Fiona,' he replied, cool as ice, 'we are losing now. All damage we deal, they give back tenfold. We are down on manpower and resources to carry out the offensive. We have to defend ourselves now if we want to survive long enough to meet our objectives.'

'That's what they are wanting, you fool,' Fiona countered. 'They want us to run and hide so they can find our bases and burn us out. We have to commit every last member of Sanctuary to one last attack.'

'What would that bring us? If we do win and drive the Inquisition from Salisbury, what then? We will have lost so many men, women, and children in that assault that all the Inquisition will need to do is send a counter-force to deal the death blow to us. We will drive them out only to have them invade again, and that is the best-case scenario.'

'What would you have us do then?'

'We have to have faith in our new Voyant.' Simmons motioned towards Rebecca. 'And when she has helped us find Zach, then we need to get to him before they do. Both she and he are now our only hope. I will not send more people to die, Fiona. We have all lost much.'

'You would have us put our faith in her?' Fiona asked, facing Rebecca. 'What does she know of loss? What does she know of sacrifice? She will bring us nothing but tears from her pretty little un-scarred face.'

Rebecca's heart pounded as adrenaline pumped through her system. Her anger took hold. Before she knew it, she was striding towards Fiona. As the patroller turned, she smiled, knowing she had touched a nerve. Rebecca, drawing a long blade from her side, did not know what came first, the lunge from her attacker or the thrusting motion from her own hands. All she knew was that Fiona was in front of her one moment, and lying on her floor metres in front of her the next. Her instincts took hold again as she forced back the rest of the patrollers with more energy. Just as she began to regain her focus, Simmons appeared in front of her with people loyal to him to protect her. Fiona and her patrollers regained their feet and stood in amazement as Simmons spoke, his hand never leaving his hatchet.

'Do you doubt her now? A Voyant's abilities start with physical movement. Then comes energy tracking and manipulation.'

'Fine,' Fiona said, 'we will give her a chance. But she knows nothing of our pain.'

'Who did they take from you, may I ask?' Rebecca blurted from behind her human wall.

'My sister,' Fiona replied.

'They took my whole family – my mum, dad, sister, brother, and gran. And as if that wasn't enough, they imprisoned and tortured me for nearly two years. So you tell me who has suffered more?'

Fiona was taken aback by the outburst. Knowing she was in the wrong, she sheathed her blade. The other patrollers did likewise and stood down.

'I know you doubt me, but I will do all I can to help you. I have suffered and will not see more people suffer and die without anyone else even knowing.'

A slow and sarcastic clap began to sound around the cavern, causing everyone to turn and ready their makeshift weapons. A hooded form glided from the shadows and spoke.

'Poetic as always from an Oldman,' the male voice began. 'Your family were very well known for that. And what could possibly go wrong with trying to find Zach? He wouldn't even think of ripping you all apart with his bare hands.' The voice reeked of sarcasm, which everyone picked up on. Simmons stepped forward, blocking the form and drawing his hatchet at the same time.

'You know full well you are not allowed here. Go now and I will try to convince Fiona not to run her blade through your treacherous stomach.'

The form laughed and lowered his hood, showing his face to everyone.

'Now, I thought you were all accepting in this place,' the smug face of Christian Jones spoke, 'especially seeing as you are losing.'

'You are as much responsible for that as we are, Jones!' Fiona shouted. 'You worked for them until you went to David Alexander, who is possibly even worse than they are.'

'Well, let me tell you a secret that will send a shudder through you all,' Christian said, his cruel, traitorous eyes focusing on Rebecca. 'David Alexander now controls the Inquisition and is closing in on someone you need, my old friend and your apparent saviour, Zach Ford.'

CHAPTER 31

'WHY SHOULD WE BELIEVE YOU?' Simmons hushed the growing murmurings from the cavern. 'You are not one of us. You are known for your lies and for corrupting others. Why shouldn't I let Fiona have some fun with you and her blade?'

'Ask your Voyant,' Christian replied calmly.

Simmons turned to face Rebecca, who had happily drifted to the back of the hall, sensing and seeing the energies mingle. Now that the attention was on her, everything stopped. She froze in fear. Simmons beckoned her to come forward. The elder walked with her. No one in Sanctuary liked or trusted Christian, so every precaution was now being taken. Rebecca had only heard his name in passing when her younger sister came back from school. None of what Katie had reported was good.

'So, Miss Voyant,' Christian began, oblivious to the circle of armed people forming around him, 'I know that you can sense things in others. I know that you foresaw the events at the cathedral, and I know there is a lot more that you can and will do. But just answer me one question: the doctor Jarvis you first met and the doctor Jarvis you last saw, did you feel any difference in them?'

'Yes.' Her answer was instant. 'I did. The last time I saw him, everything was different. His energy and demeanour weren't the same. But I did not know why or how.'

'Let me fill in the blanks for all of you.' Christian adored the sense of power he wielded and the knowledge he had. 'Two possessed people fight to the death on top of the cathedral. One kills the other, and then calls down a stream of lightning to purge his body of the demon. He does not die. But trying to purge an infection like possession is impossible.

Both men survive. But now they are having an internal conflict. They are part possessed and half human, but with a controlling residue of a demon. They either submit to the residue and become a demon or fight it and become something much worse. David Alexander has submitted and taken control of the Inquisition. His power is nearly full. Zach is still fighting it and is cracking at the seams. The moment he breaks, everyone will know of it. His power will be limitless, but only for as long as he can hold it.'

Everyone drank up Christian's words, but with a large dose of scepticism. Christian was not known for telling the truth, but on those occasions when he was truthful, he wanted something in return. Simmons thought of this as Christian finished.

'Assuming everything you are saying is true, and that is a big assumption, why would you tell us now?'

'Because whether you like it or not, I am your only way in to the headquarters of the Inquisition.'

'And why would you change sides, again, placing yourself against both him and the Inquisition?'

'I have my reasons.' Christian was not giving anything away. 'You get Zach to me and I get him to David Alexander. All you have to do is take cover until it is over.'

'Zach would rip you apart rather than help you. You know that,' Simmons countered.

'Perhaps. But I think he would be more agreeable with the right persuasion.' Christian again stared at Rebecca. 'After all, he did love a family member of one person in this hall, so why not another?'

'He is not like you, Jones!' Fiona screamed. 'Zach is loyal to his friends and those he loves. You just bounce from one person to the next and use people as it suits you. We will not be your next bouncing surface, and neither will she.'

Rebecca was touched by Fiona's change of heart towards her. Only a few minutes ago, Fiona was ready to kill her, but now she protected her. Simmons was not convinced either by what Christian was saying, but he had one move left to play.

'What would you want from us for this service, Christian?' Simmons asked.

'That when peace and order is restored, my part will be told in the stories and tales – and it will be a big part.'

'So you want glory to buff up your vanity and ego?'

The words cut Christian deep as he replied. 'I told you what you are facing. I told you everything I know, and I told you how to defeat them. I deserve a big part in the stories.' His face was red with anger, but he dared not approach anyone.

'You only did that to serve yourself for your own selfish reason, so you're selfish reward would make you famous.' Simmons continued to cut Christian deep.

'I am not selfish! I am a survivor!'

'You will have to prove that to us then. And I have the best and only way that I can think of.'

'Fine then.' Christian was calming down but was still on edge. 'I will take part in your test.'

'When our team goes to intercept Zach, you will go with them.' More murmurs began around the circle, mixed with laughter as Christian went from rage-red to fright-white. 'Then we will see if he approves of your plan or if he will leave you for dog food.'

Rebecca smiled upon seeing the confident Christian brought down to the ground with one sentence. But the growing thought of her being some kind of bait for Zach made her uneasy. She now knew why everyone hated Christian, but she did not know what her sister had seen in him, or why she had left Zach for him. She tried to bury those thoughts as Christian was led to a holding cell to prevent his escape, and as Simmons, Fiona, and the elder led her to the discussion area. Everything would need to be planned and set so they would be ready for when Zach either broke or was found. All their hopes were pinned on the hope that they would get to him first. If David Alexander got his hands on Zach, then all would be lost.

CHAPTER 32

Zach Ford's world had been turned upside down. Whereas once he saw a peaceful seaside town whose inhabitants liked the quiet of life and the company of friends and strangers alike, now all had changed. The townspeople were either members of the New Inquisition or had disappeared. Everyone Zach saw and overheard was looking for people to make scapegoats out of. Always he felt the presence of the shady enforcer who had arrived a few weeks ago. Zach had tried his best to maintain his Gunter illusion, but cracks were starting to show. As much as he hated to admit it, he knew he would be on the move again. He hated what the Inquisition had demanded of the populace. 'Be vigilant for anyone seeking to undermine our authority, no matter how big or small'; 'If you have any concerns about yourself or anyone else, seek out a bastion member to consult'; 'Any person suspected of being heretical will not have any trial or mercy shown.' It had thrown the people into madness and chaos. Now everyone was seeking to be in the Inquisition's good graces. People would hand anyone over to the Inquisition just to have a nice word said about them. It was infectious, dangerous, and very well planned.

Zach had been intending to leave for days now but had been deliberately putting it off. He had everything together, and he knew where to go and what to do and not to do. He just needed to bring himself to do it. He hated the thought of being hunted again. Everything had been going so well for him. Why had everything come crashing down around him again? He asked himself this question, but he did not know the answer. The only think he could possibly imagine regarding the whole ordeal was that there was more left for him to do.

His mood matched the weather as he strode up the hill towards the soon to be abandoned flat. Grey clouds circled in from the sea and covered the town in a thin mist. As Zach opened the door, he saw the mist descend, like a giant spectral being swooping on its prey. Even his adopted Labrador seemed on edge. Ebony had not greeted him happily liked she usually did but rather stood tense at the glass sliding door watching the mist close in. Zach made for the backmost room, where his bag was kept. All he owned was now crammed into it. A few bundles of clothes, food, water, a map, and his sabres, which were stuffed into a hidden compartment, were all that filled it. Knowing that he had done all he could do, he sat down to rest and eat. Ebony eventually shook herself out of her staring duty and joined him. As the evening drifted on, Zach allowed himself to become comfortable. He did not even notice he was sleeping until it was too late.

Zach jolted awake to a strange noise: growling. Ebony had never growled or barked since she had found him when he arrived. Now she was completely different. She was standing at the glass sliding door, body stiff, tail flat, staring into the mist and softly growling at nothingness. Zach padded to the door and looked out. All he could see was the white of the mist. The picket fence had disappeared in the whiteness. Zach put his hands against the window to improve his vision. As he scanned the area, he saw and sensed nothing. He was about to return to sleep when he noticed something on his hand: a red dot. Before he could even question what it was, his instincts went manic as he threw himself to the floor. A wave of darts flew through the door and the window. Landing with a roll, he called Ebony to him. She did not obey and was now barking as a second, more accurate wave of darts was shot. Zach took cover behind the newly upturned table, hearing and felt each little impact. He tried in vain to call Ebony. Again she would not obey.

Zach heard the glass smash as something much bigger was thrown through it. Peering around the table, he saw the smoke grenade release its contents into the room. Ebony's barks turned to whimpering, and then he could not see or hear her at all. He had no idea where his attackers were or how many there were. Only one thing was on his mind: escape. He flung himself towards the door leading to the back room, which was answered with another wave of darts, all missing their target. Zach was about to shut the door and disappear when he heard a voice.

'Zach Ford,' the muffled voice began from within the smoky room, 'by order of the New Holy Inquisition, I have been sent to detain you and transport you to a place of questioning and testing. If you come out now, no harm will come to you during the transport process.' As the voice finished, Zach could make out a figure in the smoke. The individual was dressed in a black hazard suit and a gas mask, which provided protection from the smoke. It also made identifying the person a difficult task.

'Respond now or I will take your silence as non-compliance. Then I shall be forced to continue with the same action I have taken.' Zach could see the form raise a dart gun in his direction. His attacker apparently could see through the smoke. Before Zach even had a chance to respond, darts shot from the person in the room flew past his head and body. Zach fell to the floor in an attempt to dodge the darts, only to find himself dazed and confused after his hard landing. Leaning up, he look forward and saw that the masked and suited form was now in front of him, gun raised. Zach waited for the sound of shots, but instead he heard a bark and the sound of a fast and heavy impact.

From out of nowhere, Ebony lunged at Zach's assailant, clasping her jaw around their arm, forcing them to drop the gun in agony and shock. She was small for the breed and not as powerful as the attacker was, but the dog still wrestled the person to the ground, her jaw not leaving their arm. The person shouted and howled in pain, but she gave no quarter as her teeth ripped open the hazard suit and bit down on flesh. Zach again called Ebony, but she would not come. More darts were sent into the room. One sank into Ebony's leg, but she did not notice. As Zach called her again, she stopped and looked at him for a split second. Zach then understood everything. Seeing the break in the attack, the masked person jumped to their feet and made to kick the Labrador. She saw it coming, moved out of the way of the clumsy kick, and attacked the other leg, bringing the person down to the floor again. Zach knew what had to happen. Tears welled in his eyes as he ran to the back room, slung his backpack over his shoulder, and made his escape. He turned back to see Ebony pinning the being to the ground and being hit by more darts.

All his hopes for her survival vanished as he heard two gunshots, the sound of a howl, and a third and final shot. By that point, Zach was running, tears flowing like a waterfall down his face. Summoning all his strength, speed, and composure, he disappeared into the foggy night. His only companions were the sounds of howling and gunshots. He would know again what it was to be hunted, and he vowed as he ran that the Inquisition would pay dearly for this night.

CHAPTER 33

THE CALL TO MOBILIZE HAPPENED much more quickly than Rebecca had ever expected of the ragtag group of resistance members. In what seemed like a few moments, she was bundled, once again, into an overused but perfectly decent Land Rover and was on the move. Every resource the resistance could use, now that they were on the defensive, was used to find Zach. Their break happened in the early hours of the morning. Simmons knew they had to get there first. Rebecca scanned around the Land Rover to see who else was with her. Simmons was sitting in the front with a resistance driver she recognized; Fiona sat next to Rebecca with one of her trackers sitting behind her; and another resistance operative sat in the back, guarding Christian. It was strange to see the usually arrogant Christian so quiet and nervous. Rebecca would enjoy it whilst she could. She took the opportunity to test her energy sight. Focusing on Fiona, Rebecca cast out her senses until she could see her aura. Then she began to make sense of the colours and how they interacted with everyone else's. Before she knew it, Rebecca was asleep.

Hours later she awoke to the slowing of the Land Rover and then the sound of doors quietly opening. The first thing she sensed was the odour: salty. She was by the sea. As her eyes adjusted, she saw she was right. It was a quaint little seaside town that she had never seen before. Before she got carried away with its beauty, she turned to see a more grisly sight. Everyone apart from the driver, Christian, and the other operative was slowly making their way into a cordoned-off flat. Rebecca followed and cast out her senses, checking to ensure that no one else was there. There had been quite a commotion – that much was obvious. Simmons and Fiona took the first steps in, glass crunching under their boots as they went. Rebecca followed with the tracker and looked upon the scene in sorrow. Zach had been here; her senses told her that much.

'This was where he was all along,' Simmons said glumly. 'He hid here in plain sight for nearly two years. No one knew. Can you tell where he went?'

Rebecca composed herself and tried to detect any residual energy. It hit her like a wave. Pain, sadness, anger, sorrow, and rage bombarded her. She shielded herself as best she could, but some seeped in and cast visions.

She saw Zach as if he were in the room with them all. He was crouched by the far door calling to something. She saw the darts fly past her head and into the wall, obviously meant for him. So he had been found after all. The emotions continued to bombard her, but then the vision went blurry and evaporated. Just as it disappeared from her view, she saw a faint line of energy – the energy of pure rage.

'I have a trace, but I think we should be careful,' Rebecca said, coming back to the world. 'He left here in a rageful state.'

No one in the group had any problem with leaving quickly. In seconds they were in the Land Rover, with Rebecca in the front directing the driver.

It was easy to pick up the trail. She could almost feel the rage Zach had had. He had run through fields, leapt over gaps, and climbed sheer surfaces, never stopping or resting. The trail led them miles away from the town they had been in. Finally they had to stop when the Land Rover could go no further. Everyone climbed out this time, including Christian, who was nearly sheet-white in fear. Rebecca could see the trail; it was heading straight for the sea. Before they left, Simmons and Fiona talked through a plan with the other resistance members and made ready their weapons. Fiona had her two long blades hanging from her back, Simmons had his hatchet, the driver had a pistol, and the operative drew out a shotgun. Rebecca felt very out of place. Fiona and her tracker immediately went off ahead to see that the way was clear. The rest of them moved with caution, following the energy trail.

Rebecca cast out her senses again to make sure she was going the right way. The trail lay before her. She could sense Fiona and the other tracker in the treeline watching the hill that was directly to their left. She stopped momentarily when the trail went from her sight. Breathing and focusing, she found it again. It led them deeper into the woods and closer to the sea. She could feel everyone's anxiety and nervousness, none more so than Christian's, whom the operative had to remind to move every so often. Rebecca could no longer sense Fiona or the other tracker. Assuming they were far ahead, she was about to push concern from her mind when she sensed something else.

'Others are here,' she said, trying to focus on the specifics, 'coming down the hill behind us.'

'How many, Rebecca?' Simmons asked, trying to remain calm as everyone else prepared for conflict.

'Many more than us, but their energy is strange.'

'Don't worry about that. Find the trail. Let's keep moving.' Simmons became stern and authoritative.

Just as she found the trail again and was about to move, there was a sound none of them wanted to hear: a gunshot.

'Simmons,' the driver called, 'run!' He had been hit in the chest. Blood began to drip onto the forest floor. Tossing Simmons his pistol, the driver went down and did not rise. Before Simmons could react, he saw a large body of people marching towards them.

'Follow Rebecca,' he commanded. 'Run!'

None of them needed to be told twice as they broke into a sprint, Rebecca leading the way, focusing on nothing but the energy trail. The path got smaller and smaller, and soon they were running single file. But no matter how fast they were, their pursuers were faster. Letting Simmons overtake him, the operative used the confined space and opened fire with both barrels of his shotgun. A number of their pursuers went down, but the others kept coming. The forest was getting claustrophobic as they were fumbling their way through branches, roots, and leaves. All around shots whistled past. Then finally the gunshots ceased. The forest gave way to rock and stone; they had reached the cliffs. But Rebecca kept running, leading the others, following the trail. It turned this way and that, leading them through a maze of boulders and caves, until it came to an end – a dead end.

Rebecca stopped in front of a sheer face of rock. Now they were trapped. The sound of their pursuers echoed against the stone as the operative reloaded his shotgun and took position near the entrance. Simmons stood with him, pistol loaded and ready. The first of their chasers came into view. Simmons shot and hit the target. Both he and the operative kept the attackers at bay, using the rock formations as a bottleneck. Rebecca tried in vain to find the trail again, but nothing she did worked. It ended where she stood, and she did not understand why.

As the next wave of attackers came at them, Simmons and the operative prepared to fire again. They both had their targets in their sights when they were thrown to the ground by strong hands. Both men rolled to their feet to see their pursuers jumping down the rock face behind them, swarming them like ants. It did not take long before the resistance members were subdued.

All hopes of rescue faded as Fiona and her tracker were dragged in. The tracker was dead, two bullet wounds in her chest. Fiona was alive but had a cut above her eyes. They had been ambushed too. A multitude of people surrounded them, but they did not feel like people. With humans, their energy changed colour depending on their mood. But all the people who surrounded the resistance members now had the same colour energy – and it did not move. One of them stepped forward and began to speak.

'I am the enforcer Marcus,' he began with a voice like ice. 'I have been tasked with finding the fugitive Zach Ford and to quell any resistance members I happen to find along the way. It looks like I have been blessed today. I am only going to ask this once: why are you here?'

Simmons looked around and shook his head at everyone. No one would answer.

'Very well, if that's how you want to play this, bring the operative.'

Without warning, the operative was dragged away from them, amidst the protests of Simmons, who got a swift smash to the face by a fist of one of Marcus's men.

'Do you know what phrase my men and I go by?' Marcus asked them cruelly. 'An eye for an eye. What you do to us, we repay. You killed my men, so I will repay you that courtesy.'

The operative was held in place on his knees as Marcus drew a sword from his robes. With a cruel smile, he plunged it into the operative's chest and then kicked him away. The body writhed in place for a few moments and then lay still, blood flowing from the wound like a river. Marcus looked at the group and paced towards them, not even noticing that the sky had begun to darken with thick black clouds.

'How many more of you need to be repaid then?' Marcus questioned, his patience wearing thin. 'Maybe you, girl,' he said, pointing at Rebecca. 'You were the one leading them.'

As Marcus began to step forward, the sky erupted with lightning.

His men became jumpy and skittish as thunder boomed all around them. It was then that they all heard it, a noise louder than the thunder that sounded all around, more powerful than the waves that crashed against the cliff face next to them. The noise spread fear much better than Marcus's execution had. They all heard a roar of pure rage, followed by a form landing – with a crash that shattered the stone – in front of Rebecca and the others. All the men retreated to Marcus as the huge unknown being raised itself up. It looked around and saw the dead bodies of the operative and tracker. It knew their faces. Feeding on the building rage, it roared again, brandishing its silver, sabre-like teeth. It charged head-on into Marcus and his men. Rebecca could not keep up with the speed and the ferociousness of the attack. The being either sent the other men flying into the rock face, sliced them into bits with its drawn claws, or sunk its fangs into them. No one knew where the sword had come from, but it made the attack more brutal, slicing and hacking at everyone in front of it until they were either dead or running. Then it was only Marcus.

He was not quite as confident as the being strode towards him, its body and sword bloodstained. Marcus attacked in desperation and fear, but before he knew it, his sword flew from his hand and clattered onto the cold stone. He did not even have time to compose himself before the beast sank its sabre-like teeth into his neck. Marcus howled in pain as the bite went deeper. As he became weaker from the pain, the being stopped and flung his body off the cliff face and into the sea below. Everyone heard the thud of his body hitting the rocks.

It was over. All the strange men and their leader were gone. Rebecca should have felt safe, but she had never been more afraid as their saviour padded over to the bodies of their dead.

'I'm so sorry,' it seemed to say.

Sensing an opportunity, Christian made a dart for freedom. The being, having seen it coming, blocked his escape. Christian tried to fight back, but the being picked him up with one arm and knocked him out with an earth-shattering punch with the other, before tossing him to the floor.

'Oh my God,' Rebecca said, her knees going weak, which forced her back next to Simmons. 'It's … it's …'

'It's me, Rebecca,' the being said as he began to shrink in size. Then he was almost normal, apart from the deep purple eyes. 'But not quite as you remember.'

Zach stood before them all, covered in blood but in his normal form. Everything Christian had said was true, for once.

CHAPTER 34

ZACH SAW THE FEAR IN Rebecca's face as she realized it was him. He could not even remember the last time he had seen her or any of the Oldmans, but none of that mattered now. Upon his command, the storm cloud dissipated and showed the starry night sky. He gazed at the party and thought. Simmons was injured but not badly; he would recover. Fiona was struggling to keep hold of consciousness, and Christian was out cold on the stone. It was so tempting to just roll him off the edge like Marcus, but even he might have some small use. Rebecca was the only member unscathed, but she looked exhausted. The whole group would need shelter if they were to survive the night.

Zach moved past them to the sheer rock face and pressed his hands against it. After a moment of nothing, the rock shook and split. The group behind jumped to their feet in amazement as the sheer rock face opened into a huge cave, which had been Zach's home for the past few days and likely would be the only safe place he had left.

'Come inside quickly,' he beckoned. 'There is some food, water, and warmth.' Turning, he noticed that the fire had gone out in his absence. Stretching out his hand again, he sent a wave of fire onto the dry wood. It caught immediately. The group struggled into the warmth as Zach padded out and dragged the limp Christian into his cave. Resting Christian against the back wall, Zach restrained him with some salvaged rope. He did not want him escaping again – not just yet.

'Stay here and rest. I will see to your dead.'

Before any of the group could protest, Zach stalked out of the cave into the night. He knew all of the faces that were now in his sanctuary. He could not believe that they had found him, until he thought of one particular member, Christian, who must have used his new-found friends to track him down. Zach knew he would never be rid of Christian unless he did something drastic.

…

The night gave way to morning faster than Rebecca thought possible. Both she and Simmons had been bandaging and tending to Fiona, whose condition had not improved. Whatever Marcus's men had done to her must have been severe. Zach had not returned. Both Fiona and Simmons were asleep, and Christian showed no signs of coming around yet. Being careful not to wake them, Rebecca crept out into the world. The view was amazing. The cave was right on a cliff which opened up to the sea. From horizon to horizon it was blue, not a cloud in the sky. Behind her she could see the forest they had crashed through the day before. But nothing else was the same. The boxed-in rock faces that had been there yesterday were now gone. Everything was open and clear as the salty air blew through, rustling the leaves. The bodies were gone, as was the blood. How could Zach do that?

Just as Rebecca was getting used to the view, something caught her eye down by the water. It was a figure, who appeared to be loading something big and heavy onto some kind of raft. Rebecca found a path down and began to silently climb. As she carefully descended, she cast out her senses until she felt Zach's energy. It was him down by the water. He moved the bodies of the two dead resistance members as if they were nothing and arranged them respectfully on a raft made from driftwood. Rebecca dared to go further. She hid a few times when Zach snapped around as if knowing someone was there. But soon he was finished. He positioned the raft carefully and raised his arm to the sea. It responded with a small wave that slowly moved the raft and its contents away from the shore. Satisfied that the raft was far enough away to do harm, Zach appeared to bow his head. Rebecca could hear him mutter some words, but she could not make out what he was saying. As he finished, he summoned fire to his hands and threw two balls towards the raft. Both hit their mark perfectly. The raft caught fire and drifted farther out into the blue, before it sank into the depths.

Rebecca had never been so moved by something so simple in her life. She fought back the tears as she continued to watch Zach. He remained motionless, staring out at the sea. For a second, she thought she could hear him sob. She was about to climb lower when he snapped around again. This time he saw her. His eyes were purple again; she could see him begin to grow. Before she could call out to him, Zach leapt into the air and out of sight, having moved around a rocky outcrop. Rebecca did not feel herself run at first, but she knew she had to talk to him. All hopes rested on him now.

It was not anger or rage that was gripping Zach. It was sadness and sorrow. He knew that if he could not fight it, then the anger would follow him. But no matter how hard he tried, Zach could not stop the tears from falling. He knew both of the dead resistance members. Before he was an outcast, they were good to him, and now because of him, they were dead along with countless others. Their names and faces flooded his mind, even the name and face of Katie.

Zach did not feel himself drop to his knees, but he heard the thud as his beast form took control. All these people wanted him for different reasons. He had never been loved or wanted. Everyone just wanted to use him for their own ends. It was as if he were a pawn. His own family had made him into a prison for a demon so that they could kill it along with him, their son. His friends had abandoned him on account of the word of a cruel headmaster, and the only person he truly had loved had been working with his enemy. Zach had nothing, just himself. Not even Ebony had survived. Remembering the night Ebony was killed made Zach's tears flow like a waterfall. Moments later his sadness mixed with anger.

Zach stood and slammed his fist into the rock face, sending splits all over the cliff side and causing rocks to fly in all directions. He felt not even a prick of pain as he did it again and again, each hit using his fury. Turning to the sea, he let lose an almighty roar. It was a roar of sorrow and regret, and it echoed for moments after he stopped to continue his assault of the cliff side, completely oblivious that his private emotional outburst was being watched.

Rebecca did not know what to feel as she watched from her hiding place. Should she feel sorrow that Zach seemed to be so upset about something that he was crying and roaring in sadness, or should she feel petrified of the spectacle that she was seeing in front of her? She did not know how much longer the cliff face could take Zach's punches, but it was doing well as he continued to bombard it, with no sign of stopping. She had never seen something so powerful not only in emotion but also in action. Her senses were going haywire to the point that she had to withdraw them just to see Zach. He let loose another ear-splitting roar that sent shivers down her spine. Then he hurled a boulder the size of a large car into the sea. He stood motionless for what seemed like an age before dropping to his knees again, breaking two large rocks in the process. It was then she heard him cry. He began to shrink to his normal size as the anger wore off and only sadness remained.

Her heart beating like a drum in her chest, Rebecca moved out from her place of cover and began to walk slowly towards Zach. He had not known she was there, and she hoped he would not notice her yet. She was only metres away when he snapped around again and looked up at her. His purple eyes were bloodshot from the tears, and the water trails down his face were steaming from the heat, leaving salt piles dotted over his cheeks. He pulled himself up and strode over to Rebecca. He did not stop his powerful stride even when he caught her elbow.

'Let's go and see just how much he told you,' Zach said, returning to normal.

'He has been honest with us so far as we know.'

'Then how did Marcus find you?' As Zach walked, he pulled a curious object from his pocket and showed it to Rebecca. It appeared to be no more than a red bulb that flashed intermittently.

'I found them this morning, starting at your Land Rover and ending outside the cave. They stink of Christian.'

Rebecca gasped in shock as she sensed Christian's energy all over. Christian Jones had once again shown his worth. Zach was not shocked as he and Rebecca strode together to the cave.

CHAPTER 35

EVERYTHING WAS AS THEY HAD left it once they reached the cave. Fiona was still unconscious, and Simmons was checking her bandages as well as their supplies. Christian was also still unconscious, but he was restrained against the far wall. He had shown no signs of waking either. Simmons hauled himself onto his aching feet as Zach and Rebecca returned. Zach released his vice grip on Rebecca's elbow and strode towards Christian.

'What the hell just happened out there?' Simmons asked them both. 'I'm not completely sure I know what I heard or felt.'

Before Rebecca could reassure Simmons, Zach spoke, his voice deep and sinister. 'What you heard was a lifetime's worth of anger and sorrow expelled out into the world in one go, so I can make room for some rage.' He tossed the bag of flashing bulbs at Simmons's feet. 'These belong to you, I think.'

'These went missing from our armoury the day Christian arrived at Sanctuary. Wait, that doesn't make any sense, unless …'

'Unless he has been lying to you all along. That's what he does, doesn't he?' Zach swung the back of his hand across Christian's face, but the latter remained unresponsive.

'Do you have anything to wake him up?' Zach asked, frustrated. 'He needs to answer some questions.'

Both Simmons and Rebecca scoured their available supplies but found nothing that would rouse Christian. They were at their wits' end when Zach spoke again.

'Cover your ears.'

They had only a moment to react before Zach acted. Standing next to Christian, Zach raised his right arm and hovered it over the cool rock face. He focused for a second, and his fingers began to slowly change. Using more energy, Zach made his fingers into long razor-sharp blades. He looked over to Simmons and Rebecca to check that they were ready, before he pressed into the rock and moved his blade fingers down the wall.

They noise made both Simmons and Rebecca hit the floor. The pitch was very high and it echoed around the cave and out into the world. Grinding his teeth, Zach then bared them as he moved his fingers closer to Christian's ear. It took only moments before Christian was roused from unconsciousness. But that did not mean Zach would stop. Zach ran his hand faster down the wall, making the pitch higher and the noise louder. Finally he ripped his hand from the wall, and then all was silent. Simmons helped Rebecca up from the floor. With their ears ringing, like they housed a bell tower, they padded over to the now awake Christian.

'I thought that would wake you up.' Zach laughed as Christian frantically adjusted to his position. 'You have a lot to answer for.'

'Keep him away from me,' Christian pleaded, his voice breaking in fear. 'I will talk to you two.'

'You do not have a choice whom you talk to!' Rebecca screamed. 'You answer to all of us for what you have done. Was there anything apart from Zach's whereabouts that you told us that was true?'

Christian looked at the ground, contemplating his answer. Zach made his metal fingers clink, knowing it unnerved his enemy.

'What happened in Salisbury is true,' Christian eventually answered.

'You are going to need to give us a lot more than that,' Simmons growled, tossing the bag of bulbs at Christian's feet. 'Explain these.'

'Umm, I found them, but I didn't have a chance ...' Zach did not allow his lie to end as he slammed his normal hand into Christian's stomach, winding him.

'All right, all right.' Christian coughed. 'I stole them. I had orders to carry out.'

'Which were?' Rebecca inquired.

'It doesn't matter now. I may have failed in fulfilling my orders, but I aided a brother to complete his.' Christian smiled.

'What is he talking about?' Simmons demanded.

'He means Marcus,' Zach responded. 'Marcus knows where I am.'

'But you took care of him, right?'

'Marcus is the name of the demon, not of the person.'

'Demon?' both Rebecca and Simmons questioned in unison.

'All those men you saw yesterday were possessed. Their bodies are destroyed. But the demons can be re-summoned. Am I correct, Jones?'

Christian refused to answer. He bit his lip and looked at the ground.

'Here is what I think,' Zach began, walking in front of Christian. 'You were tasked with getting the high-ranked resistance members out into the open so they could be captured and tortured. But instead, you found me. Now that your superiors know where I am, you expect to get a reprieve because I am the prize. The question is, can you giving me any compelling reason not to rip you limb from limb and mount your bones on the rock face so all can see what happens to people like you?'

'I don't have to tell you anything. When I'm free from you, I will go back into the loop and do what I do best.' Christian sat back, smug as ever.

'What if I took an eye?' Zach said, dangling his metal fingers in front of Christian. 'What person would interact with you then? What woman would drop all for you if I took an ear or your nose? You tell me what I need to know and I leave your money-maker alone. How does that sound for a deal?'

Christian shivered in fear before nodding. Zach crouched in front of him and began. 'Where is Azrael and the rest of the newly possessed Inquisition?'

'Salisbury. The whole town is under their control now. Their base of operations is the cathedral and the surrounding buildings, all newly fortified.'

'How many filled vessels does he have?'

'Hundreds – and more waiting to be filled.'

'Wait a second,' Simmons cut in, 'they don't control the town. Sanctuary still houses the resistance. That's not total control.'

'If all went according to plan, Sanctuary and all who were there would have been destroyed.'

Christian answered, 'The attack was to happen the day we left.'

'You're lying!' Simmons slammed a fist into Christian's face.

'Then why have you had no word from them?' Christian asked, his face beginning to bruise.

'He is lying, Simmons. Go get some air,' Zach commanded. He waited for Rebecca and Simmons to leave before continuing. 'What's Azrael's endgame?'

'Find you, consume you, and use your powers to take England and then Europe, with the Inquisition being the public face of his conquest.'

Zach was horrified by what he heard. Azrael wanted the world, and soon he would start his campaign. Zach could not see any way out of that apart from one.

'Is there anything else that I need to know?'

'His power grows every day, but he doesn't know if he can beat you. You are what he fears most. If he can't consume you, then he will kill you and make sure no one else will challenge him.'

'And do you have anything to say in your defence for all the crimes you have committed?'

'We used to be friends, Zach. Remember those days?'

'I remember your various betrayals,' Zach said, his voice beginning to deepen. 'I remember how you gave me to the bullies just so you would be fine. I remember the friends you stole so you would be popular. I remember the people I loved taken by you so that I would be alone. I have nothing because of you! And you will answer for it.'

Zach yanked Christian from his restraints and tossed him to the ground. Before Christian could recover, Zach was on him again, picking him up by the throat and holding him against the cave wall near Fiona.

'Now, for once you are going to do something that is good and right.' Zach made his right hand normal and set it ablaze with purple fire. 'Take this message to your master.'

'What message?'

'Death comes to him and all he owns.' Zach slammed his hand over Christian's face and let the flames engulf his head and shoulders. Christian howled in pain as his face burnt. Zach tossed him to the floor again; the flames subsided. Christian's face was horrifying. The flames had melted his skin and burnt off his hair. He looked more monster than human.

'Get out of my sight before I take more than your face.'

Christian disappeared out of the cave, holding his searing, monstrous face in his hands as he ran.

Moments later, Simmons and Rebecca returned. Simmons was still angry. 'Why did you let him go?'

'He has one more task to perform for me whilst we act.' Zach turned to them, his purple eyes glowing in the dark cave. 'We need to leave, sooner rather than later. There is only one course of action for me, and I will follow it. You can either follow me or go to safety. I don't care which one you choose, but choose it quickly.'

'What about Fiona?' Rebecca asked.

'I'm fine,' a familiar voice spoke from behind them, 'and eager to take the fight to them.'

Turning from their conversation, Zach nodded at the newly revived and uninjured Fiona.

'How did that just happen?' Simmons asked, confused.

'I will tell you as we travel,' Zach replied. Then he went to gather his belongings.

CHAPTER 36

THE RAIN CAME DOWN HEAVILY that evening, so Zach reluctantly decided not to travel, which gave Rebecca and Simmons a chance to review their supplies with the help of the newly revived Fiona. Between the three of them, they had enough for the trip to Sanctuary, with no more to spare. Rebecca could not even guess what supplies Zach would have. Since he had decided to release Christian, Zach was quieter than normal and seemed distracted. From a secret alcove in the cave, he had brought out a tattered bag which seemed not to have much in it. But he still rummaged through it every so often. He was prepared to leave at any moment. His tattered black clothes covered with a soft leather trench coat made him almost invisible amidst the gloom.

Simmons plucked up the courage to ask, 'So, how do you feel, Fiona?'

'It's strange,' she began. 'I feel fine, but more than fine, like every ache and pain has been taken from me. I feel like I can do anything.'

'Well, you were out for quite a while,' Rebecca said, joining the conversation. 'But how is that possible?'

'Jones kindly gave me the energy needed to heal her,' Zach spoke from the dark. 'She is completely healed, as if nothing happened to her.'

'Do you remember what happened to you?' Simmons continued to question.

'I remember going into the woods ahead of you, but that's it.'

'I took the liberty of shielding you from those memories, Fiona,' Zach added.

'Why?' Fiona asked, standing. 'What did happen?'

'When you need to remember, I will release the memories, but now you all need to sleep. We have a long way to go.'

They all knew that he was right, so they began to prepare for sleep. The cave entrance groaned and creaked as the stones closed over, sealing the cave. The fire was down to its embers but was still glowing bright as Rebecca settled under her jacket and fell asleep to the sound of silence.

…

The morning came quickly for Zach, who had not slept a wink, as usual. He silently opened the cave up to the world and stalked outside. The sky was as black as Zach felt. It was not a good day for travelling, but he saw no other choice. They could not stay here much longer. He began to scan the area. Casting his senses to see if there were any intruders, he sensed nothing close by. As he cast them further, they were met by a body of hostility. A mass of people were closing in. Turning, he sprinted back to the cave to wake the others. When he arrived, he saw that the fire was still barely burning. Instead of waking them directly, he sent a wave of flame into the pit. The fire erupted with heat and sound. Everyone was awake instantly, dazed and confused. Zach manipulated the fire into a sword and plucked the sword from the flames – his new weapon. He fashioned a sheath from the embers and wood and sheathed the blade, the others looking on in awe.

'We have to move now.'

'It is too late for that,' voices said from outside.

Zach whipped round, drew his sword, and strode out of the cave, the others remaining where they were. They were greeted by a huge throng of people of all ages, colours, and genders. The strangers were standing in perfect formation, not aggressive but blocking their only escape. When they spoke, they spoke in unison. Not one voice was out of sequence.

'Lay down your weapons and surrender to us, heathens. We have no wish to hurt any of you.'

'What the hell is going on?' Simmons asked, his hand hovering over the head of his hatchet.

'Stay here,' Zach commanded. 'Do not move until I say.'

Zach continued to advance on the mass of people, his sword still in his hand and burning a deep purple.

'Zach Ford,' the throng spoke, 'you are hereby ordered to surrender yourself and your companions to us. Any refusal will be met with hostility.'

'Who commands you, thralls?' Zach questioned in a demonic voice so all could hear.

'We do not understand your question,' they answered, 'which makes it irrelevant. Surrender now.'

'Why don't you come out and talk to me face-to-face? Don't hide behind your human shields like a coward.'

'This is your last chance,' the throng threatened, changing to an aggressive stance. 'Surrender now or …'

Zach did not wait for their threat to finish. He sent a wave of energy into the ground, making it shake and crack. The throng of people began to lose their balance, but none of them looked away. Zach sent in more energy. They fell to the ground, unable to get up. Then he saw his target. One man from the throng began to run. All the others stared at him, unmoving, unless they were losing their balance. Zach sent tendrils of energy out to grab the man. He was caught and wrapped in amongst the others within seconds, and then he was dragged back to Zach, lashing and cursing. As the man landed near Zach, the latter stopped the tremors and allowed the throng to regain their balance.

The man by Zach's feet was a member of the Inquisition. He wore the robes which had the emblem proudly over his heart. He struggled to put his hand back over the emblem, but Zach wrenched them apart and held them in the air with his tendrils. He looked over to the cave and nodded. Slowly the others came out and marvelled at what was happening.

'So you must be the puppeteer?' Zach asked, looking at his prisoner.

The man nodded, still trying to free his hands.

'Why are you so desperate to get this?' Zach leant forward and ripped the insignia from the man's robes.

'Give that back, heathen,' the man spat. 'You have no right to touch that.'

'And you and your order have no right to exist,' Zach hissed, striking the man across the face, 'but you still spread your evil and lies. And I am still going to touch this.'

'What is going on?' Rebecca asked, wary of the new arrivals. 'And who is that?'

'This is the Inquisition's newest attempt at capturing us,' Zach replied.

'Are you not slightly concerned by the massive number of people glaring at us right now?' Fiona blurted, her blades in hand and ready.

'Not really,' Zach replied, standing upright. 'They are just thralls. Watch.'

Zach placed his hand over the insignia. The thralls immediately stood upright, as if the order for attention had been given. He looked at them all as his rage built. These people were the few who had said no to the Inquisition, so instead of being taken and turned against their will, they were brainwashed and used as pawns. They were fodder for the Inquisition. Zach channelled his rage into fire and set the insignia ablaze. All at once the thralls fell to the ground, screaming. As the insignia burnt, Zach whirled and slammed it into the chest of the controller. He howled in pain as Zach pushed it deeper, until his hand came out the other side of the man's body. Zach's rage was nearly absolute as he threw the man over the cliff. And then all was silent.

The thralls began to slowly awake. They were confused. Some called out names, whilst others took in their surroundings. Soon they began to recognize others. Then they noticed Zach and the bloodstain on the rock. In a matter of moments, they had regained the knowledge of who they were. That's when Fiona and Simmons each let out a cry of rage. The thralls were all from Sanctuary. Zach strode over to Fiona and Simmons to calm them before he turned to the mass of people.

'We can offer you no food or shelter,' he boomed at them all. 'We will be leaving to end this oppressive rule that these Inquisitional bastards are trying to instil. We don't ask any of you to come with us. But if you do, then you will be lending your help not only to freedom but also to vengeance.'

There was a pause as the throng of people contemplated what was said. Then they responded. A roar of agreement went up through the crowd. Simmons and Fiona began to smile and welcome back the friends they thought were dead. Whilst they mingled, Zach padded to the cliff face and looked out over the bay.

How many will be dead by the time this is over? he thought.

CHAPTER 37

THEIR PLANS HAD GONE OUT the window. Instead of being on the move like they had planned, Rebecca and the others were now housing and readying a crude guerrilla army. The cliff side had become awash with people from all across the countryside. Hearing what had happened with the thrall master and what Zach was intending to do, people flocked to help. Rebecca was glad to see the members of Sanctuary again, but she was sad to hear of the road they had travelled to get there.

Sanctuary had fallen days after Rebecca and Simmons led the team to find Zach. The Inquisition attacked with ruthlessness and ferocity. Anyone with a weapon in hand was killed. Anyone who was left was converted into a thrall. None of them remembered how. Rebecca thought that it was for the best that they did not. She was glad to see the elder again, who was keen to hear of her improving Voyant abilities. She listened with great interest before ploughing on with the training again.

Rebecca could sense that Simmons and Fiona were greatly saddened by the huge loss of resistance fighters, the brave men and women who were slaughtered before they even knew what was happening. But Fiona and Simmons were constantly busy assessing who would be a capable fighter in the assault of the cathedral close. Maps, diagrams, and other confusing pieces of paper littered the ground showing their tactics. No matter how foolhardy it seemed, the attack was going to happen.

To Rebecca's surprise, Zach was hardly ever present for any of the planning. He spent his time down by the shore and away from the ever growing mass of people. It was evident that he wanted to be moving rather than waiting. She wondered what kept him there. He was far more powerful that any fighter the resistance had and also more capable against anything the Inquisition had, but before she could find an answer to her question, the elder snapped her away from her thoughts and back to training.

She was focusing more on practical abilities, in particular defensive energy. No one knew just what the defences were around the centre of Salisbury, so Rebecca was being trained to defend against anything, from gunfire to demon magic. She found it exhausting, but the elder never stopped. They could be on the move at any moment. Time was short.

Days passed. Finally Simmons and Fiona were happy with the plan. Even Zach returned from the shore to hear what had been devised. Rebecca could see his turbulent energy throb as the plan was aired.

'No matter how we do this, it will have to be a full-frontal attack,' Simmons began, long-faced. 'There is no weak point in the inner defences. We may be able to advance quickly through the outer defences, but only if we have the element of surprise on our side. We don't have the numbers to surround them, so we shall have to concentrate our attack on the smallest gate, here. Once it is down, we will have to move quickly to make it to the cathedral itself. From there it will be a battle of attrition.'

Whispers and sighs of shock and surprise began all around the maps until the cave began to echo. Simmons had known that his plan would not please. Before Rebecca could console Simmons, Zach stepped forward.

'No,' he said firmly. 'This is what will happen. I will enter the close by night and destroy this gate's defences silently. When you get my signal before sunrise, you will all slowly approach it and walk through. Begin by quietly securing these posts here and here' – he gestured to large buildings that would house guards – 'before making your way to the other gates. Attack them from the inside and the defences will be useless. This will draw any reinforcements out to you, where they will bottleneck, leaving me with Azrael and a few guards. Once he falls, his hold on the Inquisition will be broken.'

The cave was silent as the fighters deliberated. They would be outnumbered and behind enemy lines in a drawing move so that Zach could engage Azrael as quickly as possible. It was risky. Rebecca scanned the cave to see how people were reacting. Most did not know what to think. Although some whispered to those who stood around them, nobody aired a view.

'Regardless of what you are thinking,' Zach continued, visibly frustrated, 'I will be leaving tonight. We have remained here for far too long. I will not risk another attack. Anyone who wishes to come with me may do so. If not, then I will attack the cathedral in four days' time. Either meet me at Sanctuary or not at all.'

He strode away before anyone could ask a question. The atmosphere changed to astonishment. Some wanted to follow, others wanted to stay, and a few wanted to leave altogether. It took Rebecca and the elder the rest of the day to calm the inhabitants.

As the night drew in, Rebecca found Zach standing overlooking the sea. The breeze was strong and cold, but she continued to move towards him.

'That was uncalled for,' she blurted. 'Simmons and Fiona had worked hard on that plan. You undermined them.'

'If we did it their way, almost everyone who came with us would be dead before they reached the inner wall. My way is risky, but it will give them a chance.'

'You mean it will give you a chance,' Rebecca retorted.

'I will be leaving at first light.' Zach was in no mood to argue. 'Let everybody know, in case they wish to come as well.'

With that, he disappeared into the night. Rebecca stalked back to the cave to inform Fiona and Simmons. No matter how much she did not like it, she would soon be in a war.

CHAPTER 38

THE JOURNEY WAS LONG AND arduous, but no one dared to complain. Zach wore a face like thunder, which matched the turbulent sky. The storm had grown with devastating frequency over the past few days but had not broken. As cold and tired as the group was, at least they were dry. When they could, the group would stop and rest in burned-down farmhouses and other destroyed buildings. The Inquisition had been busy and relentless in destroying any opposition. Every night Rebecca would toss and turn as she heard the screams of those who had died in the buildings they now took shelter in. Zach was as silent and distant as he had been on the day they had found him.

Zach had been no help with the group. The fighters needed discipline that only he could give, but he refused to talk to anyone. He often scouted ahead of the main group for hours on end without saying what he was looking for. More often than not, the group would happen upon decimated parties of Inquisition soldiers sprayed across the path. No one said a word as they passed the bodies, most of which were incomplete. They were beyond help, even the seldom few who still groaned in agony. Rebecca did not need to cast her senses out to see who was responsible. She could see he was getting more rage filled. And she could not help thinking that soon he would explode with primal rage, at which time what was left of the resistance would be caught in the fallout, including her. But still they continued on.

That evening they bedded down in an abandoned barn a day's walk from Salisbury. The plan was to wait there for the rest of the fighters from the other, nearby resistance cells. Zach had made it known that he did not like the idea of waiting so close to their goal, but he resigned himself to the fact that Simmons and Fiona were going to do nothing else. The barn was huge, with more than enough room for the fighters who were inbound. Rebecca decided to bed down in the hayloft with Fiona. They both liked the idea of being hidden, high and out of the way. Zach had been gone for hours. Rebecca could not remember the last time she saw his face or heard him speak. When she felt brave, she would try to sense his energy. She could not see colours anymore, just violent, turbulent energy.

'Are you all right?' Fiona snapped Rebecca out of her daydream. 'You've been quiet all day.'

'I'm just tired and worried. I can't help thinking that something will go wrong or that we have missed something.'

'Everyone's feeling like that. Don't worry. Just stay with me and you'll be fine.'

Rebecca nodded feebly. The exhaustion was crushing her.

'You should get some sleep now.' Fiona spoke with a softness that Rebecca had never heard from her before. 'I will keep watch for a bit from up here.'

As Rebecca agreed, she heard the other fighters beginning to bed down for the night and set up a shift for watches. She missed her bed in her house with all her family. She never thought she would have to sleep in a hayloft with a growing number of fighters who were younger than she was. Everything had gone so wrong. She could not help but think that there was something she had not been told. As her thoughts overtook her mind, sleep found her.

Her dreams were horrible – more so because they were not her own. She was seeing through the eyes of someone else, someone angry and vengeful. She watched with them and stalked with them. Their energy was strange and unnatural, and she did not recognize it. She stalked through large halls and down long corridors, each flanked by a multitude of men and women with red glowing eyes. Every time she walked by, they bowed low. She was a person of respect and rank. Then the eyes she saw through closed and a face appeared in front of her. It stared at her for what seemed like an eternity before speaking.

'How dare you enter my mind!' It roared at her, 'Who are you?'

Rebecca tried to wake up, but she could not. She was stuck in place. The face grew larger and moved towards her, seemingly unhappy with her presence. Before it made it to her, she felt a hand on her chest, pulling her free from her dream.

She awoke struggling for air. As she looked around, her eyes first found Fiona, who appeared as if she had been awake for a while. Then she found Zach. His gripped relaxed on her as he let her regain control of her body.

'What happened?' she asked, finding her breath.

'You just met Azrael,' Zach answered, 'from the inside. That really was not a good move.'

'How did I do that?' Her head was spinning.

'I don't know, but if you can tap in, then you can do much more.'

'What?' Fiona challenged. 'Look at her. Do you think she could do that again?'

'Do not question me on something you know nothing about,' Zach said with a poisonous tone. 'If it can be done, it can be done only by her.'

'What do you think I can do?' Rebecca eventually began to feel better.

'I think you could block his vision and put him completely in the dark before we attack. It will throw him off guard.'

'How?'

'You need to distract him, any way you can.'

'I know nothing about distracting a power-hungry Inquisition leader.'

'You need to distract him only long enough for me to get there. Then you get out of his head.' He stood and looked down at her, his purple eyes glowing like sapphires. 'You do not want to be in there when I arrive.'

With that, he left the barn. Rebecca did not sleep again that night, her thoughts turning to entering and distracting the most powerful man in the country. But that was not what disturbed her most. What disturbed her the most was the fact she was convinced that he was not a man at all.

CHAPTER 39

SALISBURY HAD CHANGED IN THE years since he had been away. The town that once had been a part of his life now looked like it had suffered a nuclear explosion of biblical proportions. Almost every building they passed since they had exited the hidden tunnels was destroyed. Some still smouldered from when they were first set ablaze. Others just stood blackened against the perpetually grey sky. Since they had emerged, the large group of fighters fell silent. Zach could feel their anger and fury, but he also felt them push it to the backs of their minds. Each man, women, boy, and girl who had answered the fighters' call knew they had to have a clear mind for what was to come. It was impossible to gauge time when they eventually made it to Sanctuary. Quickly and silently, everyone made into the cave and began the final plans. Zach had hated every second of the travelling – most of all the constant planning. Everyone apart from Simmons had grand thoughts of being heroes and believed that their cause for good would easily push aside the Inquisition, but Zach knew better. The Inquisition were more in number, were greater in firepower, and had a strong defensive perimeter. Most of the resistance fighters would die. No matter how often he said this to them, they always ignored his advice. He now did not care what happened to them as long as he got to Azrael. Nothing else mattered.

'Zach,' a voice called from the planning table, 'do you have anything to add?'

Looking up, Zach saw the questioning look on the face of Simmons. Stalking over to the table, he glanced down at the map and drawings to assess them. As he suspected, the fighters had ignored his suggestion of following behind him and holding one of the smaller gates whilst he went in deeper alone. Instead they opted for a 'loud and proud' approach, which consisted of multiple attacks on each of the gates. It would spread their already limited fighters thin, thereby making them easier to kill by the soldiers they were attacking. Finishing his assessment, Zach straightened and spoke.

'Regardless of what I say, you will continue on this suicide plan,' he said, 'so it is pointless for me to comment.'

'If you have something to say, boy, say it,' a burly leader growled.

'What do you know of the foe you face?' Zach snarled, his purple eyes throbbing. 'Do you know that they outnumber us? Do you know they have superior firepower? Do you know that under no circumstance will they leave their positions until they are completely sure that you are dead? They will show no mercy to you. They will take great delight in gunning you down. This plan you have made will guarantee only one thing: your swift death.'

An eruption of shouting and swearing sounded from the planning table as everyone began to question Zach. He answered none of them but waited for them to finish before continuing.

'You have all repeatedly ignored my advice for a stealthier entry after I infiltrate the gates, saying I am a coward and so on. So let me make this perfectly clear to all of you. Your deaths mean nothing to me. The deaths of all the men, women, and children mean nothing to me. If you will ignore my advice and insult me in the process, then that is what you will receive. I will not help you, and I will not save you. Whilst you meet gunfire and death, I will be on the other side of the wall completing my mission, which outweighs the life of every single member of this resistance. Now, think very carefully about what you want to do because when the moon breaks over the building where most of you and your children went to learn about the world, I will leave. If you want to come with me and live, then be my guest. If you want to stay, sleep, and die, then you know where I stand.'

With that, he turned and gracefully padded away. He could hear the mutterings of the fighters behind and the voice of Simmons trying to appease them. Zach did not care. The moon would break in a matter of hours. He had set his plan into motion regardless of the others. He could not miss the opportunity.

As Zach rounded a corner to the living area, he felt someone tapping into his energy. He knew exactly who it was. He found her sitting crossed-legged in front of the elder who whispered commands into her ear. Fiona stood as a guard behind her. She did not notice Zach at the door. It still amazed him how much Rebecca looked like her younger sister, the sister whom he loved and was betrayed by. He still was not completely sure if he should trust Rebecca, but she was a means to an end – an end that Zach had to get to.

'I suggest that she stop now,' he said into the room, making the elder jump and curse. 'She will not want to drain herself too soon.'

Rebecca gradually came round and sat up. Zach could see she was exhausted, but she made no sound of complaint.

'I was just testing to see if I could tap in to you,' she said defensively.

'I will be a lot harder than Azrael,' Zach replied, 'and you would not want to see what is in my head.'

'No one would after that speech,' Simmons said, entering behind Zach. 'They aren't used to being talked to like that.'

'I do not care, Simmons. What is their verdict?'

'Their plan stays the same, with one change.' Simmons composed himself before continuing. 'They demand you join the assault with them.'

'No,' Zach replied. 'I said my piece, and that is where I stand.'

'I have to insist,' Simmons continued, his hand falling to the head of his hatchet. Fiona followed suit, slowly drawing her knives and moving in front of Rebecca.

Zach, having known it would come to this, had planned accordingly. Without Rebecca feeling what he was doing, he subtly broke the barriers in Fiona's mind, allowing the memories he had previously blocked to enter. It took effect instantly; a tidal wave of theretofore unknown memories filled her. She screamed and fell to her knees, covering her ears with her hands, which tightly gripped her knives. Simmons turned to her and then back to Zach, who continued to break more barriers until there were none left. Fiona continued to scream and cry, even whilst the elder and Rebecca tried to comfort her.

'What have you done to her?' Simmons demanded.

'She is experiencing everything she forgot in the woods on the day you all came to find me.'

Fiona howled as the memories entered her. Zach saw each one of them seep into her mind and felt each reaction. He showed nothing but the stony face of one betrayed.

'Stop it,' Rebecca pleaded. 'Please stop.'

'Why are you doing this?' Simmons drew his hatchet.

'All my life I have been used,' Zach boomed, his demonic voice flowing. Fiona's sobs grew quieter as he spoke. 'The only reason I was conceived was to trap demons, not out of love or affection. At the first sign of possession, my parents were going to kill me so the demon could never return. I was never loved. I was used and betrayed. My godfather abandoned me to my fate without a caring word. He sold me to people who would use me for their own gain. Even your sister' – he pointed at Rebecca – 'pretended to love me just so she could get close enough to me. Even your precious resistance is using me to get rid of their problem, not for my benefit, but so you can live happily ever after. I have been used, betrayed, abandoned, and forgotten, and now I will do what I have to do and what I want to do. I will not be used anymore. If you are going to force me to do what I will not, then a lot of people will die tonight in your little sanctuary.'

'How do you know about Green?' Simmons asked after a pause.

'I've always known. I just wanted to see if the old man had a fibre of caring in him. He did not.' Zach's tone was bitter. 'So what is it to be, Simmons? Death by Inquisition, or death by me?'

Zach summoned his sword to his hand and awaited Simmons's answer. He already knew what it was.

'You will fight with us,' Simmons growled. 'Like it or not, you will. This is not your fight but ours. We have suffered more.'

'You think so.' Zach laughed. 'This was my fight long before it was yours, Simmons. You have one chance. Let me go now and I will let you all live, at least for a few hours.'

'He's right, Simmons.' Rebecca stood and padded towards them. 'He has suffered more than we have. Why should he have to do it your way and not his? Let him go.'

Zach watched the line of thought go through Simmons's mind. Eventually the older man conceded and sheathed his hatchet. Zach lessened the flow of memories into Fiona's mind. Eventually she calmed, but she still wept silently.

'I will take you to the surface,' Simmons began, 'before the others barge in on us. We have to go now.'

Zach, not waiting for a change of mind or heart, followed Simmons. He looked back once at Rebecca and nodded. She did not know the nod contained a message. It took a few minutes for the two to make it to the main entrance, where Simmons stopped and spoke.

'You know many will die tomorrow?' he began. 'Just promise me they won't die in vain.'

Zach moved in front of him and thought. 'Simmons,' he started, 'none of your fighters have to die.'

'What do you …?'

Simmons did not finish the question, because Zach punched him in the temple. Simmons buckled and fell limp. Zach caught the fall and rested him against the cold dripping stone of the cave. Checking his pulse and mind, he was satisfied Simmons would live. He disabled the old miners' lift and climbed the stairs with ferocious speed. As he made it to the top, he glanced back into the cave and sealed it from the outside. No one would get out, and after tonight no one would need to break in. He knew it was cruel, but it was the kindest thing he could have done. It was the only legacy he would leave. A single tear rolled down his face as he finished, and then he sped into the night. In a few short hours, his fate and the fate of the trapped resistance members would hang in the balance. All he could do now was wait for his entrance.

CHAPTER 40

IT TOOK A FEW MINUTES for Zach to take up his position. The easiest way into the now heavily guarded cathedral close was through the smallest vehicle entrance. It was easy to mount a defence over it, but it would not be an effective one. The shops that lined the streets were boarded up, making it impossible for the soldiers to use them in their defensive plan. They only had a clear field of view from the rooftops. Zach had taken up position right by the sealed gate. No one had seen him as the fog of night closed in. He was as ready as he would be. He summoned his sword of purple fire that was sheathed across his back beneath his tattered black clothes. His plan was in place and he would stick to it. All he had to do was wait. He traced his route over and over in his mind. Through the gate was the first checkpoint, which was likely to be lightly defended. Around the corner would be the first barracks. Soldiers would stream from them if the alarm was raised. Another checkpoint and another barracks stood between him and the cathedral itself. If all went according to plan, all he would need to do was keep moving. Anyone who was in his way would swiftly be dealt with. All he needed was an assurance that Rebecca would do her part from the now sealed sanctuary. He heard talking and movement from over the wall. It was nearly time. He sent his final message.

...

Fiona still wept quietly in the corner of Rebecca's alcove. It felt like an eternity since Simmons had regained consciousness. He said that Zach had knocked him out. Everyone else guessed that Zach was the one who had sealed them in as his final act of defiance of the resistance. But Rebecca was not so sure.

'Moments before he left,' she had said to the other fighter leaders, 'he said he didn't care if you all died when you attacked. So why would he seal you in here so you could not attack? Maybe he was doing an act of good before he went to do unspeakable evil. That to me shows that he does care.'

She did not know why she had defended his actions. There was something in the nod he had given to her before he left. That one nod was more human than any other action she had seen from him. Now all she was focused on was comforting Fiona. The fearless fighter she had known was now gone. Only a broken girl remained. Rebecca did not ask Fiona what she was remembering; she just tried her best to soothe her with energy. But nothing she or the elder did was making any difference. Fiona still wept uncontrollably.

'They are monsters,' she said, wiping away her tears. 'Zach will be fighting monsters, not men.'

'What do you mean?' Rebecca lay down next to her fighter friend.

'They killed her.' She wept. 'Sophie. My best friend. My … my …'

'You loved her.'

Fiona nodded, her tears falling like rain.

'And they killed her. Only after they did things to her. To us. We were unnatural to them. They never stopped smiling, even when we were tied down and the knives sliced our clothes and …'

'Hush now, lass,' the elder spoke, bringing in a kettle. 'She will be avenged this night. You are a fearsome fighter of this resistance. Nothing will change that view of you we hold.'

Fiona nodded but continued to cry.

…

Rebecca felt powerless. She now knew what had happened to her protector friend, but she could not even fathom how she truly felt or how to truly comfort her. Fiona had lost not only her love but also something she would have only given to whom she had now lost. That was what enraged Rebecca more. Fiona and the whole resistance were nothing but sacks of meat to be used by the Inquisition. Rebecca left the elder to tend to

Fiona as she herself strolled the passageways. Every person nodded to her, knowing that she felt as powerless as they felt. As she rounded a corner into the main cavern, a surge of energy overtook her. She struggled to regain her balance as a familiar voice spoke in her mind.

'When the ground tremors, start the block.'

...

'Why have I not heard from any of my ground units in days?' Azrael in the body of David Alexander boomed. 'An entire battalion does not go missing in just a day!'

'We don't know, my lord,' a minion answered, cowering. 'They reported having arrived at their guard post. That was the last communication we had from them. None of the southern thrall-masters or commanders have checked in either. We are dark in the southern sector until sector twenty-nine.'

'Find out what happened to my men, Chamberlain,' Azrael commanded impatiently, 'or my hounds will feast on you.'

The hellhound at Azrael's feet jumped with excitement upon hearing of the possibility of impending food. The chamberlain shuffled off, eager to be away from death. Azrael had grown increasingly infuriated at his pitiful soldier and staff members. In the past few weeks, more had disappeared than had done anything productive, like recruit more to his cause. Their only accomplishment was the annihilation of the resistance movement, who had been a thorn in his side for too long. Finally they had been removed

'My lord,' his steward called, 'someone has arrived and begged an audience. He claims to know you.' Azrael waved his approval and watched as a heavily hooded and cloaked figure limped towards the altar. Azrael could smell burnt flesh, and hear the wheezing occasioned by pain-filled movements. But he still did not know who this form was. His hellhounds stood and growled, aware of an unfamiliar smell.

'My lord Azrael.' The being coughed, his voice unfamiliar. 'I'm sorry. I'm not as you remember me, but I'm still your humble and loyal servant.'

'I do not know you, creature. Why do you invade my time with your grovelling?'

The being stood and lowered his hood. The stench of charred flesh filled Azrael's nose, but the face was familiar. Under the flaking dead and blistered skin was a servant he knew.

'Jones,' he purred, 'what has happened to you? I ordered you to bring me Ford and the resistance leaders, and instead you return as if you have walked through a fire. I trust you have a good explanation?'

Christian recapped all that had happened to him since he had left on his long mission: the infiltrating of Sanctuary, the finding of Zach, and his being tortured for information. He had to pause to take deep painful breaths, his lungs sounding strained. When he finished, he looked at the floor and awaited judgement.

'You know that you have failed me in every way, Jones.' Azrael began rising from his throne. 'But luckily for you, I need my most deviant agent back to infiltrate again. Your life has been spared this day. But fail me again and you will pay with your life and soul. Is that understood?'

'Yes, my lord.' Christian let out a sigh of relief. 'May I beg a favour from you, lord? If you wish me to immediately return to my duties, then I humbly beg that you heal my face.'

Azrael padded to his servant and took his face in his hands. He ignored the hiss of pain and surveyed the damage.

'Remember this day, Jones,' he whispered. 'I am your lord of all power and mercy.'

Azrael poured demon fire over Christian's face. Even though his scarred servant screamed in agony, he continued until he was done. After a few seconds of whimpering, Christian rose, his face healed from the burns.

'Thank you, my lord.' He bowed. 'You are truly the most great and …'

Azrael was astounded that his servant denied him his flatteries. Turning, he saw Christian fall to his knees. His mouth moved in agony, but no sound came out. Christian keeled over as the pain continued. Too late, Azrael realized what had happened. Christian exploded in blue fire, which then engulfed the entire hall and shattered the centuries-old stained-glass windows. Azrael was swept aside by the force of the explosion. His hounds and stewards were instantly disintegrated, and his throne was shattered beyond recognition. As he rose, he heard the gunfire. Before he could boom and command, his mind became clouded. Unable to see or sense anything, he was blind, dazed, and powerless.

CHAPTER 41

ACH DID NOT HESITATE WHEN he beheld the first signs of his explosion. He drew his sword of purple fire and charged. Shattering the gate with demon fire, he sprinted through. His supernatural speed carried him to the first checkpoint, which he dealt with swiftly. The solders had no time to ready the light machine gun set up behind the sandbags. They met their end by his sword or fist. He sent bodies flying. Most were already dead, but a few were not so lucky.

Zach continued to sprint. The first barracks was his target. He could see that the doors were still sealed, but he heard the movements of confused, dazed soldiers inside. He yanked open the metal doors and flooded the room with demon fire. The soldiers burst out of every available exit. They were all ablaze in purple fire. Some charged at Zach screaming in pain, only to be cut down. He showed only the mercy that he would be given, which was none. Satisfied that the barracks and its personal were neutralized, he continued on.

He moved like a wraith in the fog, cutting and slicing through soldiers who did not even see him. Their black uniforms with the red Inquisition emblem made them easy targets in the thick grey fog. Rounding a corner, he saw the spire of the cathedral. He was closing in. Still running, he made his way to the second checkpoint. The soldiers at this one were prepared. There he was met by heavy gunfire. He felt each shot impact on his skin and clothes, but he felt no pain. His rage was his armour, and the soldiers were unknowingly adding to it. Seeing that their weapons were useless, they ran to the second barracks, which was Zach's final obstacle. He pursued them with death in his thoughts. He cut down the majority of them before they even made it, his demonic speed easily outmatching theirs. One managed to make it into the barracks and slam the door shut. Zach charged at the door, putting his full weight behind it. It caved instantly, granting him access. He was met by another hail of gunfire. One by one, he slaughtered all of the soldiers inside. Some continued with their guns, whilst other summoned swords of their own. No matter what weapon they used, it did not work. Zach sauntered out of the second barracks, blood coating his obsidian clothes. Without a pause, he stalked to the cathedral. His prize was still within.

…

Rebecca was desperate now. No matter how much energy the elder gave to her, it was not enough. She would lose the connection with Azrael before long. She fought against his efforts to stop her. He bombarded her mind with demon energy, but still she held strong. She did not know if Zach would tell her to stop or even if there was a signal. All she could do was hold his attention without giving away who she was or the fact that Zach was coming for Azrael. Rebecca was weakening fast. The elder, all but bereft of energy now, slumped against the near wall, exhausted. Rebecca barely managed to reach and sip her herbal tea before slipping into unconsciousness. It was all down to her now.

Not knowing what else she could do, she resorted to a blind attack. Summoning all her energy and that of those around her, she sent a volley of energy against Azrael. She could feel him struggle against it. Some of the energy even got through his defences and threw him off guard as it damaged his mind. But Rebecca could not hold it any longer. With her last ounce of strength, she broke the connection and threw up her defences. As she drifted into the black of unconsciousness, she whispered one thing: 'I'm sorry.'

…

Azrael picked himself from the floor, dazed. Whoever had attacked him had hit many marks. His mind was clouded and his senses were not amplified. He had next to no power left. Not knowing if the attack would continue, he was alone and confused in his throne hall of the cathedral. He staggered towards the side door and tried to force it open, finding that he had no strength to open it. Cursing, he spun round, paranoid. He heard no more gunfire, just the screams. Was that victory or defeat? He did not know. He cast out his senses. They were weak and could not see outside the cathedral, but he did find a faint life sign. He staggered towards it, desperate to feed and heal.

One of his stewards was wheezing behind a pillar. The steward had no right arm or leg after Christian's explosion, but he was still alive. Azrael did not hesitate as he began to extract the steward's life force. The sustenance was sweet. Before Azrael could finish his meal, his steward erupted in purple fire and turned to ash before him. Azrael roared in fury and then spun around, his demon sword drawn and ready. He moved to the centre of the hall, ridding himself of his heavy, useless robes, leaving only his summoned red and black demon armour. His muscles readied for a battle, but no one was there to fight.

He was about to call out when he felt a heavy impact from behind. Next thing he knew, he was in mid-air on a collision course with a pillar. Before he could right himself, he was impacted again. His face met the floor with bone-crunching force. As he was picking himself up, he felt a hand on the back of his head. His face met the floor half a dozen more times, each stronger than the last. Spitting blood from his mouth, Azrael was tossed aside like a doll. He did not wait to pick himself up but leapt and made ready. His demon face turned unusually pale as he gazed into the purple eyes of Zach Ford, the part-possessed.

...

The battle in the cathedral close had not tired Zach but invigorated him. He pulsated with rage. He could no longer feel Rebecca's energy in Azrael, but he could see she had damaged him. The once proud and fearless Azrael looked frail and fearful. Zach enjoyed dealing his damage to the demon lord who had made him suffer, but now it was time for revenge. Azrael would die tonight, and this time he would stay dead.

'You petulant whelp,' Azrael hissed, his red eyes meeting Zach's purple ones. 'What does it take for you to die?'

'More than you have, demon,' Zach replied, restraining his rage. 'You are weak now, not the imposing overlord you wished to be. You are just a pathetic demon playing at lordship.'

Azrael roared and charged at Zach, his red demon-fire sword spinning in deadly arcs. Zach blocked them all easily. He wanted Azrael antagonized, as Azrael was playing right into his plan. Sensing the right moment, Zach countered. Spinning inside of Azrael's guard, he slammed the hilt of his sword into the demon lord's face. As Azrael stepped back in shock and pain, Zach sent a purple fireball into his chest. Azrael was swept off his feet once more and sailed through the air. Summoning all his speed, Zach sprinted down the hall, faster than the gliding demon. He caught Azrael by the throat and slammed him into the cold marble floor. The floor remained undamaged, unlike Azrael. Zach retreated as the demon lord lunged upwards wildly. He had lost his sword in the flight and resorted to his fists. Zach dodged and sliced with his sword, scoring hit after hit all over the demon lord's body until black blood poured from each wound. Azrael slumped back, his energy expended. Zach, sensing his opportunity, approached cautiously. After all, Azrael was a demon lord.

'Kneel before your rightful lord!' Azrael boomed, sending bolts of demon energy at Zach. Zach darted back and blocked them with his sword, which stopped all the bolts. But Zach was failing in power. As the sword slipped out of his grasp, Zach threw up his defences. Purple fire blocked the red bolts as Zach used all his energy to stop Azrael's attacks. Knowing that the demon lord would try to feed on him, Zach resolved not to let that happen. Azrael, having found energy from somewhere, sent another volley at Zach. Both of the demon lord's hands now projected the deadly bolts. Zach was holding firm, but his strength would not last. Outside, the storm broke. Lightning illuminated the sky and thunder boomed near and far. Zach risked casting out his senses. The storm was violent but had not chosen an allegiance. That was all Zach needed. Raising his right hand, Zach connected with the storm. He sent a bolt of purple lightning through his fire barrier and towards Azrael. The demon lord did not see the attack coming and took it full in the chest. His attack ceased as he was sent flying again. Zach broke his connection with the storm and lowered his barrier. He was drained and had no weapon.

Slowly the smoking Azrael picked himself up. Zach had to do something. Leaping into the air, Zach put his full force behind his punch. It connected to the side of the demon lord's face, but Azrael expected it. Taking the hit, Azrael spun round and palmed Zach in the chest. The blow winded Zach but was not lethal. Azrael was bleeding heavily as he continued his assault. His attacks were easy to read, but each block weakened Zach. Finally Zach could do no more. Azrael thumped him again in the chest. It was Zach who was now flying. Then he collided with the floor. Both beings were drained and exhausted, but neither let up. Azrael staggered to his throne and produced a thin blade from a hidden compartment. Happy with himself, he descended towards Zach. It was then that the plan hit him.

CHAPTER 42

Zach picked himself up and prepared himself, defiance glowing in his purple eyes. Azrael strode towards him, blade ready. The demon lord gave no quarter as he lunged and swiped at Zach. Each attacked was either blocked or dodged. Zach retreated to the centre of the hall, eagerly followed by the demon lord, whose face was hungry for death. His attacks became more powerful, but Zach still managed to evade them. Catching Azrael's sword hand, Zach sent two punches to his face and then released him. The demon lord snarled in fury and continued, oblivious of the fact that he was being tricked. Zach continued antagonizing him with counter-attacks until finally Azrael reached the peak of his rage. He charged Zach whilst roaring, hoping to run him through. Zach stood his ground and made his connection once again.

He felt the blade pierce his skin twice, once as it entered his chest and the other as it broke through his back. Azrael had the look of victory on his face as he tried to yank the blade free. Zach held him there. Annoyed that he was denied the killing blow, Azrael heaved Zach into the air, the sword still in his chest. Zach let himself slide down the blade so he was eye to eye with the demon lord.

'Stupid boy.' Azrael laughed, knowing his victory was assured. 'You really thought it would be that easy. I am a demon lord. I rule all I see, and all I see obeys me.'

'There is one force you forgot.' Zach wheezed, his strength beginning to fail. 'A force more powerful than you and me.'

'And what is that, boy?'

'This.'

Releasing his right hand, Zach sealed the connection with the storm. A bright purple lightning bolt streamed to his hand. Gripping the blade with his left hand, Zach sent the whole force into the continuous bolt, which he then sent into Azrael. The demon lord twitched and shuddered as the lethal lightning charred every fibre of his demonic being. Zach relaxed as Azrael's grip on the sword failed. Then Zach fell to the floor, the blade still in his chest. Seeing that the demon lord was stunned, Zach composed himself and stretched out his hands one last time. The storm responded with two more continuous bolts. Zach breathed and spoke his completed answer.

'Nature will never answer to a demon, not even if that demon is a lord.'

He sent the full force of the storm into Azrael. The demon lord twitched violently as every speck of energy the storm had built up over the weeks was sent at him. Zach held strong as the lightning passed through him, but at one point he could hold on no longer. He broke his connection with the storm and fell to his knees. Azrael stood stone still, paralyzed by the lightning.

Zach would not waste the opportunity. Slowly he worked the blade out of his body, each centimetre opening up another wound. Eventually he pulled the blade free and shuffled over to the eerily still demon lord, whose eyes were still red and whose body showed signs of life.

'It will never be yours,' Zach whispered in his ear, hamstringing Azrael so he was on his knees. 'You die with your own weapon at the hands of a mortal. That won't go down well with your master. But I don't care. I am free.'

Summoning his remaining might, Zach brought the sword down in a two-handed blow. Azrael's head severed easy from his shell body. There was no scream, just the echo as the head of David Alexander, host to Azrael, collided with the floor. No blood oozed except that from Zach's wound.

Outside the storm broke, letting sunshine through. Normally Zach hated the sun, but for once he let it warm his blood-soaked, aching skin. He prepared for death when a voice spoke in his mind. Knowing he had one more act left in his body, Zach heaved himself up and limped to the door. The sunlight blinded him and his wound dripped constantly, but he limped on. *One last thing,* he thought to himself. *Just one.*

...

Rebecca came around suddenly and painfully. She gasped for breath as if she had never breathed before. With no words, the elder pressed a mug of tea into her hands and bade her drink. The elder looked even more frail than usual. Rebecca felt the sting of guilt. Fiona rose upon seeing that Rebecca had awakened. The resistance fighter knelt in front of Rebecca and felt her forehead. No tears were in Fiona's eyes now.

'At least you are cooler now.' Fiona smiled. 'We thought you would catch fire the way you were going.'

'Are you feeling better now?' Rebecca asked, ignoring that she was now the one in need of care.

'I will be, once you are up and about. The elder says we need to get you out of bed so your muscles can recover.'

Trusting her guard, Rebecca managed to swing herself out of the cot. Every muscle screamed its complaint, but she persisted. Putting some weight on Fiona's shoulder, she began to walk.

'Any news from Zach or from the outside?' Rebecca questioned.

Fiona shook her head. 'After the tremor, we heard nothing. The fighters are still trying to dig out. I shudder to think what will happen to Zach if they get their hands on him.'

'He was doing an act of good,' Rebecca spoke, struggling to balance. 'He meant it for the …'

The noise of cheers stopped Rebecca's words. Together she and Fiona limped into the main hall, where Simmons and the other fighter leaders were meeting. Simmons noticed their arrival and intercepted them.

'You should both go back to your rooms,' he said, panicked.

'Why?' Fiona asked. 'What's wrong?'

'The fighter leaders have voted to hunt down and kill Zach.'

'What?' Rebecca shouted, suddenly full of energy. 'Why?'

'For leaving us here to die,' the burly, bald-headed leader explained, 'and for being a demon. Just like the Inquisition.'

'Except that he is out there fighting for us right now.'

'He isn't fighting for us,' another leader said. 'He doesn't care about us. He is fighting for himself. And if he succeeds, he will leave us here to starve.'

'You don't know that,' Rebecca argued. 'He sealed us in here to save our lives. He was right about that attack. Now you can all live.'

'Live.' Another leader laughed. 'You call being stuck in a cave for the rest of your life living? I don't. I'm going to kill that son of an Inquisition whore once and for all.'

A cheer went up from the leaders, followed by a crash and a boom. Everyone turned to face the entrance tunnel, weapons ready. Fiona stood in front of Rebecca, her knives gleaming in the lantern lights. Simmons turned to them and nodded as he motioned for the leaders to remain and prepare. Together they padded silently towards the entrance gate. Other fighters lined the corridors, weapons at hand. Simmons glided past them, whispering in each of their ears. Eventually they rounded the final corner and stared in amazement. The gate was open. Sunlight poured down into Sanctuary for the first time in its history. Cautiously they climbed the spiral staircase to the surface, wary of an ambush. As they reached the top, they all allowed the sun to linger on their skin. Rebecca's muscles were soothed by the light. With a nod from Simmons, they burst out of the opening and were shocked by what they saw.

Rebecca gasped as she saw Zach lying face down in the mud, a fresh puddle of blood marking perfectly what he had done. He had moved the excessively heavy Sanctuary door by hand so that it was completely open, and he had rewired the lift so it would work normally. Now he lay unmoving in the mud. Rebecca found herself running to his side. She did not care that she was newly out of bed or that her clothes had recently been cleaned. She knelt beside Zach and carefully rolled him over. Fiona and Simmons helped. They positioned him comfortably and sighed when they saw he was breathing, albeit weakly.

'Get the elder,' Simmons ordered Fiona. Before she could move, Zach's hand reached out and grabbed her. His eyes slowly opened, revealing a strange sight. Blue. His natural blue eyes looked at Rebecca. Never having seen them before, she found that she was soon swimming in them.

'Don't get help,' he whispered. 'I just wanted to know that I did something right.'

'You can't stay here,' Rebecca explained. 'The fighters will kill you for locking them in Sanctuary.'

'There's no need for that.' Zach moved his hands, revealing the stab wound that went through his entire body. It had no more blood left to bleed.

'No!' Rebecca swore at the injustice of everything. 'We can help you. You can get better.'

'Why?' Zach's voice was failing. 'What is left for me here? What I have done cannot be forgiven by anyone. My evil doings rid the world of an evil being. There is no longer any room for me in this good and bright world. It is now down to you to make it good. All of you.' He gestured to the three of them.

Tears began to form in their eyes as Zach became pale. Slowly and with effort, he lifted his hand and beckoned the others to put their hands on his.

'Promise me here and now that you three will make this a better place and that you will always fight for good.'

They all nodded, so overcome by sadness that they could not speak. With a faint smile, Zach turned to Rebecca, his blue eyes locking with her brown ones. That moment felt like an eternity to her. She did not even hear the rest of Sanctuary from behind her as they came to see what had happened. She did not hear Simmons and Fiona talk down the fighter leaders. It was just her and Zach. Her tears fell like rain as their eyes remained locked until he was gone.

His eyes darkened and then closed, and his head slumped as life left him. Zach Ford, a boy used, betrayed, and forgotten; a boy made to be possessed; a boy who had no one to love and whom no one loved; a boy who had lost everything and more, sacrificing himself so that others would live on to make the world better; a boy who did evil things to rid the world of an evil would-be ruler and puppet organization. Now he was gone. In unison, all the resistance members knelt to honour the boy who had saved them. Everyone else knew him as something different, but Rebecca knew him for what he was: the boy who had nothing but sacrificed everything.

No songs of victory were sung that night. No revelry or drinking happened. All the resistance, instead, gathered around a single funeral pyre, united in one cause: to make the world better and fairer and to honour the boy who had allowed them all to live to do this task. As the flames grew higher, Rebecca, Fiona, and Simmons all joined hands, remembering the promise they had made. Tears began to fall as the flames overtook Zach's body. Rebecca let hers fall as she heard a voice in her head. It was familiar and spoke only two words: *I'm sorry*. A lightning bolt descended from the sky out of nowhere and struck the pyre. The fire hissed out immediately, leaving only ash and strips of clothes.

EPILOGUE TO PART 2

SIX MONTHS LATER

Aid came from all across the country, and even from around the world, when news broke about what had happened to Salisbury. It did not take long for the remainder of the Inquisition to surface and tell their terrible tale. Rebecca did not care for the stories, as she focused on one thing alone: rebuilding. Lorries and trucks from here and there piled into the historic market town and began to rebuild. It took less time than expected for the majority of the houses to be completely rebuilt. The main infrastructure was already under way. The cathedral itself was having a thorough rebuild and was being searched in case any remnants of anything unnatural remained. The resistance had long since disbanded and now helped with the rebuild. Rebecca, Fiona, and Simmons were always at the forefront of the effort, giving their ideas or energy to help the plans take shape. They had been true to their word to Zach and had spoken honestly and literally to the authorities who questioned them. It was largely voted and agreed that there was to be a memorial to Zach built in the cathedral close. A large marble statue of the boy was erected. It was a simple image of him. He stood not with a sword or holding lightning bolts, but appeared just as the boy people recognized. His part in the story of the rise and fall of the Inquisition was changed and covered up, but the people who knew now had a place to remember him.

The evening was cool when Rebecca returned to her newly rebuilt family home. It still felt strange not to have her family there. She still shed tears for them, all but her sister. It had shocked her when she found out about Katie's role. In fact, she was disgusted with her sister.

There was a small knock at the door. Fiona pushed herself in. She had changed a lot since being a resistance fighter. Now she wore a flowing orange dress that matched her naturally orange hair, which had always been hidden when she was a fighter. She was now the girly-girl she should have been in school before everything happened.

'We are waiting downstairs. Are you ready?'

'Yep,' Rebecca replied, fastening her shoes and dress. 'Let's go.'

Simmons waited in his car as the two young women came out. He smiled upon seeing how feminine they looked, but he said nothing about it, knowing better than to do that. The car journey was silent as they drove well outside the town limits. Nearly an hour later, Rebecca found herself at an eerily familiar spot, Zach's old house – at least what was left of it. It had burned down completely in the explosion. But she knew it was the best place to do what they wanted to do.

Simmons parked opposite the house. After getting out of the car, they all slowly walked towards it. Simmons was in a three-piece black and green suit, which was a family heirloom. The green matched the colour of Rebecca's dress, which was dotted with black and red. She remembered making it for Katie. But now she wore it – only for this occasion.

The only part of the house that had escaped the fire was the garden. In it was a solemn cherry tree in blossom. Rebecca had always been amazed that such a beautiful tree grew in a place of such sorrow. She walked towards it and opened the urn. Then she sprinkled small amounts of ashes around the tree and bowed her head. Fiona and Simmons did the same. No words were spoken, neither at the house nor on the return journey. Every year the three of them would return to pay homage to the real Zach Ford, the possessed boy who saved the lives on so many, when his own was forfeited.

...

The wind that blew from the mountains chilled to the bone. The cosy little mountain town was a picture of street lights and people. Even with the cold wind blowing, the inhabitants wandered from bar to bar, intent on drinking excessively.

'Jeez, it's cold out there,' a bearded, heavily layered man called, striding into the bar. 'Give me a whisky.' The barkeeper poured a generous glass and handed it to the man, seemingly not caring that the man was well into his drink.

'I'll get that, Bruce,' another man said, laughing from behind a table. 'Get on over here and sit down, you drunkard.' The other man signalled to the barkeeper, who added the whisky to the ever growing tab.

'What's it looking like out there?' Joel asked his drunken friend.

'Cold and dark like it always is in here.' Bruce laughed, raising and draining his glass, the whisky hitting the right spot.

'Had some cops come down the ranch today saying that they found bears dead in the forest. Not shot or anything, but attacked by something.'

'What do I care about bears, man?' Bruce swayed.

'Cos anything that kills bears worries me.'

'Shh. Don't worry about that now. I've got us a real mission to do. See that waitress over there?' Bruce motioned to the young brunette waitress cashing up behind the bar. 'I want her. But the barkeeper says no.'

'Well, my friend.' Joel smiled and then drained his glass. 'The bears can wait for this.'

From their hiding place outside, the two heavyset men found it was easy picking for them to pounce on their prey. Joel grabbed the waitress round the waist, whilst Bruce, who had sobered surprisingly quickly, kept her mouth shut. They pulled her into a dark alleyway off the main drag. Every time that she tried to scream, Bruce hit her. She was drifting in and out of consciousness.

'Just how I like them.' Bruce smiled, undoing his trousers. Neither of them saw that they themselves were prey.

Bruce was flung back by an unknown force, his trousers still down around his ankles. Joel reached for his gun and began pointing it wildly. It was flung from his hand by an unknown adversary. Turning, Joel saw a shadow and sent a fist to hit it. His fist stopped dead, and then he felt it being crushed. He fell to his knees as he felt blood filling his gloves. Bruce attempted to aid his downed friend but received a quick punch, which sent him, dazed, to the ground.

'Well now, gents,' their attacker spoke, 'what do we have here?'

'Nothing,' Joel pleaded, his hand continuing to be crushed. 'We are doing nothing.'

'I think she would say differently if she could talk,' the voice said, indicating the unconscious waitress.

'We were helping her,' Bruce lied. 'Getting her home.'

With surprising strength and speed, the being broke Joel's hand, making him squeal like a child. Bruce tried to run, but he was tripped and heaved back to the waitress, who was beginning to stir.

'I have fought real demons in this world,' the being said in a voice like ice, 'but I think you might be the worst. Do you know what I did to the last rapist I caught?' The being slowly drew a knife and spun it in his hand.

Bruce shook his head, petrified.

'No, of course you don't; *I* do things right.' The being pressed his face against Bruce's eyes, which were as blue as icicles. 'If I catch you doing this again, I will take more than this.'

With another lightning-quick move, the being swiped his knife across Bruce's groin, severing his manhood from his body. Bruce paled in shock and ran, leaving his crippled friend to shuffle off, weeping as he went. Returning the knife to its sheath, the being turned to see the waitress, who was now fully recovered, with her eyes wide in fear.

'I promise you, I won't harm you,' the being said, lowering his hood, showing his pale blue eyes and straw-blonde hair. 'Are you OK?'

The waitress nodded and moved herself out of the cold. Her saviour approached her and placed his long leather coat around her. She instantly warmed.

'Come now,' the man beckoned. 'Let's get you home.'

'I haven't got a home.' The waitress whimpered. 'I ran away today. That was my last shift.'

Turning, the man gazed at her, searching for the truth. Her short brown hair flowed over her freckled face and shielded her deep brown eyes. From what he could ascertain, she was not lying.

'What's your name?' the man asked.

'Hazel.'

'Hazel, if you want, you can have a bed for the night where I stay. No harm will come to you, only food, shelter, and warmth. I promise you.'

She nodded happily, knowing she had a bed for at least one night. She padded up to the man and stayed close to him as they walked onto the main drag.

Even though the snow fell thick and the wind blew hard, the man wore only a shirt and trousers, with thick mountain boots on his feet. No gloves, no hat. He did not seem to feel the cold. Taking his hand in hers, Hazel felt that he was indeed warm. But she did not care.

'Thank you, umm ... what is your name?'

'My name is not important,' the man replied, with a half-smile.

'Please. It is to me,' Hazel continued. 'How else can I thank you properly?'

'You can call me Ford,' Zach replied. 'You have to earn the right to know my real name.'

Smiling, they continued on into the night. The town of Banff in the Canadian mountains was a little bit safer for Zach Ford, the part-possessed killer of a demon lord who now only hunted the demons amongst humankind. Slowly but surely he was winning this fight, and he knew of three other people who would do the same.

ACKNOWLEDGEMENTS

F IRSTLY, I WOULD LIKE TO thank you. It is, after all, for you that I write. This project has taken longer than I care to admit but I can now proudly say that I have done it. I may never meet you or know you but still I wish to convey my thanks.

Secondly, I wish to thank everyone for Authorhouse for their sterling work in bringing this book to life. This novel has been like my child. I have been perhaps a bit too over protective of it. Through their reassurance and constant communication they have given back my confidence and helped me step by step to get to this wonderful point.

I have met many amazing writers over the years and this next thanks go to all of you. Whether I have met you in courses or just casually sat and talked with you over coffee each one of you has helped me develop and grow and I firmly believe that I would never have gotten to this point without all of you. A big thank you to each member of Phoenix Tales in particular for heling me grow.

Finally, I would like to thank my amazing wife for all of her hard work and determination she has put into me to get this and my other projects finished. She is an inspiration in herself and I know deep down that this would still be on my computer and not in your hands if it wasn't for her.

As a final note I would like to add, going for your dreams is terrifying, this I know and understand. But I implore you now, if you have a dream, passion or drive, take the leap and make it come true. Ever if it is just for yourself.

ABOUT THE AUTHOR

J.S RAIS-DAAL SPENDS ALL OF his available free time writing. This being his first published work and hopefully not the last. His love of fantasy in all its aspects mixes in with his everyday life. He enjoys Medieval Re-enactment, Live Action Role Playing and Fire Spinning. He lives with his Wife, Daughter and Menagerie of Animals outside of Edinburgh, Scotland.

ABOUT THE BOOK

LIFE HAS NOT BEEN EASY for the teenager Zach Ford. His family died in a car accident. His legal guardian renounced his guardianship. Living and surviving the trials of secondary school and home life by himself, Zach finds that each day is more gruelling than the last.

But for Zach it goes much deeper than the pressure of exams, and the threats of bullies and teachers alike. This is because Zach has a secret, a secret identity that many would want and a few would kill for.

He is not as alone as he wants to seem.

Zach Ford is possessed.

Printed in the United States
By Bookmasters